~ Bear ~

Copyright © 2019 by |

All rights reserved.

~ Links ~

Come and join me on Facebook, Instagram and Twitter to keep updated with my work!!

Just click on the links below!

linktr.ee/rubycarter

Facebook

Instagram

The Devils men have an IG account: @devilsreapersmc

Twitter

~ Dedication ~

For the sleeping angels. You will always and forever be in the minds and hearts of your Mummies and Daddies
xx

In memory of Sophia.

A huge thank you to Gio and Chris for sharing and entrusting me with your story and letting me put it out there.
Love you both loads.
You're such inspirations xxx

~

They may never have got to hold you, hear your giggles, or answer your cries, but know you are loved.

They may never have got to say your name out loud, or hear you call them 'Dada' or 'Mama', but know you are loved.

You left too early, before we could see you turn into a beautiful human, but you are an angel instead. Know you are loved more than words can say.

© Ruby Carter

50% of all proceeds from the sale of this volume will be donated to 4Louis, a UK charity dedicated to supporting those affected by miscarriage, stillbirth, and the death of a baby or child.

~ Acknowledgements ~

First and foremost I want HUGE thank you to my editor
Lauren Whale!
Girl you kick ass, you kick ass HARD! From your continued support and sensitivity throughout this process I seriously believe I don't think anyone would have been able to do it as beautifully as you.
Thank you soo much from the bottom of my heart.
And Roll on Tinhead… xx

To my girls who are my biggest support system, cheerleaders and continued help with my craziness, love you all loads xx
In no particular order: Ania Kiplan, Kym Young, Catherine Standing, Catherine Wiltcher, Grace Tudor, Bethany Worrall, Naadira at (BookedMercy) for your awesome teasers you all are honoree Devils Reapers members. xx

To my main muse and cover model **Robert Marko** a huge thank you for your continued support with anything Bear related, and letting me using your tattoos in the book. Nothing I asked was too much trouble for you and thank you again for being the face of Bear. Honestly I definitely picked the right man for the job and you are everything Bear is. Xx

Bee Bird – A huge shout out for helping me try and find the perfect Bear and your continued love and support with my books. Love ya lots xxx

H.B.Lyne – Thank you for letting me use Grinder in Bear I hope you like him. Xx

Kym Young/doll – Thank you soo much for giving me Hound, I think you will like him ;)xx

Catherine Standing – Thank you loads for giving the gorgeous name for my third biker Killian, I hope you like him. Xx

Ania Kiplan/Wonderwoman – Thank you so much for your continued support and help with my books. How you manage to do all you do and still help me with teasers and promos is beyond me. You rock! Xx

Catherine Wiltcher – To the sweetest lady. I am in completely in awe of you with everything you have endured and you continue to give me and the world sexy AF alphas, you completely kick ass!! Xx

To my readers – I am forever grateful for the amazing reviews, support and love you continue to give me and my Devils Reapers men. I hope you fall hard for Bear as I did xxx

Contents

~ About the Book ~

On the outside, it seems as though Jenna May Smith has her life together. A hard worker, she has a successful business and the most loyal friends she could wish for, but the truth is deeper than that. Damaged by the ghosts of her past, she has built walls around her heart to protect herself and push men away, never truly letting anyone in.

When she agrees to go on a date with Bear Jameson—a fiercely loyal tough guy with a soft center—she plans to make it a one-time thing, but sweet-talker Bear seems smitten and has other ideas.

As they grow closer, Jenna learns that there's more to Bear than meets the eye, and she finds herself falling for him...hard.

The magnetic bond between the two souls quickly grows too strong to fight, and they become caught in the middle of a passionate romance, but when tragedy strikes, will love truly be enough to conquer all?

In the thrilling third instalment to the Devil's Reapers MC series, Bear, the stakes of love are higher than ever. Will Bear and Jenna's whirlwind romance stand the ultimate test, or will heartbreak sever their connection for good? There's only one way to find out...

~ Chapter 1 Jenna ~

"Sis! That big-ass biker dude is here again! Want me to tell him to get lost?" Jade, my annoying—yet surprisingly lovely—younger sister, yells up the stairs leading from the bakery with a chuckle.

Bear.

The man gives me butterflies, but I am as wary of him as I am of dairy free eggs!

"Tell him I'm too busy!" I lie through my teeth as I quickly bury my head in my accounts. They don't need doing; I did them the other day, but I can't bear to see him yet. He took me out a couple of weeks ago, and in one word, it was perfect! That's the problem...

***

I am an absolute nervous wreck, darting around my bedroom and throwing clothes here, there, and everywhere. My room once looked like you could actually sleep in it, but now it just looks like a tornado tore through it!

"Jen, just leave that cute dress on; you look good in it! Trust me, that man won't be able to keep his hands off you," Jade smirks from where she's propped up against the door frame.

It's OK for her; she looks amazing in her curve-hugging Levis paired with a cute little white top covered in a sweet floral design she hand-drew. My sister definitely has Momma's genes too—all the women on

Momma's side are curvy. I am a size bigger than Jade, and fine with that, but others aren't always…

"Are you sure? He said to dress for outdoors; and I don't think this dress really says, 'ready to brave the elements', babe."

I glance at the clock. "Oh fuck, he's gonna be here in 10 minutes!"

I grab for my favorite dark blue acid-washed jeans. As I'm pulling them over my ass, Jade hurls a shirt in my face. "Put it on! Hurry! No arguments; you don't have time, Sis."

With a roll of my eyes, I do as my crazy-ass fairy godmother tells me. Anyone would think she was the older sister, but nope.

She's chosen well; the deep red peplum top hugs all my curves but isn't too dressy. Before I know it, Jade's pushing me onto my bed and shoving my black Converse on my feet. She's a blur as she sets about fluffing my hair and reapplying lipstick to my lips, then she proudly stands back with her hands on her hips and a cheesy grin on her face. She gives a little nod and waltzes out of my room, leaving me in a daze.

I hear Bear knock at the back door of the bakery, and I barely have time to glance at myself in the mirror as I am grabbing my purse before I run down the stairs to him.

When I see him waiting for me at the bottom, my mouth goes completely dry. His hair is hanging down around his face, his beard has been tidied up, and he's wearing a bottle-green plaid shirt that's open wide to reveal a black t-shirt pulled taut across his impressive chest. He has his sleeves rolled up to his elbows, and I can't help but admire the ink covering him from wrist to elbow.

I could just lick those arms…would that be weird?

I don't care; they are definitely arm-porn. Burly, thick, wiry, muscular…there are too many words popping into my head to describe them.

"Cupcake?"

Bear's voice snaps me out of my thoughts, and 1, 2, 3, I am back in the room.

"Hi," I squeak as I desperately try to stop ogling the beast of a man in front of me. My eyes snap up to meet his deep brown ones. They're as soft as a teddy bear's, but the light in them is dancing around mischievously.

Damn. Double damn. He must have caught me!

As my stare drops to his hands, I notice he's holding a little bunch of different kinds of daisies. They are delicate and sweet, although his grasp makes them seem a hell of a lot smaller than they are.

"You OK, Jenna?" Bear asks hesitantly.

"Yeah, sorry. Are they for me? They're gorgeous, you didn't have to do that!"

"Uh, yeah! I wanted to, Cupcake. You look stunning." He moves to pull me flush with his magnificent, impressive body, and I can feel every muscle ripple as he does.

He bends down so his lips are next to my ear and adds in a hushed tone, "And you smell fuckin' delicious, Cupcake."

Heat rushes down my neck, spine, and right to my core.

Yup, that worked.

"You ready to go?" Bear asks before I can recover enough to reply.

"Yeah, I am," I say, but I don't move. He's still holding my hand in his mammoth grasp, and we haven't moved our eyes off one another's yet.

Breaking the stare, he calls out to Jade, "Can you take these for your sis? Thanks, doll face."

Jade accepts the flowers like a pro and then shoves the box I prepared earlier into my hands.

I don't even remember to say 'see ya later' before Bear has whirled me through the door and stopped right by the club's jet-black pickup truck. He grabs me by the waist and swings me around like I weigh nothing, hauling me up onto the plush passenger seat and placing the container on my lap.

He settles himself into the driver's seat. "Did you bring goodies?"

My eyes widen, and I look down at the box. "Uh…I brought cupcakes and oatmeal bars, is that 'kay?" I ask nervously.

"Darlin', that sounds perfect. What did you think I meant?" he enquires with a quirk of his lip, a devilish glint in his eyes.

I can't stop the blush creeping up my neck, and swiftly whip my hair down to cover my face.

Seeing my reaction, Bear pulls away from the bakery and starts chuckling away to himself.

Jackass!

After about 10 minutes on the road, he pulls down a worn gravel track.

"Where ya taking me anyway, Bear?"

As I flick my eyes over to him, I can't help but admire him. He's such an impressive man, and those fudgin' arms are so hot! I swear they are so thick they could kill a freakin' bear.

Maybe that's how he got his name…

I mentally kick myself as I realize I have gone into my own little world again. Did he answer my question? I bet I look like a right dingus!

"Sorry, did ya say something, Bear?" *I notice that he's pulled over next to a worn-out gate with a spacious meadow behind it.*

"Cupcake, you're always going into your own little world like that. It's cute as hell. Do you realize you stick out the tip of your tongue when you do?"

He lightly brushes my bottom lip with the pad of his thumb, grazing the tip of my tongue. I swear I hear him growl his appreciation as I close my lips and softly suck on his thumb.

Bear tilts my head up to meet his eyes. "Cupcake, did I tell you that you look fuckin' dazzlin' tonight? You look good enough to eat…"

With that, he swoops in and plants a soft, velvety kiss on my lips. My breath hitches as a zing of electricity shoots down my spine. He bites down on my lip delicately, asking for permission to enter my mouth, and I willingly give him access. As his tongue slips expertly between my lips, he's gentle, but would totally be a pro if this was a sport.

He teases me, silently asking for more, and my stupid body gives in like a woman possessed. Don't get me wrong, I've kissed a few men before, but this is nothing like I've ever experienced. I know it shouldn't, but his kiss scares the shit out of me. It's life changing; I know it in my very core.

The feeling is electric, and before I know what I'm doing, I have tangled my fingers into his long mocha hair. I try to get over the center console for better access, but the gearstick digs into my inner thigh like a bitch. Unable to take the pain, I pull away and the spell's broken. I notice the truck's windows are all steamed up, and we are both panting heavily.

Before I can help myself, my tongue sneaks out of its own accord, tasting where Bear was a second ago. I freeze as I realize every square inch of my body wants to give in and 'get to know' everything about this wonderful man. I haven't wanted to 'get to know' a man like this since college…

As Bear tries to compose himself, he starts shifting in his seat. I look up, seeing that his hair is sexily mussed, and it makes a fresh wave of desire crash through me. "I planned a picnic in this big-ass park. Come on, Cupcake, I'm dying to try your cupcakes!"

With that, he jumps out of the truck and rounds the hood, his beaming smile causing his eyes to light up like the Empire State Building and making me feel like a pool of chocolate goo on a scorching hot day.

When he opens the door and helps me down again, I can't help but notice he holds my waist a little tighter, bringing me flush with him. His warmth underneath me makes the world go into slow motion, and even once I have my feet on the ground, I melt into his strong arms.

They make me feel safe…

The thought scares the bejesus out of me, but I push that aside and breathe in his scent; freshly washed clothes and cut grass with a mix of bergamot and mint. The smell washes over me, and it feels like I am being wrapped in cotton wool.

Pulling away, he takes me by the hand, and then we are off through the gate. After a 15-minute walk through some gorgeous honeysuckle, we arrive at a tree shaped like a huge arch with a picnic blanket lying underneath it covered in sub sandwiches wrapped in foil, deli meats and cheeses in a container, and a few cans of soda.

My jaw drops as I take in the huge park; the picturesque trees surrounding us, the meadow littered with flowers, and the lush green grass covering the ground as far as the eye can see. The sun is setting on the treetops at the edge of the park, making everything glow. I realize I haven't said a word yet, but as we stand at the edge of the blanket, I can barely tear my eyes from the scene in front of me.

"How did you do all this?" I whisper in surprise, my eyes finally meeting Bear's.

"I came out here and set up the whole picnic earlier. I only just left to pick you up, so don't worry, the food won't be warm." He sits down heavily, patting the spot next to him on the blanket. "Here, come and sit down, babe."

"Why? Why have you made such a big effort?" I ask him, feeling my brows furrow in confusion.

"What do you mean, Jenna? Of course I wanted to make an effort! This ain't that big, Cupcake, I just wanted you to enjoy yourself…and maybe try and get a second date. Can't blame a man for trying, sweet thang."

I say nothing at first, glancing around for anything that might give me the heads up on what the hell is going on. I chew my lip, deciding what to do next. There's no harm in enjoying this moment, I guess, but I need to set things straight—I don't want to lead him on.

Deciding to put my big girl panties on before we sit down to the picnic he's sweetly arranged, I seize Bear's enormous biceps.

Oh sweet Lord, this is gonna be hard, but I know I have to do it. He's dangerous for me. He's making me feel things, and I don't want to feel anything for a man, not again…

"Bear, there's something you need to know before going any further today. It's not that I don't like you, because I do, but the thing is…I don't want to date. I just want you to…to fuck me."

~ Chapter 2 Bear ~

"Bear, there's something you need to know before going any further today. It's not that I don't like you, because I do, but the thing is…I don't want to date. I just want you to…to fuck me."

Those words echo in my ears as I stand in Jenna's bakery waiting for her to come down from her apartment above. I stand there for at least 15 minutes, but a voice behind me stops me in my tracks just as I turn to leave.

"Leaving already, big guy?" the sugary smooth voice says, caressing my ears.

I glance over my shoulder and am greeted with the sight of a strawberry-blond goddess standing next to her shiny granite counter. Her plump red lips quirk up in amusement, lighting up her stunning face.

I turn on my heel and take in the whole goddamn view. She's dressed in a figure-hugging black t-shirt with the words *'Jenna's Bakery'* emblazoned over her ample right breast. My eyes skim over her luscious hourglass figure, trailing longingly over her thick thighs.

Mmm…

She's wearing fitted dark blue jeans with frayed cuffs and the brightest pair of thick pink sandals I've ever seen, the neon shade matching the nail polish on her cute toes.

I can't help readjusting myself as I take her in; she looks good enough to eat.

"My eyes are up here, big guy!"

Jenna's voice knocks me out of my trance, and I smile. "Can't help myself, Cupcake. Can we talk about the other week?"

"Sure, but I stand firm on what I want, Bear."

"That's what I want to talk about." I close the distance between us to take hold of her silky soft hand, linking our fingers, and tug her body into mine. It doesn't take much; I'm a big guy, 'heavy set' or whatever the hell you want to call it.

Jenna's body fits perfectly against mine, and I love the way my arm wraps around her small waist. Her gorgeous curves are in all the right places for me to grab hold of.

"Come on, baby. Let's sit down, 'kay?" I whisper into her ear.

I feel her body tremble against me I pull her to one of her cherry-red leather booths—the one I always seem to favor that faces the door.

Jenna sits down, curling up against me as I drape one of my heavy arms over her to cushion her soft body against the seat.

"How have you been, baby?" I ask to break the silence.

I don't want to fuck this up, but I stumble through my words, "Jenna, look...I, uh, I owe you an apology for the way I acted the other week. I guess I was just in shock when you said you just wanted me to fuck you, baby. You're worth more than a quick fuck, you're not one of the club girls...Jesus, I didn't mean that to sound crappy; I'm shit at this kind of stuff. What I'm trying to say, Cupcake, is that I'm trying to put the pieces of this puzzle together."

I see her sigh, and watch her eyes drop down to her clasped hands, which rest on her lap in front of her. "I know, Bear. I'm sorry, I just can't do more than sex. I'm...I'm too busy, what with the bakery and possibly expanding the business."

I can see that she's bare-faced lying to me, but I'm not mad or hurt, just curious as to why she only wants sex from me. It's not like I'm not down for arrangements like that, but I'm surprised as hell she is. She doesn't look the type to just want a 'fuck and dump' deal.

"What do you want, Jenna? Tell me so I can understand."

The insecurity in her face as I ask the question confirms it for me; she's definitely not the type of girl who does this kinda shit. What she doesn't know, however, is that I am the type of man who is as patient as they come. Just because I look scary as fuck doesn't mean I'm an insensitive bastard.

I mean, yes, I have my big-ass beard, a chest as wide as the club's table, and arms that aren't far behind in size either; my brothers don't call me a 'giant amongst men' for nothing. I'm 6'5" in my bare feet, and yes, I know exactly how I look—to both women and men.

I've seen grown-ass men cower at my presence when I walk into a room, but they never see that I am fierce, loyal as a dog, and a sucker for a damsel in distress. My brothers know that I've been fucked over a few times by girls with a sob story I've fallen for without realizing they were taking me for a ride. However, now I've seen the telltale signs, it's been a long time since anyone fucked me over. I know enough to know that Jenna isn't pulling that crap here—there is something else going on she doesn't want me to know. That's fine, I'm willing to wait to get the damn truth she's hiding.

"Bear, I want us to set up a deal. One night only to do whatever the fuck we want," she replies in a breathy, husky voice.

"Holy *shit*, Cupcake! Are you serious? You can't say something like that to me! Jeez!" I growl, trying to readjust the semi that's suddenly pushing up against the zipper of my jeans. "Not friends with benefits?" I ask, trying to hide my eagerness.

I've had no complaints in the sack, but one night with this beautiful specimen of a woman? Shiiit, I'm going to have to pull out my A-game and all the stops to show her that one night won't do.

"No, just one night. That's all I'm asking you for. You need to be OK with that, or this can't happen."

Why is she so opposed to more than one night? I get the whole not wanting a relationship thing, but just one fuck? I don't get the reasoning behind it at all. What's more, I know I ain't letting go. If she thinks she's just getting one night, she's in for a rude awakening.

"How about this, babe? I will agree to one night, but if you want more after, you need to tell me why you only wanted it to be a one-time thing. That's my deal; take it or leave it, Cupcake," I challenge, a grin stretching over my face.

She takes a deep breath, picking at her cuticle before nodding. "Fine. Deal. I'm not going to be coming back for more, but I'll give ya an A for effort, big guy."

"We'll see about that, darlin'. We'll see," I chuckle. My gaze roams back over the gorgeous strawberry-blond goddess sitting next to me, fitting perfectly in the curve of my arm like she belongs there. I can't help my eagerness to take things further; we've been chatting and flirting for weeks and she's driving me nuts.

I lean down and watch her hold her breath as my lips hover over hers. Her sweet sugary scent envelops me like she's a siren of the sea. My eyes flick to hers, sparkling green and heavy-lidded. I run the thumb behind her back softly over the bare skin where her shirt has ridden up, then pluck at her ruby lips with my other thumb and forefinger.

"Fuckin' perfection, Cupcake," I whisper in a growl. My lips finally capture hers, and she gasps in surprise. I take the chance to intertwine my tongue with hers, and before long, they're tangling and dancing with one another, pushing and demanding for more.

Her scent is surrounding us inside our own little bubble. It feels as though she's slipped into my very blood, and I swear she's taken root inside of me. I have never tasted anything so sweet and perfect as her lips. She tastes like strawberries, sugar, and honey. I know what I want, and like a lot of bikers, once my mind is made up, I don't change or give up for no one. Like I said, I am a patient man, and I am willing to work to find out Jenna's secrets.

"So..."

Fuck!

I curse as my phone interrupts me, blaring out Guns. I snatch my phone out of my cut's inner pocket, knowing who it is before I hit the answer button.

"Yeah, boss?"

Seconds later, the voice of Axe, the Devil's Reapers Prez, comes through my phone. "Bear, where ya at? I need you back here for church in twenty."

"I'm just at Jenna's, boss. Do you need me to pick up anything for Dani?"

"Oh yeah, good thinkin'! Could ya grab me something with peanut butter if she has it? Thanks bud. See ya in a while."

I turn to ask Jenna for something for Dani, but she's already up out of the booth, swaying her ample hips up to the bakery counter. Its chrome gleams in the light as I watch her place cupcakes and thick slices of cake in a cardboard box decorated with pink and cream stripes. Closing the box, she gently places one of her bakery's stickers on the lid to seal all the goodies in.

I slide out of the booth and stroll over to her, brushing my palm down the small of her back to skim over the juicy butt that's been tempting me since I walked in here. I smile as I feel her relax into my touch.

"Thank you for this, baby. What do I owe ya?" As I link my other fingers between hers resting on the counter, I notice how my sun-kissed tatted skin contrasts against her creamy, pale arm; my large, scarred, inked hand engulfing her petite, angelic one.

I look down, and my eyes land on the full bust that's peeking outta her polo shirt, teasing me. I realize she hasn't answered my question, so I give her a slight nudge, pressing my chest to her back.

"Oh shit, sorry Bear! Did you say something?" she blurts out in surprise, tearing her eyes from our joined hands.

"It's OK; I just asked what I owe you for the cakes."

"Nothing, it's on the house. You've met Dani, and we all know what happens if she's hungry—I think the phrase 'hangry' was created because of hungry pregnant women." She chuckles to herself, and I can't help but laugh along with her. It's not a delicate giggle; it's a deep belly laugh.

"Babe, I'd take a group of drunk and pissed bikers over a hungry Dani any day. Are you sure? At least let me grab some coffee and cake for the rest of the men to say thanks."

"Nope! Not needed. I wouldn't do it if I didn't want to."

"OK, babe. Look, I'd better go, otherwise Axe is gonna have my ass. We have club business to attend to." I bend down, place a soft kiss on her silky-smooth cheek, and whisper, "Catch you later, 'kay?"

I hear her breathing hitch as my beard brushes back and forth over her cheek, and the sound is so intoxicating I barely hear her reply to me.

"OK Bear, I'll see you later."

I reluctantly pull away, striding to the door. As I pull it open and walk through, I holler over my shoulder, "Cupcake, name the time and place and I'll be there with fuckin' whistles on my balls!"

~ Chapter 3 Jenna ~

"Cupcake, name the time and place and I'll be there with fuckin' whistles on my balls!"

Seriously? Oh my god! Well I guess I did tell him, didn't I? Shit, I already have butterflies swarming in my tummy thinking about it. Jesus!

I'm standing there in a daze, not sure how long I've been gawping at the door, when it reopens again.

Zara strides through it; one of her ear buds in her ear and her crossover bag slung across her chest. Dani's right, this girl can throw on anything and look fab. Today she's wearing black frayed jeans and black sliders with a gorgeous bright pink leopard print tank top that fits her figure perfectly.

"Hey babe! How ya doing? I could do with my regular before I head into work, I'm fuckin' worn out." She glides into the booth closest to the door and sags into the seat.

"Hey hon, sure thang. I'm good; I hope everything's OK? I'll get your drink and goodies right away."

Once I've prepared Zara's drink, I grab her usual blueberry muffin and place a cube of the new brownie recipe I want her to try on her plate.

"Here you are, hon. Enjoy."

"Aw, Jenna, did I ever tell you you're amazing? God, I need this coffee badly, I've hardly slept."

"Oh good Lord, Zara Hart, not you too! I hardly see Dani because of her being…what, 26 weeks pregnant now? Are you?"

Zara's eyes widen, and she nearly chokes on her coffee.

"WHAT?! Oh, hell no! I'm not ready for kids! Flex and I are great the way we are at the moment. I know he *wants* kids, though. I see him being all sweet to Dani, and it just makes me love the big lug even more...but no, it's not that. The clubhouse was so loud last night! I seriously don't know how Dani does it. Wrench, Dagger, and Tin were doing fuckin' flamin' shots like they were water. I know I can drink, but fuck!"

Zara finally comes up for air, takes a massive gulp of what she calls 'brown gold', and quickly pops the little brownie bite in her mouth. The sound that comes out of my friend as she does should be saved for Flex...or at least her favorite toy, 'Mr. Jimmy Dickfinger'.

"What d'ya think, hon? Any good?"

She gives me a wide-eyed nod, her right palm clasped dramatically over her chest as she chews slowly, savoring the bite. Once she swallows, she answers me. "Oh my God, Jenna! What was in that brownie? It tasted incredible; chocolatey, rich, creamy...oh God, babe, you gotta gimme another! My whole mouth filled back up with saliva just thinking about it." She smacks her lips, still trying to taste my newest creation.

"Well, I'm glad you liked it, you're the first taster. It has stem ginger cubes, crushed graham crackers, maple syrup, and three different chocolates in it."

"Mmm...So how're things with you and Bear? Any more dates lined up?" she asks cautiously, taking a quick sip of coffee and peering at me over the rim of her cup. I see a mischievous hunger for information in her eyes.

"Oh, we're all good, but no, no more dates. I'm just not ready for a relationship right now."

Or ever, but that's no one else's business but mine…

"Why, what happened, Jen? Did he try to get too hot and heavy? Wouldn't you give Pooh Bear any of your honey? Is that it?" She bursts into fits of laughter at this, making me laugh along with her. She's one crazy chick, but I love her like a sister.

"Ha-ha, very funny, Miss Hart! No, he behaved, but we may or may not have kissed."

"Ooh, how was it? Gimme the deets!"

I roll my eyes as I realize she's not gonna drop it; she's looking at me like a dog with a bone. I can't help the nervous smile covering my face, and I try and fail not to stumble over my words. "It…it was…*awesome,* Zar'. That man sure can kiss."

I let out an uncontrollable sigh, and Zara grins.

"WOOHOO! GO POOH BEAR!" she whoops from her seat.

I glare at her as she finishes the last sips of her coffee, quickly stuffs the last bite of her blueberry muffin in her mouth, and glances down at her phone.

"Oh fuck! I need to get to the shop before my moody brother gives me shit again." She snatches her bag up, swinging it up over her shoulder, then leans down and gives me a little hug. "All right, biatch, I'll catch you later. Message me; we need another girls' night out again. Maybe bring your sister if she wants to come?"

Before I have time to reply, she dashes out of the door.

***

6 days later...

I know we said only sex and only one time, but Bear has been all up in my goddamn space since our talk. He's been ordering the same thing every time; black coffee and an order of pancakes with bacon and maple syrup. He thinks I haven't realized, but I feel the heat of his eyes on me when my back's turned every damn day. I swear, if he stares any fudgin' harder, he's going to burn a hole in the back of my head. It's Friday today, and he's been in here doing this for the past 4 days in a row.

I grab the coffee jug and stalk over to where the big guy is casually slouching in his usual booth, one foot resting on his other knee.

"Hey gorgeous, how's things?" he asks. I feel his eyes roam up my body from my toes to the top of my messy bun.

"I'm fine, thanks," I snap curtly. "Out with it, Bear, what the hell are you doing?"

"Whatcha talkin' about, darlin'?"

"You've been here for 4 days in a row; what's up?"

The big guy starts chuckling to himself, at first softly then growing louder. His beautiful smile stretches so wide that I can see a faded scar running from his eye along his jaw to his beard. It makes him look more real, raw and rough around the edges...

As I see his lips move, I come back into the room. "What?"

"I said, are you keepin' count?" He sits up, slowly brushing a finger over the back of my hand, which rests on the table, and his voice drops to a hushed murmur.

"Maybe I can't help counting down the hours until you give me a time and place. I can't wait to get you on top of me, Cupcake."

Oh sweet fudgin' hell, what the fuck am I meant to say to that?!

"Um…uh…I…I…"

Sweet baby Jesus, my mouth is suddenly like a humongous ball of cotton wool.

"And you know what else?" he says in a deep animalistic growl that reaches into my panties and vibrates against my button, "I. Can't. Fuckin'. Wait. To. Taste. Every. Inch. Of. Your. Body. You name the time and place, but know this, Jenna. Once we go there…*and we will* go there…I will fuck you like a rag doll, so hard that you won't know which way is up and which way is down!" He hisses the last part out through his teeth, nostrils flared.

I stare at him in shock. He's like the hungriest Bear you ever saw—the 4-legged kind or otherwise. I watch him swallow hard, wetting his bottom lip. His tongue brushes the thick, glossy beard that shimmers in the light.

My eyes lazily follow the direction of his tongue.

FUCK!

This Bear is wild, rough, and making me throb and tingle for him.

He's just cemented what I've been thinking all along.

This man—this gorgeous, furry-faced man who makes my heart race and my panties soaking wet—is *definitely* going to be under me before this week's through…

~ Chapter 4 Bear ~

"Maybe I can't help counting down the hours until you give me a time and place. I can't wait to get you on top of me, Cupcake."

I hear her sharp intake of breath at my words.

Mmm, that's it, gorgeous. Stop pretending I don't have the effect on you that I know I do.

Why won't she give in and let this happen?

"Um...uh...I...I..."

"And you know what else?"

Fuck it! I'm gonna tell her exactly what I want, and how I know she's going to love everything I do to her.

I lean in further to get my point across to the gorgeous beauty in front of me. "I. Can't. Fuckin'. Wait. To. Taste. Every. Inch. Of. Your. Body. You name the time and place, but know this, Jenna. Once we go there...*and we will* go there...I will fuck you like a rag doll, so hard that you won't know which way is up and which way is down!"

I can't tear my eyes off her angelic face as I watch her flush from her neck to her forehead. I can see her struggle with herself, her stunning misty green eyes becoming glossy. Her lips part, her breathing becoming so quick and shallow it sounds like she's panting with need for me.

God, I'm desperate to sink myself into her body! I swear I can smell her arousal, and it's making my dick as hard as steel. It's aching, pulsating for her. I try and readjust myself, my dick pushing up against my zipper hard enough to leave teeth marks.

I barely hear her husky whisper of a response as her stunning eyes lock on mine. They're so dilated that they're nearly black with lust and need as they shine back at me. "OK, Bear."

I watch her struggle to tear her gaze from mine. She does eventually, flicking her eyes down to look at the table. She sets the coffee jug down in front of me and grabs one of the paper napkins from my table. Taking a pencil from her pocket, she starts scribbling on it, then slides it under my nose. Written on the stark white napkin are Jenna's digits.

Fuck yeah! Wild fuckin' horses couldn't keep me away from this woman right now.

My eyes meet hers again, and I give her a big shit-eating grin, then grab her wrist hard enough for her to fall into my lap, fitting against me like she was carved especially for me. I can't wait any longer to lock lips with this sexy-as-hell creature. I let go of her wrist and slide my hand against the column of her slender, silky neck, pulling her in to give her my lips.

As my lips graze hers with a feather-like touch, I hear her let out a huge sigh, and she relaxes into my hold. I take that as my cue to continue with the kiss, starting to deepen it as I keep a hold on the back of her neck. As her mouth opens, I slide my tongue in to meet hers. The kiss stays soft and gentle at first, but after a minute or so, the dance of our tongues starts getting more vigorous, and the she-cat who's on my lap starts squirming against my hard-on.

Fuck!

I reluctantly pull my lips away from Jenna's and risk a look at her. Her eyes are still closed, and she's touching her lips—in shock, I think.

I rest my forehead on hers and breathe in her sweet scent, staring at her plump, swollen lips. My words escape me in a whisper that only we can hear. "Cupcake…I can't believe I'm sayin' this, but we have to stop kissin'."

"Why's that, big guy?" she replies in a raspy voice that goes straight to my dick.

"Because, babe, if you keep wigglin' that gorgeous ass on my dick, you're gonna end up unmanning me right front of the whole fuckin' bakery, and probably half the town."

Her eyes spring open in shock at this, wide as little bush baby's. I swallow the chuckle dying to escape as the color drains from her gorgeous face.

"Oh, shit! Shit! Bear, let me up!"

"Hold up darlin', let me just readjust myself," I smile, shifting in my seat. "Okay, you're good to go now. I'll be outta your hair soon, just gotta let myself calm down. But I will be messagin' you later, Jenna."

I let her go, instantly missing the feel of her soft, warm skin under my rough, callused hands. She slides off of me, cautious of the erection that's now clearly visible through my jeans.

"Did you want some more coffee before you leave?" she asks, shyly looking at the coffee pot she left on the table.

I notice her pale pink lipstick is smudged from my kiss. My fingers itch to touch her again before I leave, so I reach out and graze the pad of my thumb against the smudge mark to wipe it away.

Jenna leans into my touch and sighs, but the sound of the door opening and closing snaps us out of it. She refills my coffee cup, not waiting for my response.

"You go back to your customers, darlin', and I'll message you later. I've gotta get back to the clubhouse soon."

"'Kay. I'd better go, I'll see ya around."

I watch her turn away and sashay her delectable fuckin' ass all the way up to her next customers.

Yeeeaaah…I'm definitely going have to wait a while until I can get up to leave, otherwise the little old ladies in the booth behind me are gonna get a good eyeful of my manhood…

***

Later, around 8pm…

"Yo, Bear! Want a beer?" Dagger shouts over the music blaring through the main room in the clubhouse. It's a classic AC/DC tune, part of a typical night at the club. As much as the club life's crazy as fuck, I love it. I wouldn't change a damn thing about it. I grew up in the club, prospecting from the age of 20.

I was homeless on the streets of Tennessee when I got spotted down a back alley by Axe's dad, who was Prez at the time. He took me in, and gave me a roof over my head, food in my belly, and a reason for living. My club and my brothers are the only real family I've ever known. I went from my birth mom to a placement with Child Services, but it wasn't long before I skipped that hell-hole—the streets were kinder than my so-called 'foster parents'.

Shaking my head to get rid of the memory, I stroll over to Dag, the Sergeant at Arms for the club, who has his usual crowd of women watching him. For an older man, he's in pretty good shape. A lot of the club girls call him a silver fox, but you can't see a strand of gray in his copper hair. Granted, he's not as big or heavy as me, Flex, or even Axe, but he's still fit.

Me and Dag are close, as brothers go. We tend to stick together—including in the bedroom. It's as hot as hell watching your dick disappear into a woman's mouth as she takes another man's deep inside her.

"Hey, Dag! A cold one sounds fuckin' fantastic to me!" I shout over to him as I approach the bar. He's perched on a stool chatting to Tinhead, our prospect, who's behind the bar.

"You both all right? What ya been up to?" I ask as I slide into the seat next to Dagger.

"Ah, nothin' much, Bear, just waiting on the others to drag their pussy-whipped asses in for church," Dag sniggers before taking a deep drag of his beer.

"Dagger, you're just sore because you ain't found a special lady who would put up with your grumpy old ass yet!"

Tinhead loves diggin' at Dagger, but we all know he don't mean a thing by it.

Dagger points his beer bottle at him. "Thing is, Prospect, I don't want an Ol' Lady. Don't get me wrong, Dani and Zara are family, but I don't need a full-time woman. The club girls are perfect for getting this old dog's dick nice and wet! On that note, brothers, I'm gonna go get some before church."

He downs the rest of his Bud and staggers over to Brandy, who's sittin' nearby and chatting with the other club girls, Jewel and Candi.

Dagger stands in front of her and gives her a quick flick of his head, and they're off down the corridor to his room.

"Jesus! That man's dick's gonna drop off, I'm sure of it! Where you been, anyway, Bear?" Tin enquires.

Why do I get the feeling he already knows the fuckin' answer?

I turn from watching Dagger walk away and catch his eye. "Out with it, Prospect."

"Just asking a simple question, brother." He carries on wiping down the countertop, stacking the glasses at the back of the bar, but then the little fucker turns to me and says over his shoulder, "Color suits you by the way."

"Huh? What ya goin' on about, Tin?"

"The lovely shade of pink you're wearin' really makes your brown eyes pop, Bear!"

Ah fuck, Jenna's lipstick! I must've been wearing it on my face riding through town too.

"For fuck's sake!" I growl, leaning over the bar to look at myself in the mirrored wall at the back.

"Chill ya balls, man! It's barely noticeable, I only saw it in this light. Jenna OK then?"

I grab a handful of the napkins on top of the bar, douse them with my beer, and start wiping my lips furiously.

"Huh? What was that about Jenna, Tin?" Zara calls as she and Dani walk through the doors followed by their men—Axe and Flex walk behind them, talking amongst themselves with their eyes locked on their women in front of them.

Dani's got a proper baby bump now, and she protectively rubs her tummy as she and Zara come up to me and look between me and Tinhead.

"Hey ladies. You OK? I was just asking Bear here how Jenna was."

"We're all good, thanks, Tin. Ooh, has something happened between Pooh Bear and Jenna?"

Zara thinks she's fuckin' hilarious callin' me goddamn Pooh Bear. I just shake my head at her; she's like an annoying little sister.

"Fuckin' Pooh Bear, Zar'? Really?" I mutter under my breath.

"I don't know, doll. You would have to ask the man in question about that." Tinhead rounds the bar and goes to the back room to escape the conversation without another word.

Lucky fucker.

"Well, Bear? What's happening with you and Jenna? Give me all the deets."

"Yeah, are you treating our girl right and all?" Dani pipes up, joining in the conversation.

I'm gonna have to slap Tin upside the head for this shit. "Ladies, I ain't sayin' anything. If you want 'deets'," I draw quotes in the air with my fingers, "y'all will have to chat to your girl for them." I say.

"If *you* won't tell us, *I know* I will get the info outta Jenna," Zara says smugly, rounding the bar to grab herself and Dani a drink.

Pulling out my phone, I decide to give Jenna the heads up, grateful for the excuse to text her.

Me: - *Cupcake, hope you're OK? Just wanted to let you know Zara n Dani are probably gonna ask you about us… B*

I slide my phone in my back pocket just as Flex slaps me on the back.

"You OK, bro? The prospect givin' you shit about Jenna? He did the same to me with Zar', remember? Best fuckin' thing he ever did; now look at me!" he says with a grin. I gotta admit, since he's actually locked Zara down, he's been smiling more.

"Yeah, yeah. I hear ya, man…" I'm interrupted by my phone vibrating against my ass, and I dig it out of my pocket.

Cupcake: - *Is this Bear?*

Me: - *Of course it's Bear! You got other men calling you Cupcake that I need to know about, babe?*

This time, her response is lightning fast.

Cupcake: - *No. Only you :P What's this about Zara and Dani asking about us? x*

Me: - *Tin was asking about you…I may have had some of your lip shit on my lips. You didn't tell me it rubbed off on me, cheeky witch ;) Damn straight only me!*

I glance back up to carry on chatting with Flex, but he's staring back at me with a raised eyebrow and a knowing grin on his face.

"What's up, VP?"

"Nothin', Bear. I don't think I have ever seen a man stare that intently at his phone. Well, except maybe me and Axe. Hope you're ready for it, Bear." He grabs his beer and sits down next to Zara, wrapping his arm around her and whispering shit in her ear.

Cupcake: - *What you up to tonight Bear? X*

Me: - *Gotta go to church soon, then I'll probably have a ride out to unwind and crash. What about you, darlin'?*

Cupcake: - *Ooh, sounds nice. I've decided to name my time and place…*

Cupcake: - *tonight at mine… x*

Me: - *Fuck yeah, baby! I'll be there after church, OK? Is your sister out?*

Cupcake: - *Sounds great, big guy…can't wait. Yeah, why? x*

Me: - *Big guy…you wait until you see what I'm packing, babe ;) I want her gone because I'm going to be makin' you scream my name all night!*

Cupcake: - *Is that so? Maybe I'll be making you scream my name all night…especially with that big thick cock in my mouth…;P xx*

DAMN! This woman is determined for me to blow in my pants like a fuckin' kid!

Me: - *Baby, you can't say shit like that! I'm picturing it now!*

"All right, everyone in church now!" Axe calls.
I quickly readjust my semi.
Sweet Jesus, this needs to go down! Think of Doc's stinking socks...his wrinkly balls.
I keep picturing them and feel the pressure in my jeans lessen.
Yeah, that definitely seems to be working.

***

"So, are we all agreed it's all hands on deck regarding a playground out the back of the clubhouse?" Axe asks us proudly.
Around the club's church table, 'Ayes' go around the room, mine included. It makes sense if ya ask me, what with Axe and Dani's little one coming in a couple of months. The way Zara is when she's looking at all the baby shit with Dani, I bet there will be another kid around here soon enough—in fact, I'm surprised she's not already pregnant.
"Right, in other business, I reached out to the other chapters regarding the annual rally. They've all agreed to have it here this year—I don't want to be away from Dani too close to her due date. It will be in 8 weeks' time, all weekend, y'all know the deal."

"Sounds great to me, Prez! I'm lookin' forward to seein' the rest of the chapters—it feels like years since we last saw 'em," Dagger says.

"This rally's gonna get messy! I can't fuckin' wait!" Tin pipes up.

The whole of the club start talkin' amongst themselves, and I can hear Dagger, Tin, and Wrench chatting about all the new free pussy that will be coming with the other chapters. Normally, I would be as excited as them, but tonight, all I can think of is what I'm gonna do when church is finished.

Axe brings the gavel down, pulling me out of my thoughts.

BANG! BANG!

"All right, all right! Has anyone else got anything to say?"

The word 'no' echoes around the table on repeat, and then Axe slams the gavel down with such force it makes the thick table shake.

Before anyone else can move, I'm scraping my chair back ready to go and see the red-haired angel that's been swimming around my head all day.

"Yo Bear, you want a drink?" Axe shouts from behind me.

I wave him off. "Nah, I'm all good, Prez. I've got somewhere to be."

I grab and turn my phone on, quickly sending a message to Jenna:

Me: - *Just out of church, are ya still up?*

Cupcake: - *Yeah, I am. Xx*

Me: - *Spread those pretty thighs and play with that little bean of yours.* ;P

Cupcake: - *Bear! You did NOT just say that?! X*

Me: - *Damn straight I did, Cupcake. Do what I say and there will be a reward in it for you. I'll be there in 10. I expect that pussy soaking!* ;P

Cupcake: - *What kinda reward? I thought it takes 30 minutes to get here from the club? X*

Me: - *You'll have to see, babe. Get playin', gorgeous, I can practically taste you from here. Oh, it does, but I have something to drive faster for. See ya soon babe.*

I grab my lid from my room and squirt some of my aftershave into it, then step into the rowdiness of the main room and holler; "Catch y'all later, I'm off out!"

As soon as I get to the main doors, I hear Tin shout, "Say hi to Jenna for us!"

I flip him the bird behind my back, both not bothering to give him the satisfaction of seeing my face and eager to see the gorgeous redhead who's had me riled up since this afternoon.

~ Chapter 5 Jenna ~

I've been staring at my phone for what feels like an hour, but when I snap out of my trance and look at the time displayed in the corner of my cell, only 15 minutes have passed.

Fudgsicles, I'd better get moving!

My room's perfect as always, but I quickly readjust my figure-hugging black tee dress, lowering the plunging neckline even more. I can't believe this is actually going to happen. I reapply the deep red lipstick I chose for tonight, and quickly look in the mirror to make sure I haven't got any lipstick on my teeth.

KNOCK, KNOCK!

Oh Jesus!

I fluff up my long waves and try to take some big deep breaths in and out to calm myself. I know I told Bear that I only want sex, but that doesn't mean that I'm in my comfort zone…

I stride my way the door and decide to take the bull by the horns, swinging it open. Standing there is the huge beast of a man, helmet in hand and cut still on, a black t-shirt stretching over those thick, burly arms. My nose is filled with the sweet smell of fresh air and his scent.

"Hey," I whisper in greeting as my gaze meets his big chocolate eyes.

"Hey, darlin'."

My mouth has suddenly gone dry, my palms sweating like a bitch. I'm nervous, but not of Bear.

I admire his chiseled arms and the neatly trimmed, long, thick beard that reaches the middle of his chest, then my eyes drift to his gorgeous full lips, which are stretched out in a stunning smile.

"Darlin', are you still with me?"

"Sorry, Bear. Come in."

He does, ducking under the door frame. The smell of leather and fresh air is even more intoxicating as I close the door.

Is it normal to get wet from smell alone?

Bear takes off his cut, then starts looking around for somewhere to put his stuff.

"Here big guy, let me take them." I snatch them from him and try to scurry away like a scared little mouse, but before I can, his huge arm wraps around me. Bear has to practically double over to reach my ear, and I feel his beard tickle my outer ear.

When he speaks, his gruff, growly voice vibrates through to my inner ear, making me shiver and tingle all over. "Jenna, you don't have to do this right now. This is your decision, remember? I'm happy just watching TV with you, darlin'."

Oh God, why does he have to be so sweet

I try and calm my racing heart, then swivel around in his arms so my body is pressed up against his immense chest, and whisper against his soft, warm lips, "I know I don't have to, Bear, but I want to…"

To prove my point, I lean further into to his hold and give him the softest of kisses, his beard tickling the skin under my nose and cheeks. It quickly deepens and one of Bear's hands strokes down the plane of my back whilst the other one squeezes my ass cheek so hard it's nearly painful.

He growls into my mouth as our tongues continue their slow, deep dance, and I unconsciously start rubbing myself against the hard bulge in his pants. Bear grabs underneath my ass, and I drop his stuff and instinctively wrap my legs around his waist like a spider monkey.

He breaks away from my lips long enough to pant, "Bedroom, babe?"

"Behind me, second door on the left," I breathe in reply.

In 5 strides, he's opening my bedroom door with a swift kick, his giant biker boot slamming against the pine.

He carries me through and kicks the door shut behind us, slowly letting me slink to the floor until my bare feet sink into my plush cream rug.

"Jenna." Bear says my name hoarsely after a minute, and I suddenly realize I'm staring at my rug and pretty pink toenails. I peek up through my eyelashes and see the big guy in a battle stance. His shoulders and chest are broader than my door frame, and his magnificent arms hang by his sides. I can hear him breathing from here.

I finally lock eyes with him, and, to my surprise, see that he's nervously licking his lips.

"Babe..."

Before I know what's happening, Bear's in front of me; one gigantic hand wrapped in my loose curls, tipping my head back, the other pressing my lower back so I'm pushed up against his warm, solid body.

He dips his head, and I instinctively take his lips. They are softest I've ever felt, and I love the coarseness of his beard. We kiss with such hunger I swear he's trying to consume me, and I can feel him creeping into my veins…

When we finally pull away from one another, panting, I can't help the next word that pops out of my mouth, "Wow!"

I mentally curse at myself. *God, I sound like a child…*

"Wow indeed, darlin'," he chuckles, lazily fingering the outline of my dress and tracing the seam that goes across my breasts. His touch sends shivers up and down my body.

"Gorgeous," he murmurs to himself as he leans down and kisses the top of each breast, then lazily licks from one to the other, making my breath hitch.

"Bear...that feels so good."

"Mmhm, I know, darlin'…do ya wanna get out of this pretty dress before I tear the fucker off you just to get that stunning body of yours?"

My pussy clenches at his words.

Oh Lord, does he have to be so sexy?

"As hot as that sounds, the dress cost a lot." I say breathlessly.

I step back out of his hold, immediately missing the heat of his body, then reach around me and unzip the dress, letting the straps drop down my arms, but keeping one arm underneath my bust. My eyes don't leave Bear's, and I watch his nostrils flare as I gather all my courage and let my dress fall to the floor.

Bear growls, his eyes roaming up and down my body. Even though I have my black lace Victoria's Secret panties and bra still on, I have never felt so naked. Bear can see all of me, right down to my soul, and the feeling both scares and excites me.

"Baby…your body is stunning. You look so pure, like an angel."

After what feels like an eternity, I finally find my voice. "You're wearing too many clothes, Bear." He goes to pull his shirt off, but I grab his wrist to stop him. I don't know where it comes from, but I hear myself purr, "Let me."

His crooked grin makes his eyes dance mischievously and darken with lust.

I tentatively reach and pull his t-shirt up painfully slowly, my knuckles lightly grazing the dusting of hair over his chest that tickles my palm as I caress him. He helps me tug it over his head, and suddenly he's standing there in all his glory, sculpted like a work of art. He might not have every woman's dream body, but no one can deny Bear is magnificent. He's covered in a sea of colors from his tattoos, broken only by the long deep chestnut beard that reaches down past his neck.

My eyes can't stop feasting on this amazing man; I could never tire of looking at the tattoos that cover the top of his chest, reaching across his pecs and down his impressive arms.

Yup, like I thought, they're definitely lickable.

"Babe, you OK? You've not said anything for a long time." I don't miss the rawness in Bear's voice, so gruff it's clear he's really struggling to contain himself.

"Yeah babe, I'm good…more than good." I flick my eyes back up to his and absently rub and wet my lips. Sure enough, I hear Bear groan.

"Cupcake, get on the bed. I need to know if you taste as sweet as you smell."

My legs finally move, and I hop onto my bed. The mulberry blanket feels soft and fluffy under my skin as I lay back with my legs bent, leaning back on my elbows to really appreciate Bear in all his glory. He steps right up to the edge of the bed and slowly starts popping the button on his jeans, tugging his zipper down.

Before I know it, he's naked as the day he was born. I decide to sneak a quick peek between his legs and gasp at his long, thick cock…

I've not seen many dicks, but how is that thing gonna fit inside me? Forget 'bear', he's hung like a fuckin' horse!

I lick my lips and swallow nervously. "Wow, Bear, you really *are* a big guy! Maybe we should ask the club to change your name."

His cock bobs up and down as if in agreement, and I swallow my snigger. If I wasn't so wet at the sight of it, I would laugh at the comical timing.

Not the time, Jenna…

"Baby girl, now's not the time for you to be makin' jokes." Bear drops to his knees and pulls my legs open and to the end of the bed in one swift move, leaning in and inhaling as he runs his nose from where I know I am wet right up to my button.

Kinky bastard…

"Mmm, baby. Let's get rid of these, shall we?" he rasps from the top of my mound. Before I can say anything, he rips my pretty panties from me, and the cool air in my apartment hits me.

"Hey, they were new!" I squeal.

"*Fuck,* babe! You got the sexiest little pussy I ever saw!" Bear growls.

The next thing I know, he has hooked my thighs over his vast sinewy shoulders so my feet are draped down his back, and his face is in between my legs. His tongue takes a slow swipe at my glistening pussy, making my back arch off the bed.

"I FUCKIN' KNEW IT!" he yells, my thick thighs making him sound muffled.

I go deathly still as dread fills me, hardly daring to squeak "What?"

Bear flicks his lust-filled eyes up to mine, and I can see a glistening line of wetness over his long beard where he licked me. "You taste fuckin' incredible, sweet as a cupcake."

Before I can reply, the gorgeous man delves back between my legs, tracing the tip of his tongue inside me and moving it in and out in slow, deliberate strokes that make me ache.

"Ahh, Bear... don't... stop."

He hums against my clit, and then bites it lightly before kissing and licking it. Jesus, I'm so drenched I can hear myself. I open one eye and see Bear's eyes fixed on my face as he licks me out.

Sweet Jesus, it feels amazing; like I'm his personal popsicle. I'm tingling with anticipation as I feel my climax building. I'm right on the tip of the cliff, dying to go over. I grab hold of Bear's thick brown hair, pulling and yanking, but Bear quickly pulls out of my hold.

"No! Don't stop, baby!" I cry out, not recognizing my own voice.

I know this may be the norm for most of my girlfriends, but a gorgeous man making me feel special and cherished is definitely a first for me. His mouth feels like perfection against my skin.

"Baby girl, if I let you cum without me inside you, I will shoot all over your nice rug. I don't know about you,

Cupcake, but I don't think that's how you want this to go down tonight," he says with a sexy smirk.

He gets off his hands and knees and stands up to his full height, and I see that he's about to burst. There's precum shining off his cock, and his balls look full.

I try and gather up some courage before sitting up so he can see me better. I tease him by running my finger over the edge of my lacy bra, circling each cup, then I flick my wrist and undo my bra. It pops open, releasing my big heavy boobs. My nipples are painfully hard, and I can't help but bite my lip as I look back down between that gorgeous man's legs as he strokes his impressive erection.

"Sweet mother of God, Jenna! Baby. You. Are. Fuckin'. Gorgeous. Damn, darlin'!"

He climbs on the bed beside me and immediately takes my face in both his hands. He starts kissing me passionately, consuming more of me with each kiss. Our tongues tangle and brush each other, and we can't seem to get enough.

While Bear caresses my face, I take his hard, pulsating cock in my hand, barely able to wrap my fingers around the girth, and stroke him slowly.

Mmm, God. He's red hot, and feels so soft...

I go to cup his balls, but that makes Bear jerk and pull away from my lips.

"Fuck, baby girl! You're definitely trying to unman me before I get inside you," he pants against my lips—a sure sign he's struggling to hold back. "Hold up."

He gets up off my bed and starts shuffling around in his jeans. The next second, he's tearing at a condom packet with his teeth.

Mmm, I would love to be that fuckin' packet right about now.

I watch this impressive man unroll the bright red condom down his huge, painfully hard cock, then he settles back between my legs, nudging his immense erection at my entrance. I can't help feeling like I'm the luckiest girl in the world right about now.

He takes both my hands in one of his gigantic ones, pinning them above my head. "I gotta have your hands up here, baby otherwise you're gonna make me bald before we're done tonight."

I can't help the giggle that escapes me, but it's swiftly cut off by a moan as Bear swivels his hips, grinding the head of his cock right onto my throbbing clit. He leans down and takes one of my engorged nipples into his mouth, sucking and nibbling it as he's grinding himself against me, making my body quake.

Before I know it, he's pushing inside of me inch by inch. He's slow at first, letting me adjust to his size and making me bite back a moan as my breath hitches.

"Fuck! Sweetheart, you're so tight! It musta been a long time, but you gotta relax your grip on me, babe!"

I wish I could, but his girth is huge inside of me.

He starts to pull out, nearly reaching right to his tip.

"God, you feel so good, Bear," I sigh.

In reply, he pushes himself back inside of me, making my hips lift off the bed of their own accord to meet his thrust and encourage him to push himself deep inside of me.

His gorgeous face has a look of deep concentration on it, and I know he's holding himself back from doing what he and I really want.

"Bear. Fuck me," I demand in a sultry voice.

"But Jenna…"

"No. Fuck me. Fuck. Me. Hard!"

He searches my eyes for uncertainty, but when he can't find any, he gives me a devilish smile and rears back, pulling out right to the tip of his throbbing cock, then slams back inside, right to the hilt.

"Fuuuck! Baby…you're so…tight! So perfect!"

I wrap my legs around his waist and hold onto his strong back, meeting his every thrust. I can feel the pressure building again, edging me closer to my release.

Bear's lips find the sensitive spot between behind my ear that sends tingles up my spine, making me twist my hips to rub my clit up against him.

He must know what I'm trying to do as his thumb finds my nub and swipes it over and over again, building my need as our fucking refuses to relent.

"Fuck me harder, Bear!" I cry out, digging my heels into his firm, delicious butt. He doesn't stop moving, fucking me with everything he has as I'm writhing underneath him, trembling and twisting as I meet his every movement…

"Ohh fuck. Beeeeaaarrr!"

He leans down and plucks one of my dusky nipples with his tongue, sucking it into his hot, wet mouth and nibbling it.

"I like that," I whisper in his ear.

His hair hangs over his shoulders, framing his handsome face like he's a dark angel.

"So good…" he groans as his movements start to become more urgent and jerkier. He's gotta be close too. "Sweet fuckin' God! So fuckin' good! Baby!"

I arch my back off the bed, pushing my breasts into his mouth more. I scream hoarsely as I come apart underneath this heart-stopping, leg-quaking man.

He grunts, and finally roars above me, cumming. I watch every muscle tense, making his strong face look even more handsome than before.

"Fuuuucccck...Jenna!"

Bear collapses onto me, and we both pant heavily, gasping for air. He rolls me over to rest on top of him whilst he's still inside of me, and the sting and feeling of being completely full are amazing.

I sigh contentedly, laying my head on his soft but strong chest and listening to his still-racing heart We lay there for what feels like hours, breathing hard; he really gave me a workout.

"Jesus, Jenna. You feel amazing, but I really should get up and get cleaned up so I can hold you...maybe have another round. What d'ya say, gorgeous?" he chuckles, winking at me mischievously.

"OK, big guy. I'm game, you've twisted my arm."

I roll to let him up so he can clean himself, and he gently pulls out of me, causing me to hiss from the stinging.

"Shit, sorry babe. I didn't realize you were so fuckin' ti...What the? Why the ever-loving fuck is there blood over the condom, Jenna?"

~ Chapter 6 Bear ~

"Jenna? Why is there blood over my condom?" I demand. I fuckin' know why, but I want her to say the words out loud. No wonder she was as tight as a fuckin' fist!

Her eyes are wide, and a look of pure terror and embarrassment covers her gorgeous crimson face as she nibbles on her bottom lip. "I…I…I am…*was*…a virgin," she stutters.

Her saying it out loud makes me feel like absolute shit. "FUCK! Why the fuck didn't you tell me, Jenna? Didn't you think I deserved to know I was taking your fuckin' virginity? I *fucked* you. I fucked you hard! Shit!"

I grab the back of my neck, gripping and tugging at my hair.

I can't look at her right now…it hurts to look at what I did. I pivot on my feet, go to her bathroom, and make quick work of disposing of the bloody condom, tying it up and quickly throwing it in the trash can. I grab one of her washcloths, rinsing it in hot water to clean her up.

I go back into her bedroom, finding her eyes still as wide as they were when I left her. She's pulled up her bed sheet around her beautiful breasts, and her eyes are watery and bloodshot as hell.

"Ah fuck, baby girl. I didn't mean to make ya cry. I'm just pissed you didn't tell me."

"Why? Do you regret it?" she whispers brokenly, sounding small and scared.

"Sweet Jesus, no! Never; but it should have been special. I should have taken you slow and gentle; it's everything you deserve, darlin'."

She just shakes her head at me, causing a fat tear to slide down her flushed cheek, then crawls cat-like to the end of the bed to get to me, the sheet falling away from her stunning body as she does.

I can see marks all over her flawless skin, and the sight makes me wince internally. There's a red rash between her thighs, and her breasts are covered with bite marks.

"What you gave me was perfect…"

"I fucked you *hard*, Jenna." I interrupt sharply. "You should have had flowers, candles, and all that kind of stuff."

She reaches up, grabbing the back of my neck and pulling me down to her eye level. "You listen to me, Bear. If I told you I was a virgin, you would have done exactly that, and I didn't want that. You would have gone slow and sweet on me when I wanted exactly what you gave me. I wanted to experience real, deep, dirty fucking, and you gave me exactly that. To me, *that* was perfect. I wouldn't change a damn thing."

What the fuck does a man say to that?

"Jesus, Jenna…" I grab the back of her neck, pressing my thumb underneath her jaw to lift it so her swollen lips meet mine. I capture her sweet lips and swallow her moans, our tongues tasting each other. Before I can help myself, I swipe my thumb up from her sweet hole to her swollen button, and she hisses out, making me pull away from her soaking centre.

"Shit, babe! Sorry, I just couldn't help myself."

"It's OK, big guy, I'm just still a little sore, that's all."

"Oh shit, I forgot! Lie back I'll take care of ya." I pick up the forgotten washcloth, head back into the bathroom, and run the hot water again to reheat it.

As I return back into Jenna's room, I see that she's propped on her elbows. She stares at me, then at the cloth in my hand.

"Just lay back baby, I may not have been able to go gentle with you for your first time, but I'm gonna look after you afterwards. Don't fight me on this, Jenna."

She gives me a sweet smile and a quick nod of the head.

"Good girl," I praise her, kissing the inside of her smooth calf. I'm careful to be gentle, wiping in between her legs and kissing as I go, working slowly and carefully. I keep my eyes locked on her all the time, watching her sigh and relax in my hold as I work.

"Bear…come back up here, sweetheart," she says when I'm done with the sexiest rasp in her voice.

I ain't saying no to this sexy siren—I don't think anyone in their right mind would call *me* 'sweetheart', but it sounds pretty damn perfect coming out of her mouth.

I crawl up to her on all fours. She's lying down with her hair fanned around her, the rose gold tone striking against her pale blue sheets. The light from the moon peeks through her bedroom blinds, casting an angelic glow over her stunning face.

I stare down at her, taking all her in. She's absolutely stunning. Her sparkling eyes dance with mischievousness, and as she licks her lips, I see she's trying to hide it from me, but I've had enough encounters to know the signs when a woman is turned on.

Something's different about Jenna. I don't know if it's because I just took her virginity like an animal, or that she's completely different to the women I am normally interested in, but the sight of her makes my breath hitch.

Her dusky pink nipples are still pebbled, and she's rubbing her thighs together. She looks a classic movie star, with curves in *all* the right places. There's a slight curve to her stomach that I find sexy as hell, and her thick thighs felt amazing wrapped around my waist when I was balls deep inside of her. She makes my fuckin' balls and dick ache at the same goddamn time...

Ahhh, fuck!

I feel her lips wrap around my dick, surprising me.

"Darlin'...fuck..." I throw my head back, my long hair tickling my bare back as I feel her take the tip of my dick inside her hot, wet mouth. She sucks me in little by little, pulling me deeper into her sweet mouth. It feels like fuckin' heaven, I ain't gonna lie.

I reckon it's the closest I'm gonna get to going to the real place with all the fuckin' shit I've done in my life.

Jenna brings me back to the here and now by licking the big vein on the underside of my cock. The little she-devil is fisting me tightly, trying to gain more momentum to take me deeper into her mouth. "Oh baby. Fuuuck! That's it. Right...like...that...darlin'."

Her motherfucking tongue is magic, making everything heightened. Her other palm starts rolling my heavy balls in her hand, then she gently runs her fingernail along the seam of my ball sack, sending an electric zing up my spine.

I thread my fingers through her thick, mussed-up hair and give it a good yank. "Fuck!"

She keeps licking, sucking more vigorously, and I push my dick further down her tight throat until I can hear gaggin'.

"Relax your throat, baby."

She does as I ask like a good little Cupcake, and I instantly feel every groove in her tongue against the base of my cock as she tries swallowing it whole like it's a fuckin' sausage.

Her teeth graze across my dick lightly— normally I hate a chick doing that shit to me, but fuck, it feels good...

The little minx leans back, still taking me all the way in her mouth. Her eyes don't leave mine as she starts rocking her hips, playing with herself and moaning without breaking eye contact. Her eyes shine brightly, a flush creeping down her neck.

"FUCK!"

If that isn't the sexiest thing I have ever witnessed a woman do...

"Jenna, I'm gonna cum! If you don't want it down your throat you need to pull off, babe."

The sexy bitch doesn't relent, determined to suck the cum right outta me. She has a devilish look in her eye, raising an eyebrow as she carries on sucking me and finger fucking herself while I watch.

"Yes, babe, fuck your pussy over me. Once you cum, I want you to put those fingers you've had deep inside that pretty little pussy into my mouth!"

She hums in agreement against my dick and sucks harder, tipping me over the fuckin' precipice with such force I feel my cum shooting into my naughty virgin's mouth.

I can't help the roar that escapes me. "FUCCCCCCK! JENNA! YES!!"

My Cupcake was definitely fuckin' right that I would be screaming her name. I bet Mrs. Montgomery is getting a hell of a lot more than she bargained for next door.

Like hell this is gonna be a one-time thing! Nah, that ain't how it's gonna go down if I can help it...

"I'll have a meat feast with sweet potato fries on the side, a Diet Coke, and…hmm, can I have a slice of your apple pie for afters too?"

I raise an eyebrow as Dani reels off her order—she and lil' peanut must be hungry.

"Babe, are you seriously gonna eat all of that? Good job it seems like only your boobs are getting bigger, and I bet Axey boy is lovin' that!" Zara giggles.

Poor Dani goes bright red, and we all laugh along. She does look amazing, wearing a gorgeous jade-green skater maternity dress that fits nicely under her growing bust and flows over her baby bump. She's forgone her leather cut with *'Property of Axe'* decorating the back, claiming it doesn't go well with what she's wearing, but I think it's more to do with the fact it won't go over her boobs. Her hair looks to be getting thicker and longer by the day, and she has a lovely glow to her skin—though she swears it's just sweat.

Zara is wearing her signature black vest top and skinny fitted jeans, a slight curl to her ivory-blond hair. She's started wearing it like that more and more since she and Flex got hot and heavy with each other—or should I say, when Flex decided to finally pull his head out of his ass? To say he gave Zara the run-around is putting it mildly, but since she told me why, I totally get it; I don't think many people wouldn't feel guilty about their wife's death if a rival club had something to do with it.

I'm so glad my girls have finally found who they were meant to be with; I can see their happiness in the way their eyes shine when they talk about their men.

"Don't listen to her, Dani," I pipe up as I scribble down her order, "she's just jealous of the gorgeousness that comes with being a curvy chick."

I stick my tongue out childishly at Zara, and she laughs. "Damn straight I am! I wish my little mosquito bites would grow, for fuck's sake!"

She grabs her chest dramatically, and I just shake my head. "You have *not* got mosquito bites, they're just smaller than mine and Dani's. Anyway, I'm sure Flex doesn't say shit about your boobs."

She rolls her eyes at me and smirks, "Fine, they aren't *exactly* mosquito bites, but they aren't as big as your or Lil' Momma's tatas."

"HA! Zara Hart, did you just call our boobs tatas? The last time I did that, I clearly remember you saying, and I quote 'What are we, in high school?'"

"Whatever, girl, I'm just trying not to cuss as much ready for when lil' peanut comes."

Zara turns from Dani back to me. "Jenna, can I order a Greek wrap with halloumi and a large Diet Coke?"

"Sure thang girls, I'll grab your drinks and be back in a minute." I leave my friends to it, knowing I will catch up with them properly soon.

As I make my way back over to behind the counter, my gaze hovers over at the bakery door and then the table that Bear favored over a week ago. I can't believe it's been a week since I gave that gorgeous man my virginity.

***

By the end of the night, we fall into a heap on my bed—I don't have the heart to ask him to leave after he's made me feel like a million dollars. His massive, enticing body is pressed up against my back, his huge arm slung low on my stomach an inch away from my pussy. I'm still sore and wet from all the times he made me cum before I basically begged him to fuck me again. He felt amazing inside me; my pussy is still fluttering from the invasion.

Everyone says your first time is perfect and magical, but let me tell ya, it's really not. Don't get me wrong, it was special because Bear gave me the proper experience, but it did fuckin' hurt—I can almost feel the sharp shooting pain of Bear entering me as I think about it.

Once the pain and soreness subsided, though, it felt so good—better than I ever thought my first time would. He took me again and again, first with his tongue and fingers, and then finally pulling a second orgasm out of me once he entered me. By that point, I was that far gone that he could have been doing anything to me; I just needed to cum.

"What am I changing my name to?" I hear Bear mumble against my neck.

"What?"

"You said we should ask the club to change my name. What would it be if not Bear?"

Oh, Lord…

"Nothin', it doesn't matter."

He nudges me, pressing his semi against my ass.

How the fudge can this man still get it up?

"Yes it does. It mattered that much that you brought it up earlier. Come on, darlin', tell me."

He's removed his head from my neck and is now propped up on his elbow. He has a hand under his head and is staring down at me.

God, he looks like Michaelangelo carved him out of marble. The moonlight shining through the bedroom window casts amazing shadows over his magnificent body.

This gorgeous man has just given me one of the best experiences of my life, so I am going to pull my big girl panties up and tell him.

"I think they should call you jam jar."

He sniggers. "Why the fuck should I be called that? Because of how heavy set I am?" he asks, a dirty grin spreading over his handsome face.

God, he's not gonna make this easy for me, is he?

I feel my face burning up as I mumble out my answer. Next thing I know, Bear jolts up and roars with laughter until tears are near enough streaming from his eyes. I can't help laughing along with him, the sound is infectious.

He stops laughing long enough to repeat what I just said before bursting into fresh peals of even harder laughter. "I should...be called jam jar...because…because of my GIRTH?!"

***

"You OK, sis? You're in la-la land again..."

Oh shit, I must have been daydreaming again! I need to stop doing that…

I'm staring at the drinks I've poured for the girls when Jade bumps my hip with hers again. She has a knowing look across her smug face, one eyebrow raised so high it's nearly touching the bakery ceiling.

"Yes, Jade, I am fine, just thinking about stuff. How's the display counter looking? Does it need restocking?" I ask, hoping to distract her. She knows I've been on edge for the past few days, unsure why I haven't seen Bear around. I know I wanted a one-time thing, but I still wanted to see him here.

I go to walk off to the girls when my sis says to my back, "Still not heard from him, huh? Just text the big lug! Ask him what he's been up to."

I spin around to face her. "It's fine, Jade. It was only a one-time thing; he doesn't owe me anything. Just leave it, 'kay?"

"OK, Sis, I just like him is all. Don't tell him that though, OK?"

I don't answer her as I continue to the girls' table with their drinks, trying not to think about him.

"Here you are, ladies. Where's…?"

I don't get to finish my question before I'm interrupted by Kelly storming through the bakery like a bat out of hell, gasping for breath.

"Oh my God, I'm so sorry girls! I got caught up in traffic, and then these two old ladies in front of me decided they wanted to walk so slowly a freaking tortoise could catch them up the whole way here! What did I miss, anything interesting?"

"Hey hon, you want a soda?" I ask the flushed, panting Kelly. She's looking stunning as per usual, her olive skin not needing a scrap of makeup and her thick wavy jet-black hair bouncing around her petite figure, stopping just above her 'big donkey booty', as she calls it.

"Oh hells yes, Jen! Can I have an extra-large one?"

As her big hazel eyes meet mine, I smile back at her. "Of course, hon. Hold up and I'll join y'all; just let me go grab your drink and take your order."

"Thanks, Jenna! I'll just have whatever Dani's having, please."

I go back up to the counter, grab an extra-large soda for Kelly and let Jade know to make double of Dani's order.

"Thanks, Sis. I'll be taking my break now, OK? Come get me if you need me, but I think Maggie should be in soon."

Maggie's my intern, and a little sweetie. She's 21, and curvy like me and Jade—we joke that she's our adopted blond little sis. Poor girl has an abusive drunk for a dad, and her Momma left when she was 3, but that's all we know about her real family. The only time I see happiness in her eyes is when she walks through my door and sees us. She's been working here for 3 months now, and all the regulars love her; she's like the bakery's little ray of sunshine.

I hope that one day she'll tell me her full story, but all I can do at the moment is to keep her close and make sure she's safe.

I get to the girls' table, place the drink in front of Kelly, and plop down next to her, opposite Dani and Zara. "What did I miss?"

Zara is first to speak up, shooting me a coy smile. "Oh, I was just telling the girls that you and Bear had some naughtiness the other day, and we were wondering if it's gonna continue?" she smirks, a little twinkle her eye.

My mouth drops open and I blink at her for a few seconds before squeaking, "What? How did you know? I never said…" The words have barely left my mouth when the realization hits me like a freight train.

Jade!

I turn my head, giving my sister dear the worst evil eye she ever saw.

She catches me looking and does a shy little wave as she winks at me.

"We will talk later," I mouth before turning back to the girls as Dani and Kelly squeal.

"Jenna, what the hell? When were you going to tell us?" Dani demands, her eyes wide as she grins like a Cheshire Cat, absently caressing her baby bump.

I debate my next words carefully. It's not that I don't trust my friends, I just don't want them getting their hopes up. "It doesn't matter. It was just a one-time thing, that's all. There's nothing to tell. So, how's work going?"

Dani shakes her head. "No you don't, missy. Your name isn't Zara Hart; I want answers."

"Hey! Meanie," Zara pouts, pulling a fake grumpy face.

"What? It's true, you're great at deflecting."

Dani looks from Zara back to me, learning over the table. "Anyway Jen, tell us the details, come on. It can't just be a one-time thing! Did he say something?"

"It is, hon. That was the way I wanted it, and Bear respected that. No, of course he didn't say anything; he was a perfect gentleman."

I'm met with silence. As I glance between my friends, their faces look stunned.

Kelly's eyes are wide, her mouth gaping open like she's a freaking fish. "A one-time thing? Are you serious? Girl, if it was me, I would be climbing Bear like a goddamn tree all night every night! That man is FINE!"

Kelly giggles, and we all laugh along with her. She's a sweetheart, if a little ditzy at times.

"Kel', I can't believe you! Yes, I'm serious; I wanted one time and that's what I got, but I will say this...I did climb Bear all night."

Squeals, screeches, and fits of giggling erupt around the table. Dani goes beet red, and Zara howls her head off, before gasping, "You go, girl! Are you sure Bear knows that, though?"

"Oh yeah, of course he does! He agreed to it, but I haven't heard from or seen him since to check we're still cool. I don't want it to change our friendship."

I stare down at the table, tracing circles on the plastic top.

Dani places her hand on mine across the table, making me look up. She has a small, sweet smile across her face, and her features are soft. "Honey, I think that ship sailed once you slept with him. These bikers go after what they want, and trust me, Bear wants you. He'll make it more than a one-time thing, that's for sure."

I let out a big sigh I didn't realize I was holding in. "Oh fudge! That's what I was afraid of...Don't get me wrong, I do like Bear...a lot...but I just don't want a relationship."

"Dani's right, sweetie. If you did climb Bear like a tree, trust me, *he will* be back for more," Zara says, waggling her eyebrows and shooting me a sly grin that instantly makes me feel guilty.

"Maybe you'll get your answer sooner than you thought," Kelly chimes in. Confused, I flick my eyes over to hers and follow her gaze to the bakery door.

There, standing in his leather cut with a freshly-trimmed beard, his shoulder length hair hanging loose and adding to his gorgeousness, is the man who makes my heart stop.

Bear.

~ Chapter 8 Bear ~

"Yo Bear, long time no see!" Tinhead yells from his usual spot behind the bar. I've been away at the chapter in Georgia for 4 days, trying to iron out the details for another 'green' shipment after losing Tiny— the Sergeant at Arms from the Alabama chapter—in an ambush at our last meet.

Axe has been nervous about there being bugs in other chapters ever since, so I agreed to take a trip down there with Brains to scan the whole of their clubhouse before Axe would talk to them—he insisted it needed to be over the phone; he didn't want to leave Dani for that long while she was pregnant.

I've been on the road for a whole day, and I am fuckin' beat, not to mention disconnected—I had to leave my personal phone at the club and use a burner while I was away in case of bugs.

"Yeah bud, good to see ya. I'm just gonna clean up, pour a drink for me, will ya?"

I need to have a hot shower, crash in my own bed, then see Jenna. It's been fuckin' hard not seeing of talking to her for so long, especially after our night together.

***

I'm sitting nursing my drink after my much-needed shower when Flex slaps me on the back, joining me at the bar and grabbing a bottle of Bud from Tin. "Bear, I heard you were back! You all good, brother? Axe wants a low-down on what you and Brains found; you got 10?"

"Yeah, sure thang. Once I've finished my beer, I'll join ya, then probably hit the hay; I'm flagging." That's an understatement; I could fall asleep on this bar right now—I'm barely holding my head up.

"Sure. We won't be long."

Flex knows me well enough to tell exactly when I'm tired and just want to unwind; I get quiet, which is usually his job. I've had to put up with his somber ass for years what with losing his wife and the whole turmoil over Zara. I'm sure it's only a matter of time before Flex asks her to be his Ol' Lady, but God knows how she put up with his moody ass long enough to make him see that he could move on after his wife dying.

That was tough to watch—I see Zara like a little sister, and Flex didn't make it easy for her, but I'm glad she didn't give up or let him get away with the shit he pulled.

Once I'm done with my beer, Flex and I walk into Axe's office, and he tells me Brains has already crashed, leaving it up to me to talk to the Prez. I ain't surprised, Brains hardly slept while we were at the other chapter's clubhouse. He's a creature of habit; he likes his own pillow and bed and needs everything in its place. I guess that's why he loves making and fixing computers so damn much; every little piece has a place and purpose in those too.

Me and Tinhead can relate to it much more than the rest of the brothers, what with Tinhead coming from an Army background and me living on the streets for years and loving the structure and hierarchy of the club. I needed the authority as a kid, and now I thrive on it.

Axe shuffles over to hug me. "Good to see ya back, Bear. I won't keep ya long, brother, I can see you're close to dropping. So how was everything at the chapter? Everything seem OK?"

"Yeah, I didn't see anything out of the ordinary except that most of their club is on the green. One of them was smoking it so hard I thought the skinny bastard was gonna turn into a spliff."

Axe slams a fist into his desk. "For fuck's sake! I had my suspicions, but what the fuck is wrong with them? What don't they understand about not gettin' high off your own supply?! Fuckin' hell, I'm gonna have to sit down with Grinder about this shit, stupid young punk. I don't want the cops sniffin' around them, it won't take long for them to link it back to us. There's always somethin' with this fuckin' club."

"I know brother, I know," Flex sighs. "Look, let's hit the hay. I gotta get back to Zara, and you have to see your Ol' Lady; we can catch up properly in the mornin'."

"Yeah, I guess you're right. Fuckin' hell, I didn't think I would see the day both of us settled down. When are ya gonna ask Zara to be *your* Ol' Lady? You not gonna lock that down?"

"What the fuck, Axe? Course I am, I'm just gettin' my shit together first. As soon as that cut goes on her, she and I are both gettin' inked, she just don't know it yet."

"Well I'll be, never thought I'd see the day!"

We're all glad Zara pulled Flex outta his funk, even if did take years. Him being a shell of his happy, cocky former self was so hard to watch; not only as a friend, but as a fellow human being.

"Prez, VP, we good? I can go over the details in the morning if you need," I suggest.

"Yeah, sure thing Bear, go get some shut eye. You look how I feel, and I bet you feel even worse!" Axe chuckles, slapping me on the shoulder.

I don't need to be told twice before I haul my big ass to bed.

***

The next day...

I slept like a baby, but I feel like I could sleep a hell of a lot more.

I wonder why they say that; ain't babies only meant to sleep a few hours at a time or some shit? I overheard Dani talking to Zara about it, telling her she'd read it in one of those stupid baby books. All I'm gonna say is they didn't have baby books in the cavemen days, and we all got here all right.

Once I'm up and dressed, Brains and I head into Axe's office to talk to Axe and Flex about all the finer details we saw while we were at the Georgia chapter. Needless to say, they weren't best pleased by most of it. Axe is goin' to reach out to the other surrounding chapters for advice—he doesn't know much about Georgia's new Prez.

***

I get back on my bike, loving the feel of freedom as I ride. I'll never tire of it; even when I'm 80. I'm free from all the years of being on the street and being called a street rat, scum, filth, and a junkie. I never felt free until I came into the club, but now the road is my playground. The wind whips around me, a welcome break from the warm, sticky, Tennessee air.

It's around 2pm by the time I pull up outside Jenna's bakery. I saw Kelly racing through the crowds on the sidewalk and rushing through the door on my way down here, which can only mean one thing—all the women are in there.

Fuck!

I wanted to catch her on her own to check she's not pissed that I haven't spoken to her for a week. I sit on my Fat Boy scanning the streets and sidewalks for a while, checking nothing is out of the ordinary, then debate going back to the clubhouse, but I shut down that thought as quickly as it comes.

Hell no! I want to see her.

I jump off my bike and pull off my lid, then yank the bakery door open. I'm instantly hit with warmth and the sweet smell of sugar mixed with the bitter aroma of coffee. The bakery is filled with the buzz of conversation and the low hum of the milk foamer on the coffee machine that I can see Jade working.

I scan the bakery like a homing beacon and quickly find Jenna sitting with all her girls surrounding her in one of the booths, Kelly leaning into and talking to her.

Kelly flicks her eyes over to me, making Jenna catch sight of me in the doorway, a look of pure surprise and shock spreading over her stunning face. She looks breathtakingly adorable, smiling from ear to ear with her hair up in a high, curly ponytail.

Her rosy cheeks flush as I stride over to where she is, not giving a fuck that the girls are there. To be honest, they're just blurred lines at the edge of my vision whenever Jenna is around.

As I finally get to her side of the booth, I can't help but smirk. "Hey Cupcake. Ya missed me?" My fingers are twitching with the need to touch her, so I caress her cheek with the back of my hand, making her shiver.

Jenna blushes harder, the pink tint reaching from her neck all the way up to her cheeks. With a slight nod of her head, she finally answers me, "Yeah, I guess so, big guy. Do ya want a drink? Something to eat?"

We continue to stare at each other, ignoring the girls until Zara yells loud enough for the whole damn bakery to hear.

"I SAID, Pooh Bear has got bear cub eyes for our girl! They're all huge and soft; too cute."

As Jenna bites back a snigger, I keep my gaze fixed on hers, not bothering to look at Zara. "Well I think Flex needs to spank ya ass a lot harder. Don't think we don't hear you screamin' and shoutin' his name!"

As the girls burst into giggles, Zara shrieks, "Oh God, the shame! I can't believe you, Bear! Seriously?!" and covers her bright red face with her hands.

I bite my lip to hide my shit-eating grin and nod at Jenna. "I'll take a black coffee and a slice of today's special, babe."

She reluctantly pulls out of my grasp and slides out of the booth. Now there's only a hair's breadth between us I can see her breathing hard and licking her lips.

"I'll just go grab them, Bear," she says breathily, walking away.

I wish I could sink my teeth into the round peachiness of her gorgeous ass; I bet it tastes as juicy as the rest of her...

Fuck!

Now is not the time or place to be thinking of Jenna's sweet pussy. I try to discreetly hide my semi as I stalk behind her like she's my prey, watching her slender back as she pours my drink and goes and grabs the special of the day, which she places in front of me with my coffee, trying to hide a mischievous grin.

I look down and see that the special is the girliest cake I've ever seen, a triple-layered red velvet cake with red sprinkles on top of the cream cheese frosting. I cautiously pick up what I swear is the smallest fork she has in the slabs of meat I call hands and dig it into the cake, holding the bite close to my face. My eyebrows are raised as high as my hairline, I'm fuckin' sure of it.

"Something amusing, Cupcake?" I ask, putting the bite of cake into my mouth and waiting for Jenna's response.

"Actually, big guy, I was thinking how funny it was that you came in and asked for the special today and not yesterday—which was an apple and cinnamon pie—or tomorrow—which is double chocolate brownies...Maybe it serves you right for near enough ghosting me." She says the last part in a hushed voice with pursed lips.

I rub her swollen ruby lips with the pad of my thumb as the sugary, creamy sweetness of the cake hits my tastebuds, bursting into the most incredible flavors.

"Mmm, now that's some good-tasting cake." I cup the back of Jenna's head to bring her closer to me, stroking her jaw with my thumb. "Like hell I been ghostin' ya; I've been outta state on club business. I decided to come back here and see if you want round two, because as much as I like your cake, darlin', I would much prefer to be eatin' something else... I can still feel your vise-like grip holdin' me while I do it..."

I hear her sharp intake of breath as I let my words sink in, and then I capture her juicy lips greedily. I've been needing them since I left her last week.

I nip at her bottom lip, demanding permission to her mouth, and in a moment, my tongue is dancing with hers. I can taste the sweetness and sunshine of her mouth, a flavor that's pure Jenna. As I reluctantly pull away from my goddess and her luscious lips, we are both breathing hard. The next thing we know, there's a chorus of whooping and whistling, making Jenna freeze. We both know it's Zara freakin' Hart and most probably Jade, Dani, and Kelly too.

"She's *your* friend," I chuckle against her lips before leaning back. "All right, I gotta go, babe. I have to get back and help Dagger with his bike, but I wanted to see you first."

She gives me a coy smile and a little nod of her head as I get up, and I can still see the blush covering her skin as I walk away.

"Cupcake!" I call over my shoulder, grinning, "I'll see ya tomorrow, same time, same place. Mrs. M will have somethin' else to listen at the wall for!"

With that, I'm out of the bakery door without a second glace—although I know that if I do look back, she will be blushing from the top of her cute little ears to her pretty feet.

~ Chapter 9 Jenna ~

Oh my God, I can't believe he just did that! It's bad enough we had a hot making out session over my counter in front of at least 20 people—including my sister and *all* my girls—but he also had to go and make that comment about my freakin' next door neighbor listening in!

I just stand there for a few seconds in shock, staring at the door, then flick my eyes over to my sister, who looks like she's humping the counter and has a cheesy grin on her stupid face. I look over to the rest of the girls to see that Dani is being typical Dani, blushing and giggling, Zara is wiggling her eyebrows up and down and grinning at me like a mad woman, and Kelly has pretended to faint, her mouth hanging open like she's trying to catch flies.

Yup, that's basically how I feel whenever I'm around Bear. Hold up, did he just say he'll see me same place, same time...TOMORROW?!

"Well, well, Sis, I don't think he did get the message about your little encounter being a one-time thing," Jade mumbles as she slides behind me to serve the next customer.

I walk back over to the girls in silence, plop down in my seat and lay my head on the table.

"Jenna...I don't think he's going to take no for an answer, sweetie," Dani whispers across from me, laying her hand over mine.

I let out what feels a huge breath. "I know, my sister said the same thing. If things were different and I met him in college, I would be there in a heartbeat, but, I just can't...*don't* want more. How do I tell him that? I don't want to crush him and lose him as a friend."

"I know, but Bear isn't like those frat boys, hon," Zara says gently once she's composed herself, her face softening. "He's experienced, older, and he won't play games. From what I've heard from Flex, he's been played himself, and I don't think he would do that to you. If he did, do ya really think we wouldn't call him out on that shit? Lil' Momma here would chew him out good."

I can't help the giggle that escapes me as I think of Dani givin' him hell. She confessed she was shy in front of the men when she first met them, but now she has Axe, she has an amazing strength and confidence that most girls would only wish for.

"I say you get back on that Bear and ride him long and hard, like you've never rode him before!" Kelly chimes in. "If he can't take no-strings, don't feel bad; he's a big man who can look after himself...and if not, I don't mind making him feel better."

I whip my head around in shock and laugh. "Only you, Kelly! You crazy-ass bitch!"

"I'm just saying, girl! Was it good?" she enquires with wide, curious eyes. She leans closer to me, still staring, and the other girls unconsciously do the same.

"Well...YES! I can't lie, even though he was my first, he was amazing—"

I don't get to finish my sentence before Zara is screaming at me across the table "WHAAAT?! Your first? You mean, *your first*, your first?!"

"For fudge sake, girl! I don't think the pastor in the church around the corner heard you! Yes. My first time."

I am yet again met with deathly silence until Dani finally speaks up, "Sweetie, are you serious? You gave your V-card to Bear?"

"Yeah, I did. It was everything I wanted...and much more." I reply in a soft voice.

Dani sighs sympathetically "Oh, honey. If it wasn't your V-card and just sex, I think it would be a lot easier, but he's a biker; if he's taken your virginity, he ain't gonna want any other man near you. Trust me, I thought Axe was bad, but Sue told me once that Bear reminds her of Doc, and he was really protective over her. He'll be your personal man repellent."

"Oh God, today's just full of revelations! Well, he knows the deal." I pull out my phone. "I'll just send him a message to remind him of what we agreed, and that will be that."

Me: - *Hey, you did remember our deal, didn't you?* x

"All right, I've texted him to get some answers, but I'd better get back to work. Do you girls need anything else?"

The girls shake their heads, but Zara puts a hand on my shoulder to stop me. "Jenna, if you need to talk, we're only a call away, but we really need a girls' night out soon."

"Yeah, sure thing hon. That would be great." Shooting her a grateful smile, I turn around to go back behind the counter when my phone buzzes in my hand.

Bear: - *Cupcake, what are ya talkin' about? Yeah, we said one time...but I didn't say how long that the one time will b. I'll see ya @ urs tomorrow. :P*

Oh, for God's sake...

Later, around 10:30pm...

I finally roll into the apartment after work exhausted. This afternoon was crazy busy; went so fast I didn't get a chance to reply to Bear earlier. I pull out my phone.

Me: - *Bear, you agreed one night was it; I told you why I couldn't do anymore. Can't we just be friends? X*

I stare at my text messaging app, willing him to respond. It says he's received it, but when nothing arrives after a minute, I decide to just lock my phone and grab a shower before bed. I fumble into my bathroom and am immediately swamped by memories of looking at Bear standing here in his birthday suit, tattoos running up and down his body like a second skin...

I briskly turn on my shower full blast, needing the scalding water to ease the ache in my muscles from a busy day at work, and step under it. Before long, my eyes are closed, and my head is propped against the tiles as the water cascades down my body and the image of Bear in all his glory pops into my mind again.

I feel the familiar tingle between my legs, and can't help squeezing my thighs together, which only increases the sensation. Everything about the man is like pure sex, from the way he walks to how he smells.

My hands have a mind of their own, and the left starts plucking at my painfully erect nipples as I imagine Bear standing between my legs, butt-naked.

His big hands are covered in ink, and I picture the bluebird covering his right hand, along with a big red heart and the word '*Trust*' written underneath it on a banner. I remember how the hand wrapped around his 'jam jar' and he stroked himself so vigorously it looked near enough painful.

My own right hand reaches between my legs at the gorgeous image of Bear between my thighs. Before I know it, my fingers are dripping, spearing me. My slick hole is still tight, but God it feels so good. My hips buck off the tiles as I bite back a moan. I'm panting, gasping, a shuddering wreck as I remember.

Bear's face in between my legs…

Bear kissing me passionately…

Bear plucking my nipples…

Bear's thick, juicy cock entering me for the first time, then again and again…

With that thought, I come undone, letting out a strangled moan. I'm unable to hold it in any longer and scream until my lungs burn.

"Aaaahhhhhh! Beeeaar!"

I flop back onto the tiles of my shower, shuddering from the aftershocks with my fingers still deep inside of me. I squeeze down on them and clench my thighs together, giving myself another orgasm, though it's smaller this time.

Spent, I pull myself up reluctantly and make quick work of washing the rest of my body, suddenly very aware I need my bed. I get out, hurriedly toweling my hair and body off as I step back into my bedroom.

I hear my phone ringing, then it cuts off. It restarts a few seconds later, and I check the clock sitting next to it on my nightstand.

11:30? Fuckin' hell, how long was I in there?

After a moment's hesitation, I rush over and answer the phone without checking the caller ID.

"Hello?" I ask breathlessly.

A familiar gruff, gritty voice comes over the speaker. "Cupcake? Everything OK?"

"Oh, Bear. Yeah, I've just been in the shower and ran to grab my phone, I didn't know who it was," I explain, blowing out a big breath I didn't know I was holding in.

Fudgin' hell, what is wrong with me? Here I am trying to play it cool as a cucumber to the hottest man ever, and I'm panting over the phone!

"Babe, hold up." I hear Bear walking and what sounds like him kicking a door shut, then he speaks. "You still there, Jenna?"

"Yeah. What's wrong?"

"I gotta know, babe, why the hell did ya answer the phone like you've just been fucked?"

"Oh my God, Bear! I did not!"

"Darlin', you sure did. You sounded exactly like you did after I took your virginity and you'd been screamin' my name all night," he growls out in a low rasp.

Just like that, I'm a big pool of goo again. I flop back on my bed with towels still wrapped around my head and body.

"Jenna, have you been fuckin' some other guy? Nah…I don't think that's it; you've not been home long." I hear the smile in his voice as he asks, "Come on, darlin', has someone been a bad girl?"

"No, and even if I had, why would I tell you? What do you mean I've not been home long, Bear? How do you know?!"

"Doesn't matter how I know, I just do. Now, lemme guess...you've just showered...aw, has Jenna been playin' with her muff pie? You can tell me, darlin', I can still taste ya on my tongue...Mmm—"

"Yes! I played with myself, OK? Are ya satisfied?" I snap. I can still feel my arousal, wet between my thighs.

God, if he was here...

"Darlin', I would come over, but I've been drinkin'," he says, reading my mind. "Fuck! I'm hard as steel thinkin' about it. What was that text about?"

"Don't worry about it. Which part, big guy? The part where I said you agreed to just one night? You *did*," I exhale in frustration.

"Jenna, like I said, I did say 'one time', but I didn't say how long it would be. You want it too, you even just admitted that you played with yourself in the shower...So what were ya thinkin' about, babe? You know you can tell me anythin'."

Realization hits, and I swallow hard.

Oh crap, I've never done this before! I did watch a lot of pornos in college, though...

Bear's gruff murmur interrupts my thoughts, which is just as well. "Were ya thinkin' about me takin' you deep and breakin' into your tight hole?"

I'm silent, and after a second, he groans. "*Fuck*, you were! That's why you won't say anythin', ain't it?"

"Maybe..." I say, feeling myself redden.

"Well fuck me sideways, darlin', I'm dying over here. I wanna be back in between those stunning legs again, and have them wrapped around my waist while I'm deep inside that pretty pussy."

I bite back the moan that's threatening to escape, but it does, and Bear growls.

"Ahh, fuck! Jenna..."

I hear rustling the on other end of the phone and clench my thighs back together. "Bear...what ya doin'?" I breathe.

"Darlin', I know you were a virgin, but you gotta know how fuckin' adorably innocent you are sometimes. What d'ya think I'm doin', sexy? Listen."

There's more rustling, followed by *thwack thwack thwack thwack*.

Bear takes a ragged breath. "Can you hear that? That's me jerking myself off, baby, all because of you. Fuck, tell me what you were thinkin' about in the shower."

"Mmm...I was thinking about you...about the other night and how you were with me...about you licking and sucking."

I hear another sharp intake of breath over the phone, followed by a guttural growl. "Fuck, Jenna...what else darlin'? Give me the details. Are you still wet?"

I hum, and then I don't know who responds, but she definitely isn't Jenna May Smith aged 26. "I was thinking about how you used your mouth and fingers on me that night, making my body come alive under your touch," I say huskily. I decide to get more comfortable and prop myself up on my pillows, peeling off my towels before I can chicken out.

I take a deep breath, and my fingers find my pussy again. My lips part, forming his name as my middle finger swipes my core. "Beaaaar..."

He must sense the shift in atmosphere on my end, because his next words are slow and deliberate. "Jenna, are you touchin' yourself for me? Dip a finger in for me, darlin'; tell me how it feels."

"I have already, and I'm dripping, Bear, it's so hot and wet. Oh God, I can practically feel you inside me. Ahh…"

"Yes, baby. Fuck that pretty little pussy. Know I'm the one who's been in there stretching you to fit only me. Imagine me pluckin' on those sexy nipples."

"Ahh, Bear! I've got my eyes closed and I'm imagining you in me…fuckin' me, filling, stretching and pounding me with your wide, thick, juicy cock. I hope you're strokin' it with those big, strong hands. Mmm, I wish I was suckin' you off right now Bear, you taste amazing. Do ya wanna know something?" I ask in a low voice. I keep fucking my fingers, feeling my orgasm building.

I can hear Bear struggling to control himself as he breathes into my ear. "Yeah, darlin', I'm fisting myself hard as fuck. Tell me, baby, give me somethin' to send me over the edge."

"I'm picturing you fuckin' me and then me takin' you deep in my mouth, right to the back of my throat. I'm imagining you making me choke on that thick cock as you fist my hair tightly, then cumming hard in my mouth…all over my tits, my stomach and my pussy, marking me as yours…"

"Fuuuccckk! Jesusss! Ahhhhhhh!"

Just like that, I have made the sexiest man ever cum so hard I think he's lost his voice. He's panting heavily down the phone, and the sound of his ragged breathing sends me over too.

"Ahhhhhh, Bearrr!"

My body flutters and contracts as I come apart, then we are both just listening to one another's breathing. I decide to tell Bear what's on my mind, choosing not to listen to the voice of reason in my head for once. This may make things a lot harder, but for once, I don't care. "Bear, I have to tell you something."

"What's that, darlin'? I don't think I have ever cum that hard with my hand before. All that about me markin' you with my cum...*fuck.* You need to hear this. I don't care how long you need, but one time can't be enough! It's not nearly enough, Cupcake."

"That was my first time having phone sex. I hear you, but I said..."

"Jenna, I know what you said, baby, but did you not just cum screamin' my name so loud that Mrs. M heard you? Are you tellin' me you don't want as much pleasure as you deserve, darlin'? You can't deny you want me..."

I mull over his words. He does make a good point, and he intrigues me more than any man has for as long as I can remember; I need more time to work him out.

"Bear, you sure are getting ahead of yourself over there. Just because you have a jam jar in your pants, don't try getting a matching swollen head, will ya? I can't do a relationship. What about...friends with benefits?"

I can't believe I just suggested that, but I didn't think I would be the type of girl to have phone sex or lose my virginity to a biker either.

Who knows anymore? Maybe I should listen to Jade more...Oh God, I must be losing my mind...

"Now you're talkin'! Let's just have some fun, no pressure on either end. I'm gonna come over after you shut up shop, OK? I need to crash; you wore me out, you sexy little beauty. See ya tomorrow night, darlin'."

"Night, Bear."

As we end the phone call, I can't stop the smile spreading across my face. I feel just like when Billy Johnson told me he liked me in 4th Grade.

I'm gonna try and channel Jade and my Momma; I can hear them saying, *"Stop thinking so much, Jenna! Go with it!'*

I just hope this doesn't explode in my face like last time...

~ Chapter 10 Bear ~

"No, I asked for no mayo! Jesus, pass me a knife, Jewel, I'll scrape this shit off myself."

Jewel tosses me one, and it skims the skin of my knuckles.

"Thanks, doll!" I shout, twisting back around in my seat to face the prospect.

"OK Tin, what were ya witterin' about?"

"I was sayin', did you tell Jenna that you asked us to watch over her last night?"

"Nah, I just told her I knew she got home late, that's all. Don't worry about that, I'll deal with the fall out."

Fuck, just thinkin' about us arguin' and then having hot angry make up sex has got me all hot under my cut.

I'm just biting into my three-meat sub when Axe comes into the kitchen with Flex, grabbing his own sub. It's back to club girl cooking now Dani has upped her hours at the ink shop, which the Prez isn't happy about.

No other woman would tell Axe Cole no—well, except maybe his Momma, but she's no longer around—but Dani stepped up to him and informed him that she wants to work for as long as she can. Dani is such a confident woman now Sue has showed her the ways of bein' the Ol' Lady, but when I first met her all those months ago, she could barely look me in the eye—she kept callin' me 'Mr. Bear', which was funny as hell.

"You all right, boss? VP?" I offer them both a hand slap and a pat on the back, and as we pull apart, Axe nods.

"Yeah Bear, all good. After lunch, we're gonna have church early."

"Sure thang, Prez. How're Dani and the baby gettin' on?"

"Fine, thanks."

Axe's face looks pretty tight, and early church means that whatever is going on, he ain't happy about it. I flick my eyes to Flex's and find the same look, and Flex confirms my thoughts by giving me a curt nod.

Fuck, I thought shit was going to settle down! I don't think we could take another hit after Dani bein' abducted and Flex finding out about his wife's killer!

We need a break right about now, but club life is never a walk in the park. It's hard, dark, and dirty, but I love the family tightness, and I live and breathe this club.

We all traipse into church, taking our seats at the huge wooden table. Axe sits at the head, Flex to his left, Dags to his right, me next to Flex, Brains next to Dagger, Doc next to me, and Wrench and Tinhead sit at the end of the table, not really having a place until they've been patched into the club.

Once we're settled, Axe slams his gavel down on the table to start church.

"So, I talked to Grinder and his VP, Hound. They *have* been using green, but he swears to me it's not the green we gave them to distribute. I'm unsure if he's lyin' or not, so I need some of you to go to the Georgia chapter to check it out for me. I would come, but I don't like to be away from Dani right now unless I really have to. Flex, Bear, are you down for going? Take one of the prospects with you. If you find out they *are* smokin' our supply, you shut that shit down and bring back whatever's left with you."

"When d'ya want us to leave, Prez?" I ask.

Fuck, please not tonight! I need to see Jenna!

"Tomorrow, first thing. Leaving here around 6 means you'll pull up to their club around 12. I need you to be there for as long as it takes to get some answers, OK?"

"Sure thang, boss," I reply, relieved.

Axe's brow furrows for a moment, then he speaks again. "Wrench, I need you here to check over all the bikes, vans, and cages with Manny. I want Tinhead going with Flex and Bear. All agreed?"

There are a chorus of 'Aye's, then Axe inquires, "Is there anything else anyone wants to bring up?"

After everyone says no, Axe hits the table with his gavel once more, ending church. As we all filter out, I hang back to chat to Axe and Flex, who are staring at me warily.

"Everythin' OK, brother?" Flex asks.

"Yeah, yeah, everything's good. I'll be at Jenna's tonight, so I will see ya back here in the mornin', ready to go."

I swivel on my heel, but only make it as far as the door when Axe replies, "Is this somethin' I should keep an eye on, Bear? Do you want me to get Doc or Wrench watchin' over her when you're gone?"

I turn back around and look back at them. From the smirk on his face, it's clear Flex already knew what I was gonna say.

Damn that Zara!

"Nah, she's all good. I'm sure Zara and Dani will check in on her, and she has a little sister."

"Ah, good. Is this all new? First I'm hearin' about it."

I can't help the big-ass grin on my face as I reply, "Yeah, it's all new. She's sayin' shit about only wanting a one-night stand, but that shit's gonna change tonight."

"What the fuck? Seriously? She don't look like the type to be wanting that. What's her story, Bear? She running from anyone?" Axe inquires, frown lines across his tanned face.

"Jeez, Prez! I don't think so. She digs her heels in when she's determined, that's for damn sure. It took some coaxing to even get her to go on a date with me. Nah, she ain't running from anyone but herself."

That seems to placate Axe, and after a minute, he gives me a small smile like he's in on a secret I don't know about and flicks his head to the door, signaling I can go.

I don't waste any time leaving the room, grabbing my lid, and jumping on my bike ready to go over to my Cupcake and her little muff pie.

As I do, I can't help but think on Axe's words—I know she ain't running from anything, but there is something I want to know. I need to crack the code that is Jenna.

***

I park my bike up behind the bakery, knowing I can check on it if I need to because Jenna's bedroom overlooks the back. The sticky hot humidity clings to my arms even at this time of night, and the smell of warm pavement blows in the air, but no matter how hot it gets in Tennessee, I wouldn't be anywhere else.

I check my cell and notice it's after 8pm, which means Jenna should have closed the bakery and be upstairs. I notice I have a missed call and three texts—one is from my cell provider, and one is from Flex, telling me to bring all the regular luggage for our trip; code for bringing all the normal gear we take for protection. Even though we're staying within the club, it's not unheard of for a chapter here and there to go rogue or make alliances elsewhere, and it's best to err on the side of caution.

The last text is from Zara under the name best suited for her:

Lil Troublemaker: - *Pooh Bear, don't you go hurtin' my girl now! I know what you're like with women, I've seen them all come and go. If you hurt her, I will spit in every scrap of food I make for the club. ;-D x*

What a fuckin' nut! That girl knows what buttons to press.
I just chuckle to myself and type out a quick reply:

Me: - *Like I said before Flex don't spank ya enuff. Speak later.*

Lil Troublemaker: - *Don't u worry Pooh Bear, he spanks me plenty! :P U don't seem awfully bothered by me spitting in your food…I can make pretty big loogies.*

Me: - *Not worried 'cause it's not gonna happen, I don't plan on ever hurtin' Jenna. C u soon.*

Lil Troublemaker: - *Aww Bear, ur too cute. Good, keep it that way x*

I send a quick message to Flex to remind him to spank Zara more or fill her hands and mouth with somethin'— it's what I would do to Jenna, that's for damn sure—then I knock on the black-and-chrome back door to the bakery and hear Jenna's heels clicking on the tiles on the other side, followed by her sweet, smooth-as-honey voice.

"Who is it?"

She doesn't even realize how sexy she sounds, but I have to adjust my damn dick like a horny punk-ass kid.

"Cupcake, it's me. Open up, darlin'."

I hear the clinking of metal as all the locks are undone, then the door opens slightly. I see that stunning gaze stare back at me for a second, until she relaxes and pulls the door wider to reveal her full gorgeous self, stepping aside to let me in.

As I step through the door, Jenna presses her back up against it to make room for both of us, and I lean into her soft, curvy body. I grab the lock behind her and start to lock up again, her beautiful eyes never leaving mine. As I finish locking the door, I lean down and run my nose up the column of her neck until I reach underneath her earlobe to place a small kiss there, nipping it with my teeth.

"Jenna, don't open this door again unless you know who it is for sure, OK darlin'? I'll get Wrench to come over in the morning to put in a peep hole." I feel her sigh and relax against me, and suddenly feel like I'm 100 feet tall.

"Don't worry, I will be more cautious. Promise," she whispers, her soft breath tickling against my neck.

"I know you will, darlin', but let me, OK? Call it peace of mind."

I lean back to gage her reaction and see the softness in her eyes even in the dim light. She licks her lips nervously. "OK, Bear. Thank you, that would be great."

I bend back down and kiss her soft forehead and just breathe in the sweet sugary scent that is all Jenna.

My lips still pressed against her head, she leans into my body and fists my black Devil's Reapers t-shirt tightly like she's worried I'm goin' somewhere.

Hell, no.

"That's my girl. Now let's go make this good girl dirty," I say softly. She shivers, and it's all the answer I need.

We stumble up the stairs to her apartment, me groping her like a horny virgin, and she tries to unlock the door, but her fingers shake so hard she can't put the key in the door.

I should help her out, but I'm too busy caressing her braless breasts through her thin bright pink vest top.

"Here, babe." As chivalry wins out, I reluctantly let go of her boobs, pop the key in the lock, and do the honors. With a turn of the key and a yank of the door handle, we push ourselves into her apartment.

I haven't even stepped through here yet and I can hear the tinkling of The White Buffalo playing softly in the background. The lights are down low, and candles shimmer around the room, making it warm and inviting. The warm, sweet smell of something baking in the kitchen fills the air. I flick my eyes back to Jenna, who's looking beautiful—breathtaking, even—yet nervous. The gentle yellow glow surrounds her standing in her cute as fuck PJs. Her perky nipples are pointing at me like headlights through her shirt, her bottoms cut off at her firm thighs.

"Cupcakes?" I ask with a smirk, trying to bite back a laugh, as I jerk a thumb back to the kitchen.

Jenna stares down at my hands...well, unless she's checkin' my dick out. It's pushed up against my zipper, and I swear the fucker is going to have teeth marks down it.

"What?" she squeaks, looking deep into my eyes. "I said, are you cooking cupcakes? Whatever it is smells so fucking good." I start to pretend to rub my stomach, pulling a sad face, which in turn makes her relax and giggle.

"No, not cupcakes, Bear. I'm trying a new pie recipe, mixing some fruits you wouldn't normally put together. You OK?"

She walks to the kitchen and grabs my cut outta my hands, hanging it off the back of the chrome-and-cherry-red barstool at the breakfast bar.

Jenna's taste is nothing like mine; she seems to make everything look pretty with a lot of color, but I would have this whole apartment covered in black, chrome, and leather. Simple. Jenna has cream walls with colorful paintings hanging on them; some of flowers, others landmarks in sunset or sunrise. There are pictures of her and her family, and one of her, Dani, and Zara from a night out at Ol' Jacks.

Her apartment door is a replica of the purple one in *Friends,* I remember her saying, and there are sweet orange flowers on her breakfast bar.

"Well, whatever it is, darlin', it smells incredible. It's making my mouth water, but not as much as you wearin' those itty-bitty pajamas, damn. Turn the oven off, I'm not hungry for pie anymore."

I readjust my cock, and her eyes flick to where my hand is, eyes bulging outta her head.

"Bear, the pie's got another 5 minutes before it's done," she tells me breathlessly, licking her plump rosy lips.

"Cupcake, you and I both know I can *do a lot* in 5 minutes, so let's not waste any more time standin' around."

I stalk up to my beauty and pull her up against my raging hard-on, wrapping my hand in her silky, wavy hair. It even smells of strawberries, good enough to eat.

Her breath hitches and one of her little hands finds the hem of my shirt. My dick throbs as soon as she lays one of her warm, soft hands on my stomach.

"Bear..."

I pick her up underneath her luscious butt and turn us around. "I know, darlin'. This is gonna be quick, jump up on the counter for me."

She does, and as if reading the dirty thoughts running through my head, she pushes down her PJ bottoms and leans back on her elbows, her head just missing her kitchen cabinets. She looks absolutely precious, but not at all like the innocent-looking Jenna I first met. No, this woman has definitely found her inner sex goddess, and I feel like beating my fists on my chest like a gorilla for being her first. Damn!

I instinctively drop to my knees, and as if reading my thoughts, she bites her bottom lip hard and then opens her stunning legs like a flower in springtime. I'm dying to get a taste of the sweetest nectar there is.

"Yes, Jenna, perfection," I growl, lowering my head.

I hear her soft moans and gasps each time I take a swipe at her sweet nub, and I just want to consume every single part of her.

I continue my onslaught on her pussy, and Jenna takes a strong hold on my hair—she's gonna rip it out by the root at this rate.

Shit!

Her moans and gasps are gettin' quicker now, and I can feel she's on the verge of exploding on my tongue. As long as I can hear my name, I'm happy.

I fill her with two of my fingers, going knuckle deep. As the beeper on her phone goes off, Jenna Smith temporarily deafens me from the orgasm ripping through her like a tornado.

Yup, tonight is definitely the night I am gonna get her to cut the bullcrap. I ain't giving up until she tells me exactly why she doesn't want a relationship—I don't buy her BS about being busy, not when she reacts to me like this.

Nah, even if I have to pull it outta her, she *is* gonna tell me.

"Oh my God, is it that good? Do you want another slice to make sure?" I can't believe Bear has eaten nearly half of the pie I made; I don't think I've ever seen anyone put away as much food as him! He's all man, nothing like the college jocks I used to like. Even with his mouth full, he's sexy as hell.

"Jenna, it's fucking delicious! You can't sell this pie, babe." he grins, making the creases near his eyes stand out, which in turn makes me melt inside. Together with the couple of crumbs in his long beard, it makes him look cute as hell. I want to tell him, but I don't think this big bad biker would appreciate being called cute.

"You just said it was delicious! Why can't I sell it in the bakery?"

Bear wipes down his face and beard, licking his lips to savor every last crumb. "Yeah, it fuckin' is. I don't want you selling it in the bakery because I want you to make this pie just for me." He leans back in my armchair, propping his foot up on his other knee, that gorgeous smile on his face again.

"Oh really?"

"Yes, really Jenna."

I roll my eyes and shake my head at his possessiveness. As I look back up into his big teddy bear eyes to tease him some more, there's a look in them I've not seen from him before, like he's observing me.

"What's up, Bear? Why are you looking at me like that?"

I watch him tap his finger against his lip, a look of curiosity in his eyes, "Cupcake, can I ask you somethin'?"

"Of course, what is it?"

"Look, I know it ain't my right to pry and all that, but I gotta know...ah, shit—"

I hold a hand up to interrupt him; it looks like he's in physical pain. "Bear, just say it, will ya? It's painful to watch you struggle."

He sighs heavily, running a hand through his hair. "Okay, babe. Look...I need to know what the deal is with not wanting more from what we have. What's the story, Jenna?"

I wasn't expecting that at all, and my heart sinks. I hate lying! One, I'm shit at it, and two, I hate the guilt. "I already told you, I'm too busy with the bakery. I can't do anything serious right now, I'm sorry."

"See, that's what I don't get, babe. The bakery is just as busy as it has been since I've known you. You're a crappy liar, too; you couldn't even look me in the eye! I could understand if the feelings weren't reciprocated, but I know that deep down, you like spending time with me," Bear says with a smug, cocky grin.

I go to correct him but find myself opening and closing my mouth like a fudgin' fish.

He leans over the arm of the chair until he's inches away from my face. One eyebrow is arched, challenging me to deny it.

Damn him!

"Yeah, so what? I enjoy your company, but that's it."

"*Bullshit*, Jenna! You don't realize you have a tell, do you? You nibble on your bottom lip every time you answer a question with a lie. I know you more than 'enjoy' my company, too; I doubt you moan and cum on command for Dani or Zara."

I choke on my sip of red wine, my neck and face reddening to match the contents of my glass. I can't help fidgeting nervously, shuffling my feet and quickly crossing my arms.

"Jenna, you ain't making yourself look any less guilty. Come on, just tell me what the real reason is; no more crap about being too busy."

My eyes drop guiltily from his face and stare at my fists in my lap as I try not to let the tears that are gathered in the corners of my eyes fall. I try to find my voice, but I can't seem to get the words out, even though I'm screaming them at Bear in my head.

Through blurred vision, I see a pair of black biker boots appear by my legs, and the next thing I know, Bear tips my chin up to look at him. I instinctively shut my eyes as quickly as possible, but that makes the tears that were threatening to escape run freely down my hot cheeks.

Bear settles himself next to me on my couch, wraps me up in his big arms, and shifts my body so I am sitting on his lap. My head is pressed against his thick chest, and I can hear his strong heartbeat. Bear grabs my soft gray blanket off the back of the couch and drapes it over me, cocooning us—it feels so good to be looked after like this.

I feel him rest his chin on top of my head, and he starts rubbing the back of my arm with his huge hand. "Jenna, darlin', please just trust me."

I think about my first time and look back down at the word '*Trust*' emblazoned on back of the hand that's holding me tightly, and it hits me that I already do. I take a deep breath in and decide to bite the bullet, even with tears still slowly dripping down my face.

"His name is Brent Johnson. He was the quarterback of the college football team—tall, tanned, and the guy all the girls wanted. It started with having to sit next to each other in class, then became what I thought was harmless flirting."

Bear sits up straighter, stiffening. I look up at him and see his nostrils are flared with aggression, his gaze hard as steel.

"It's OK, Bear. He didn't hurt me—well, not physically anyway. This isn't like Dani and her ex, I promise. Just listen, OK babe?" I place my palm gently over his cheek, his beard tickling my hand.

My touch makes Bear's eyes soften, and he nods gently and places a soft kiss on the inside of my wrist.

"As I was saying, he was flirting with me. There was this big summer dance coming up, and Brent talked about going—I said I would see him there. On the night of the dance, I was so excited. I had the cutest sunshine-yellow vintage dress with little white hearts on it, and I couldn't wait for Brent to see me in it. I got a ride with a few of my girlfriends, and when we arrived; the dance was in full swing, with everyone dancing around and strobe lights lighting up the whole hall. I scanned the crowd and saw Brent standing near the giant speakers next to the stage the band was playing on with a few guys from the football team and all the popular kids. I went up to talk to him, but he completely blanked me, so I left him to it. When the first slow dance came on, he walked up and asked me to dance with him. After we danced, I asked him why he had ignored me most of the night. He nodded to the corner where his friends were standing with a smug look on his face, and the football team and cheerleaders cut off the speakers..." My voice cracks and I trail off, fighting a fresh wave of tears.

"What happened, Jenna? Tell me so I can understand, please." Bear pulls my body tighter to him, and I gather up all my courage and strength. This is the first time I've told anyone in what has to be 7 years— he's the first person to know outside my immediate family. I let out a big breath before I continue.

"Loud enough for everyone to hear, he announced that he only talked to me and danced with me because he felt sorry for me, because, to quote him, 'Who the fuck would want to fuck you? You're a fat whale who will always be...'"

"A virgin!" Bear spits, finishing my sentence for me. "That fuckin' little prick! So that's why you won't take the chance on us? You can't still believe that shit, darlin'? Have you seen how gorgeous you are? You ain't a virgin anymore," he informs me with that mischievous grin I love so much.

I shake my head. "You don't mean that, you're just lying to make me feel better."

"Jenna, do ya really think I would do that shit to you? I love your body, it's sexy as hell." As if to prove his point, he lifts my shirt and starts kissing and licking his way down my boobs to my rounded stomach, pulling my PJ shorts down my body. "Mmm...absolute perfection. Gorgeous. Sexy. Sweet. Beautiful."

I moan softly under his lips. "Ah...I can't think about anything when you're doing that, Bear. This isn't fair! Of course I don't think that, but I need to protect myself...ahh! Do...you...get it?"

Suddenly, I'm on my back on my dark gray L-shaped couch, and Bear's wide shoulders are between my legs. I feel his beard rub against my thighs and pussy, and then he takes a few licks, lapping up the honey that's still there from our countertop fun.

"Fuuuck!" My clit is still so sensitive that I tug on Bear's hair from the roots, making him hiss.

"Easy, darlin'! Still sensitive, yeah? Grab my wallet off the floor."

Rolling over to reach it, I pass it to him, but not before getting a good sniff.

Mmm...

"What the hell? You sniffin' my wallet?"

"Yeah, I love the smell of leather," I smile shyly as I roll back to face him. It smells amazing. "You think I'm a bit kooky now, don't ya?"

He grabs a condom out of his wallet and tosses it back on the floor. "Yeah, you are, but that's one of the many reasons why I like you. Now spread those luscious legs again; I need to show you exactly how non-virgin you are now."

I oblige, my pussy quivering and pulsating for him and his 'jam jar'.

Bear drops his jeans and boxers. As they fall on the floor with a soft sigh, his cock bobs up and down on its own, near enough hypnotic. As he strokes himself, I lean on my elbows, fist his t-shirt in my hand, and yank him down between my legs.

I need him inside me. *Now!*

***

The clock on my nightstand reads 02:38, and I remember I'm in bed with Bear snuggled up behind me—he wore me out, the beast. One of his arms is slung over my stomach, the other under my pillow.

I still can't believe I told him about Brent fat-shaming me. I want to let Bear in, but I can't help the urge to just keep protecting myself, even though I know Bear would never do that to me.

"I can hear you thinkin' from here, darlin'. What're you thinkin' about?" His rough voice vibrates against the back of my neck, sending tingles up and down my body. I twist around to look at him so that I'm nose-to-nose with him.

"I'm just thinking about the fact that you're the first person I've told outside of my immediate family about what Brent did to me."

"Babe, you haven't gotta worry; I would never do that shit to you. Just thinkin' about what that fuckin' pussy did to you has got me raging mad. Does he still live around here?"

I can just make out Bear's nostrils flaring in the darkness, so I put my hand up to his face and lean into his burly chest "It's OK, big guy, things are better now."

I feel him relax under my touch, and he replies in a whisper. "I know, Cupcake. Kiss me, babe, I need your lips on me." He caresses my face, cupping the back of my head gently as his thumb brushes my jaw.

Who the fudge am I to deny the sexy-as-fuck man in my bed?

I push my naked body up against him, and my lips instantly find his in the dark.

His lips brush mine softly at first, but and soon we are eager and wanting more from one another. I tangle my tongue with his, and one of his hands glides down my back and takes ahold of my ass. He squeezes almost to the point of pain, but it feels so good it makes me tremble.

We break apart from each other's lips, gasping.

"Wow!" I exhale.

"Jenna, I know you only wanted one night, maybe friends with benefits, but I would love more with you, darlin'. Even our bodies fit together," he chuckles.

"You would bring your jam jar dick into it, wouldn't you?"

"Fuckin' hell, is that gonna stick around?" he asks.

I catch the slight insecurity in his voice, and suddenly I know exactly what he's asking. "I don't think I can put my all in just yet Bear. Can we take it slow, just see each other for a while?"

The next thing I know, I'm flat on my back and being eaten by my very own big Bear.

Fuckin' hell...

~ Chapter 12 Bear ~

"Motherfucker!" I bolt out of Jenna's bed like my ass is on fuckin' fire, then scramble around her room to grab my clothes and try and shove them on as quickly as possible.

Fuck, where are my boots?

"W-what's going on, Bear? Everything OK?"

My gaze flicks to the princess who just woke up after I've been spoonin' and kissin' her all night. She makes the cutest face when she's in a deep sleep—her button nose crinkles up. I can't get enough of her.

"Ah, shit! Babe, I didn't mean to wake ya up, but I need to get to the club. I forgot to tell ya last night—I gotta go to the Georgia chapter on club business, and I gotta be back at the club by 6. D'ya know where my boots are?"

She nods her head, sighs, and rolls outta bed, grabbing her bed sheet. I follow her into the living room.

"Found them, Bear, they're here!" she announces.

I sense something's up, and I don't think it's just because it's still early—she should be getting up soon to get the bakery ready.

"What's up, babe?" I pull her body so her back is flush with my front, leaning down to place a kiss on her shoulder as she leans into me.

"Nothin'."

"Come on, Jenna, be honest with me. What is it?"

She lets out a big sigh, looking at me nervously. "I don't want to mess you around, but I don't want to label this yet either. Can we just go on a few dates and keep getting to know one another?"

"Cupcake, we will go at your pace, OK?"

She just nods her head, her strawberry curls bouncing around her feather-soft shoulders. I turn her around so I can look into her eyes, then grab my boots off the floor, shoving my feet in them. I snatch my cut off the back of the kitchen stool quickly and lean down to give this gorgeous woman a kiss.

"We good, yeah?"

She bobs her head up and down, and I wrap my large hand in her tangled hair, stooping down to meet her lips. I suck on her bottom lip.

Mmm, even in the goddamn morning she still tastes as sweet as fuckin' honey.

I tweak her nipple through the bed sheet, making her yelp and giving me access to her mouth. My tongue dances with hers, both of us soon craving more. I quickly break away.

"I really am going to be late; Flex will have my ass. I don't know how long we're meant to be gone—Axe mentioned 4 days, but I'll message ya, OK darlin'?"

She nods breathlessly, "Yeah, of course, babe. Go."

I can't help but give her another quick kiss on those baby soft lips.

She's so beautiful…I am not gonna fuck this up.

With that, I'm on the road back to the clubhouse.

***

I can't stop replaying everythin' I found out over in my head. No wonder she wasn't up for a relationship straight away with that bastard abusing her trust. How the fuck could he do that in front of the whole school?

His words swim around my head, *'Who the fuck would want to fuck you? You're a fat whale who will always be a virgin!'*

I'm still raging as I pull up outside the clubhouse. I drove so fast I'm still early, so I head inside to grab a quick shower and the saddle bag for my bike.

***

After taking a quick hot shower and throwing on fresh clothes, I still have 15 minutes to spare before we gotta get going. I round the corner to the door I need and rap on it.

KNOCK, KNOCK.

The door eventually swings open to reveal a half-naked Brains with one eye open, squinting.

"What's up, bro?" he asks, yawning into his fist.

"Brains, can you do me a favor? Can you find everything you can on this name for me?" I pass him the slip of paper I have in my hand.

He glances down at it and nods. "Yeah, sure thang bud. You want standard or advanced?"

"Advanced, I want everything; his bank details, what he wipes his ass with, and what time he goes to bed. You feel me?"

Brains replies with the only answer I will accept, "Sure, Bear. I'll gather as much as I can and let ya know what I found when you're back from Georgia. Is that OK, or do you need it before?"

"Nah, unless there's something you think I should know about, keep it until after Georgia."

"Cool, cool. Catch ya later, OK?"

"Yeah, sure thang Brains. Thanks, bro."

I leave the clubhouse and find Flex and Tinhead saddling up their bikes. I walk over to them with my saddle bags in hand, ready to go.

"You OK, Bear? I see you turned up on time after your sleepover at Jenna's," Tinhead yells.

"You cheeky bastard, prospect! You'd better watch it, you ain't been patched in yet."

Tinhead grins. "Yeah, yeah; you all want me in the club, otherwise I would have been gone by now."

"You two finished arguing like two high-school girls and ready to get going? Sooner we get there, sooner we can get back," Flex calls, mounting his bike.

"Yeah, I'm ready to go, just give me a second," I say as I quickly attach my saddle bags, shove my lid onto my head, and sit on my baby, kicking up dust.

I text a message to Jenna:

Me: - *Hey Cupcake, forgot to say the club's got a big rally coming up in a few weeks, if ur up for it. We're just about to leave the club now, so will probably text when we get 2 Georgia. :) x*

Cupcake: - *Ooh that sounds fun! OK big guy, I'll come :) Ride safely babe. P.S. My bed sheets smell of u x*

I can't help the stupid smile that covers my face when I read her reply; she doesn't realize how much of a big part of my life she is already. I'll message her back once I'm in Georgia, or she'll never get up to open the bakery.

"You good?" Flex's voice says over the radio system built into our lids.

I nod in reply to him and rev the engine, feeling my baby rumble and vibrate between my thighs.

Ahhh…I fuckin' love my bike.

We pull out of the clubhouse gates as Wrench holds them open for us, and start the nearly 6-hour journey to Georgia. It's gonna be a long-ass ride, it's scorching hot—the heat is making waves on the tarmac already.

***

After 5-and-a-half hours of riding, the sweat is dripping down my back from the heat. We pull into the Georgia chapter clubhouse gates and are greeted by Killian; the prospect I met last time I was here.

He can't be much older than 21—23 at most. He's slim and tall, with hair so blond it's nearly white and pale blue eyes. He's lean too, a good little fighter from what I've seen of him. Hound, the VP, is Killian's uncle, but you wouldn't think it—Hound is as proud of him as any parent is of their child.

We park our bikes up and take our lids off, placing them on our handlebars, then Tin and I start walking over to the clubhouse doors. The Georgia chapter is a lot like ours, quite modern-looking, clean and neat—the club girls and Ol' Ladies must keep it like this; I doubt Grinder and Hound got time for that shit.

Grinder, the young president of the Georgia chapter, comes out to see us, shaking my hand. "*Hola, hermano*, you're back! Was your ride OK?" For someone who can't be older than 24, he's a cocky shit.

He's half-Mexican but born in these parts, and he's got a fat spliff on the edge of his lips, puffin' on it like the magic fuckin' dragon.

I quickly glance at Flex at the same time as he glances at me, and we share a look that says, *'Fuckin' hell, stupid kid'.*

He comes to a stop right in front of Flex like he's no-one—maybe because he's still sitting down on his bike.

Sure enough, he backs up as Flex swings his long legs off of his Sportster 1200 and straightens himself up. I can't help but smile. Just because my VP ain't as heavy as me don't mean he ain't scary; he's tall and menacing, especially when he stands up and spreads his legs in a power stance like he is now.

"Who are you, *hermano*? *¿Eres Hacha?*"

"No, he's not Axe. He's Flex, our VP. I take it you're Grinder?" Tin translates for us.

He just shrugs as Flex and I look at him with puzzled frowns. "A brother in the Army was Mexican, he taught me a lotta Spanish."

I nod. He might come in handy here, which is probably why Axe sent him.

Grinder nods and grins. "Come in, *hermanos*, I'll get Killian to get you all drinks."

"What are you drinking?" Grinder asks Flex as we walk, and I size him up.

Grinder's about 5'11" and has close-cropped black hair and a fairly close-shaven beard. He's got his cut on with a pale gray t-shirt underneath, and I can see what looks to be a full sleeve of tattoos on one arm and the bottom of a half-sleeve on the other. There are wooden beads hanging around his neck, and just looking at him is making me feel fuckin' old.

"We'll have three Buds. All of us need to use the bathroom, then we need to talk." Flex answers for us all, staring down at him. Grinder may be the Prez here, but Flex has years of knowledge that demand respect, and he knows it.

Grinder nods. "*Sí, hombre*. I'll wait at the bar for you."

He turns to me, "Bear, *hermano*, you know where the bathrooms are at."

***

After cleaning up and finishing our first Buds, we grab fresh ones and follow Grinder and Hound into Grinder's office. Looking at Hound, you would think we were separated at birth, being equally big motherfuckers, though his hair is red where mine is dark. It's a good job we didn't end up in the same chapter, or we would have been named Tweedle-Dum and Tweedle-Dee.

As we walk into the Prez's office, I notice it looks brand new; modern where ours has history, and there's a modern-looking club table—Axe's Dad had ours made. The room is nice, with clean white walls and black decorations, but the only sign it's in a Devil's Reapers clubhouse is the Devil's Reapers MC emblem printed on a huge banner above the desk.

"So, what are you here about, *hermanos*?" Grinder asks from his place at the head of the table.

Hound sits to his right, arms crossed across the wide chest his well-worn royal-blue t-shirt is stretched to fuck to cover. Meanwhile, Grinder has his feet propped up on the table, lounging back in his chair, the cocky little shit.

Flex steps forward, clearly determined to cut the bullshit, but talking in code to be safe. "I'm here representing Axe, my Prez. He sent me to tell you that you need to move the plants we sent you to pass on to your friends fast and stop keeping them for yourselves, or he wants them back." Flex's eyebrow is raised to the fuckin' ceilin' in challenge. It's clear that Prez or not, Grinder ain't showing he's loyal to the colors he's wearing, and my VP won't stand for that.

It takes a little while for the penny to drop, but when it does, Grinder takes his feet off the table with a thud and leans forward. "Fine. We were just testing them out for the customers. I gotta say, they are some *great* plants you got there. Once I pass them on, I will pass the coin back down to him, *¿bueno?*"

Flex glares at him, analyzing him, then nods. "Yeah, all good, but don't pull this shit again, or we won't give you any more plants, OK?"

"Yeah, I'm hearing you, Flex. Listen, as we have already opened a bag of the *plantas*, we can't exactly pass this batch on to our *clientes*. Why don't we finish the—?"

Flex cuts him off. "No. I don't think you're understanding me, Grinder. I get that you're new to the Prez position, but you've lived the club life since you were a kid. To help you out, I'm gonna tell ya this how this *is* going to go down. You *are* gonna give your customers the plants; whether you have used some of them or not, get it gone. If the pigs come and find them, you're gonna cost the whole club money. You get the plants out of here, and we'll get outta your hair once it's shifted. Filter the money down to us, OK?"

Grinder starts rubbing the back of his neck with his hand, and I know in my gut that he's not telling us the whole story.

What the fuck is he hiding?

A moment later, he answers my question. "Yeah…that's the thing, Flex. You see, there are no more plants for the customers, because we moved them onto other customers of *our own*."

~ Chapter 13 Jenna ~

I don't feel right, and I haven't for this past week—I think I'm coming down with a bug or something. I need to get the air-con cleaned again; it's been on constantly recently, and it might have bugs in it that are making me sick or something.

I drag my ass downstairs to help Jade with the customers; usually it's the other way around, but today I'm counting on her.

When she sees me, Jade rushes over. "Sis, what the heck are you doing down here? Get back upstairs, Maggie's coming in 5 minutes."

"I know, I know, but I can do something if it's not dealing with the food. I can do the register. Are *you* OK? You haven't got a tummy upset too, have you?"

"Jenna, for the love of God, get your ass back up to bed. We're fine; if I really need you, I will call you, OK?"

I give up—my little sister is forceful when she wants to be; Bear jokes stubbornness must run in the family.

I feel a sudden pang of longing for him—he's called when he can, but it's been days. He can't tell me much about what's going on, but I know it's something to do with the Georgia chapter. He's meant to be coming back this morning and said he would pop in, but I'll have to tell him not to.

"OK, OK, I'm going, but I will do the accounts, so there." I stick my tongue out at my sister and stomp back up the stairs.

"I'll be up around 11 to check in!" Jade calls after me.

Once I'm back in the apartment, I decide to make myself some ginger tea and grab a few crackers to nibble on, then lay back on my couch.

***

ZZZZ, ZZZZ, ZZZZ
Oh, what's that noise?

I peel my dry eyes open, realizing I must have fallen asleep. A touch of my cup tells me it can't have been for very long, my tea is still lukewarm. I take a long sip and sigh.

Mmm…

It feels like it's already helping. I might try and have a cup of peppermint after.

I unravel myself from the throw on my couch and grab my phone off the coffee table. Once I unlock it with my fingerprint, I see I have a missed call from Bear and 2 texts. I decide to open the texts first and call Bear back in a second.

Bear: - *Hey darlin', on the way back, will message ya when I can. B*

Bear: - *Babe, hope you're OK? We've just stopped for a break and sum food but will be back at the club in the next couple of hours. B*

Smiling at his concern, I tap out a quick reply:
Me: - *Hey big guy, sorry I missed your call, I've not been feeling well. I fell asleep on the couch, so I'm*

gonna get into bed. Hope you get back to the club safely x

I put my comfiest PJs on and snuggle deep into my bed, then my phone rings again. I grab it and see it's Bear again, and my spirits are lifted just by seeing his name on the screen.

I answer quickly, "Hi Bear, you OK?"

"Hey darlin'. Yeah, I'm good, are you? You sound sick." His gruff voice makes my body come alive; the sound goes straight to my little bud, driving me crazy.

"I've had a sickness bug for nearly a week. Every time I think it's going it comes back with a vengeance. I think I just need to sleep it off. You back at the club already?" I ask, trying to stifle the yawn I'm holding in.

"Nah, we had to stop again, Tin drank too much black coffee..."

As he trails off, I hear Tinhead shout, "It's not my fault the coffee they served was like gas!"

Bear and I chuckle together, but when he speaks again, his voice is full of concern. "Your sister isn't sick too, is she? Just take it easy, OK babe? Once we actually get our asses back to the club, I'll come over as soon as I can."

"Don't worry about me, Bear. I'm a big girl, I can look after myself."

"Jenna, I *do* worry. I know you can look after yourself, I've seen that with my own eyes, but I will still be over once I check in at the club. All right, I'd better get going; Pissy Pants Prospect is back."

He roars out a laugh at his own joke, making me giggle along with him.

"OK, speak to you soon."

As soon as I end the call, I can immediately feel my eyes getting heavy. I place my phone back on my bedside table and plonk my head on the pillow. I'm already beginning to feel light, weightless, even...

***

Much later...

What the fudge is that pure heat on my back?
I peek an eye open a crack to look at the clock on my bedside table and see it's 3:17pm. I go to roll over, but quickly realize I can't move thanks to what feels like a dead weight wrapped around my waist. I glance down and see a very familiar heavily tattooed burly arm, the hand tattooed with the word *'Trust'*. I swear it's trying to tell me something.

I notice he also has a tattoo on three of his knuckles; an anchor, a key, and a ship's wheel.

As much as love admiring this gorgeous man, I can't help but wriggle to stretch out my body.

"Darlin...you awake?" I hear Bear grumble into my neck, sending shivers through my ear and down my body, tickling me inside and out.

"Yeah, I am, what are you doing here?" I ask as I roll over into his arms and see the gorgeous face I've missed so much. "Hi," I say shyly.

"Hi yourself, beautiful." Bear reaches up and caresses my face in his big hand, running his thumb under my chin and tilting it up so we are eye-to-eye. "How are ya feelin', babe?"

"I feel a little better since my sleep, thanks. You don't have to be here, ya know."

He leans down so we are nose-to-nose and eye-to-eye, then places soft kisses on my forehead, nose, and lips, lingering on the latter. "Cupcake, I know I don't have to, but I want to be. Your sister's got the bakery under control, but I offered to get Tinhead to help. She didn't seem to go for the idea; she grumbled some shit about him being a player."

I can't help but just lean into him and roll deeper into his waiting arms.

Mmm, I love his aftershave and the smell of his leather cut.

"You still have your jeans on babe, why?"

"Darlin', I couldn't get in butt-naked now, could I? Or is that what my little Cupcake wanted? Missed me, have ya?" He jokes with a grin.

I blurt out the words in my head, making him stop in his tracks and grin proudly. "Yeah, I have."

I decide to lay back down on top of his t-shirt covered chest, sneaking my hand up under his shirt. His skin's so soft there, and his slight sprinkling of chest hair is downy as a baby's.

I wonder if he moisturizes…

I can't help the snigger that comes out of me at the thought.

"Somethin' funny, beautiful?" he asks, rubbing my shoulder with his thumb back and forth in the most hypnotic way.

"Um…I was just thinking about how soft your chest was…and wondering if you moisturize."

I start cracking up at my thoughts again, and Bear chuckles along with me. "Jenna, have I told you you're a nut? Fuckin' *moisturize*?!"

A long, comfortable silence passes between us. It feels comforting, and as safe as I always do with Bear. I know what other people think of him and the club, but he's like a big fluffy marshmallow inside. Yeah, he's covered in tattoos and has a big long beard, but I've never felt this comfortable around any man who isn't family.

"You OK, darlin'? You went real quiet then," he asks as he plays with my crazy-ass bed hair. I love when my hair is played with—it immediately relaxes me.

"Yeah, just enjoying you playing with my hair—it's nice, but I do need to get up in a minute."

"I know. I don't think I've ever done this before, you know," he replies, a hint of insecurity in his voice.

"What? Lay in bed with a girl? I thought I was the virgin, not the other way around!" I giggle, poking him in his rock-hard stomach.

"Ha-ha, the girl has jokes! Cheeky little cupcake, ain't ya darlin'?"

He tickles the back of my arms before his fingers dart to tickle under my armpits. "NO! Don't you dare! I hate to be tickled!"

"Oh damn, baby, you shouldn't have told me that," Bear chuckles lightly, continuing his onslaught.

I squeal, trying to roll away. "NO! NO, BEAR! Stop, please!" I ask, pleading with my eyes too.

He smiles down over me, his gorgeous dark hair hanging around us like a curtain. "OK, babe. Go freshen yourself up, I gotta get going soon—I need to get back to the club for church. You sure you're going to be OK?"

"Yeah, I'll be fine, don't worry. The bakery's been so busy I've been working extra hours; I'm just burnt out. Stop worrying, OK?"

I slide out of bed, and on the way to the bathroom, I glance over my shoulder at Bear sprawled out.

Damn, the man looks good anywhere! Clothes or no clothes, he's damn fine!

Just then, a more practical thought pops into my head, and I spin to face him. "Bear, how did you get into my apartment?"

He just lays there and smiles, his head propped up on the arm he has tucked behind his head. "Jade let me up. I told her I was comin' to look after you, and got major sister points for it, too."

I walk into my bathroom and shut the door, then shout through it, "And how did you look after me, exactly?"

"Well, darlin', I kept you warm as you slept, like your very own personal teddy bear. I've also put some of Sue's homemade chicken soup in your fridge, and I got ya some Reese's cups for when you're feelin' better too!" he bellows back while I wash my hands.

I swing the door open to see him standing at the end of my bed, shoving his thick arms into his cut. I stalk him slowly until we're toe-to-toe, then stand up on my tippy toes and tug on his thick beard, bringing his lips flush with mine. At that moment, my tummy problem dissolves and disappears, my tongue wraps around his, and I nibble on his bottom lip. When we part, he's breathless.

"Whoa, what was that for, babe? Whatever it was, I'll be sure to do more of it."

"Just being you, Bear. You're so sweet and lovely."

His eyes go wide in mock surprise and he shushes me with a finger. "Jenna! Don't go tellin' anyone that! I'm meant to be a big scary biker man, you know that."

"I know, but you don't scare me, Bear."

Well, not in the normal sense anyway...

***

Bear leaves to go back to the club, and about an hour and a half later Dani and Zara come over from the shop to check on me. We are all sitting in my living room drinking tea—although Dani has the decaf she hates so much, sipping it and making a face every few seconds.

"So, your sister tells us that Bear was over for a while...you must be feeling *much better* now?" Zara grins, waggling her eyebrows suggestively.

"He brought over chicken soup from Sue and my favorite candy…oh, and he got into bed with me while I was sleeping and started spooning me to keep me company."

Dani and Zara's eyes are near enough bulging out of their heads now.

"He *what*? Oh my God, that is too cute! He wanted to look after you! *I love* Sue's chicken soup; it's just amazing," Dani says with a smile that lights up her face.

"I know; I would have been completely freaked out if it was anyone else, but seeing Bear was just what I needed."

I tell them how I've been feeling, then Dani asks a weird question. "Babe, have you been peeing more than normal?"

I think on it for a second, then nod. "Yeah, but only for the past couple of days. Do you think I have a UTI? I can't seem to shift the stomach flu either."

"Have you got sensitive boobs too?" Dani asks warily.

"Yeah, but that's cause I'm due...FUCK! I'm late! I'm *never* late, girls! I'm like fucking clockwork!"

I can't be! We were careful; we used condoms!

"Calm down, Jenna! It's probably just stress because you've been so busy with the bakery, that can bring it on early or make it late sometimes. It's happened to me before," Zara says, wrapping her arm around me to comfort me.

"Well, hon, there is only one way to find out. Do you want me to go down the block and grab one from the drugstore?" Dani says from the other side of me, rubbing my back.

Zara smirks. "Dan, I think they'll send you straight to the prenatal vitamin aisle; it's not like you need more confirmation than your growing baby bump."

She gives me a quick hug. "I'll go. Don't worry, OK?"

I nod slowly. "Thanks, girls. What would I do without you?"

***

"He's literally going to hate me, isn't he?" I ask the girls sitting in my bedroom somberly as I pee on the stick.

God, I feel physically sick, but I don't know if that's because I'm nervous or I'm pregnant. Jeez!

"Jenna, Bear could never hate you, I've seen the way he looks at you with his big doe eyes. Just be honest with him; as they say on the boxes, those things don't work 100% of the time," Zara says as I come out of the bathroom after washing my hands.

Dani pats the middle of my bed, and I settle myself between them as we wait for the little window to change from the hourglass.

"This has to be the longest 3 minutes ever!"

I exhale a long breath, then start counting in my head.

1, 2, 3, 4, 5, 6, 7, 8, 9, 10, 11...

The alarm on my phone eventually beeps, and I go to grab the test out of the bathroom and come back into my bedroom without looking at it.

Both girls meet me at the bathroom door, looking at me like they're waiting for the lottery results. I slowly turn the stick over in my fist, and there in my hot, sweaty hand is the best, most life-changing result you could ever get...

I just hope I won't be the only person thinking that...

"I'm pregnant!"

"He's here, boss! Yo Bear, everything OK at Jenna's?" Flex calls as I roll through the clubhouse gates.

I pull off my lid and answer my VP, "Yeah, she's just sick, I think she has some kind of bug. I stayed with her until I knew she was OK. What's up?"

Flex nods, then sighs. "Axe has just got off the phone to Grinder. The situation's tricky—did you know Grinder and Hound are cousins on his Dad's side? It was Hound's Pops who was the previous Prez."

"Whoa! No, I didn't know that. What did Axe say?" I ask as we walk through the clubhouse doors.

"I don't know, but he started shouting for you—I think he's pissed. I don't know what's up with him today."

"That's not like him, bro." I reply, pushing down the handle of the office door.

I open it to see my Prez staring at his phone. "Prez, you wanted to see me? Is everything OK?"

Axe looks up at me. "Bear, come in, brother. It's a cluster fuck if I'm honest. Nothin' to do with you, just Grinder and Hound being sneaky. There's always something with this damn club. Both of you sit down, I've just messaged Dags to get in here too."

As Flex and I take our seats, I can't help my leg from bouncing up and down nervously.

"Fuck's sake Bear, can it, wouldja?" Flex snaps. He turns toward the door as Dagger comes swaggering in with a telltale bounce to his step.

Flex groans and turns away. "Jeez Dags, could you zip your dick up at least?" he chuckles as Dagger sits next to him at the table, readjusting his dick in his pants.

"What? Just 'cause you have it on tap with Zara don't mean the rest of us aren't allowed some fun! A man's gotta get his dick wet when he can, brother. I may be older than alla y'all, but I can still fuck like you young'uns."

We all roar with laughter at this, making Dagger look at us all warily. Dagger's a man of few words—some of the girls call him moody, scary, and intense—but I've always got on well with him. When he does talk, whatever he says is usually funny as fuck.

Axe clears his throat. "All right, now you're covered, Dags…" He shakes his head, smirking at Dagger. "So, you all know what went down with Grinder at the Georgia chapter. Well, I got back on the phone to him again, and I found out he and Hound are cousins, Hound's Pops being the previous Prez."

"Why is Grinder president? Couldn't he pass the gavel onto his own son?" Flex asks before I can.

"Apparently Hound doesn't want the gavel, even though he was meant to be next in line after his Pops stepped down."

Whoa, I definitely wasn't expecting that! That's unheard of in this club; we're all about tradition.

"Anyway," Axe goes on, "it turns out the customers he was telling you about were some big local dealers Grinder's Uncle Striker failed to hold up his end of an 'exchange' with when he was Prez. To keep them off his back, he had promised that the next time quality green came through the chapter, they would get it. Grinder fucked us over to keep his uncle's promise, but I told him we still need paying."

"What a fucking shitstorm! Have they got the cash to do it?" Flex asks Axe.

No way, that green was worth at least 10K!

As a grin as dirty as the ones he gives his Ol' Lady spreads across Axe's face, I realize just what they're gonna be paying in—and fuckin' hatin' it, too.

"Nope, but they will be paying in something they have plenty of..."

"Harley parts!" I bellow, laughin' my head off. "Fuckin' Harley parts!"

They're like gold dust with a skilled mechanic like Wrench, and while Grinder clearly doesn't know that, the others sitting around the table do.

"Prez, that's fuckin classic! A return fuck-over!" Dagger announces, a smirk that matches Axe's covering his face.

"Exactly! It'll teach him to fuck *us* over—just because we're in the same club don't mean I gotta like his stupid ass. When he calls back with an offer—which will be next to nothin'—I'm gonna mention that we know they have a lot of Harley wheels, mirrors, and seats, and we'll be taking them all for compensation. They can bring them with them when they come to the rally in 2 weeks' time."

"Fuckin' brilliant, boss! I know for a damn fact Wrench can get them cleaned, fixed, and sold on in no time. If there are too many for him to do on his own, we can rope Manny from the repair shop in to help him. Fuck yeah!" I declare.

"When are you supposed to hear from him?" Flex asks, a twinkle of mischief in his eyes.

"He's meant to be calling back by the end of this week. All being good, we'll easily double the money we would have got for the green."

Axe leans back in his chair, looking a lot more relaxed than he was when I came in—he musta just realized how good he's got it.

"You good now, Axe?" I smile.

"Yeah, now I know I've definitely got him by his little boy balls. Bear, how well do you know Hound?"

"Not too well, Prez; just that he's a man of few words, like Dagger. Doc might know more, or even your Pops."

He nods. "Yeah, no problem. I'll talk to Doc, then maybe reach out to Pops."

***

A week later...

We are all called into church around 2.30pm, and Axe tells us the first order of business is making a call to Grinder to find out why he hasn't called back with an offer, even though it's way past the deadline.

As we all sit around the table in our usual places, Axe puts his burner in the middle of the table, switches it to speaker, and dials. It rings out once, but when Axe tries again, Grinder's voice fills the office.

"Yo, who is it?"

"It's Axe. You forget something?" the Prez grinds out, stalking the length of the room and cracking each knuckle as he speaks.

There's a second of complete silence on the other end, then the sound of noisy breathing comes through the phone.

"Fuckin' hell, is this kid stupid or what?" I mutter to Dags, shaking my head.

"Look, Axe, I was meaning to..."

Axe slams a fist into the table loud enough for Grinder to hear, cutting him off. "Look, shithead, we might both be presidents, but you need to give me some goddamn respect, not pussy excuses!" he bellows, hunched over the table to yell into the phone.

"OK, OK!" Grinder replies quickly. "I ain't got the cash to give you for the green, all right? I know tha—"

"OK, you haven't got the money, but you still owe us, so how about this? You have a ton of old Harley parts in your warehouse out back, correct?"

"Y-yeah. What about 'em? Do you want some?" Grinder stutters.

Axe chuckles, then clears his throat. "Nah, I want it ALL! You're going to bring the seats, the mirrors, the handlebars—*every single thing* in that warehouse—with you to the rally next week. Deal?"

"Why do you want all that junk?" Grinder asks.

"That's no business of yours; just bring it all. You don't want me to have to come down there and collect it all, because I won't be leaving just with old parts!"

Axe slams his finger down on the end call button, cutting Grinder off before he can argue.

He'd better bring all the parts, otherwise I know we'll be going down there with several cages and the truck we keep out back for storage and long-haul journeys, probably taking the warehouse and some of their own bikes for the trouble…

***

Day of the rally...

It's been 2 weeks since I've been able to actually spend some time with Jenna—we've just been calling, texting, and video chatting. I've gone into the bakery when I could, and she's seemed better than the last time I saw her, but I couldn't spend much time with her—I've been too busy working with Wrench to get the club up to scratch. She says she's fine, but things have been so busy at the bakery I don't think she's stopped.

I pull out my phone and send her a quick message:

Me: - _Hey darlin', still up for comin to the rally this afternoon? Looking forward to seeing u. B_

Cupcake: - _Yeah, Zara n Dani have told me what to expect...What time does it start? Looking forward to seeing u 2 big guy x_

Me: - _What exactly did they say? Sometimes it can get rowdy, n u might see sum shit u aint used to, but we wait until all the kids are away from the club for that. Everyone should be getting here @ 3. B_

Cupcake: - _They said exactly that! OK, see u then x_

Around 12pm...

The sun is burnin' down on me and Wrench as we work like fuckin' dogs in the backyard; clearing all the weeds and dead shit, mowing the lawn and trying to make it look nice.

Dagger and Tinhead are over at the far end of the yard making new benches to replace the woodworm-infested ones we threw out this morning. Tinhead's working the bar again tonight—we've built one outside to make it easier for him and the club girl who will be helping out with drinks. He's gonna be busy; there are meant to be at least 4 chapters coming today, not including ours.

The sweat drips down my back, and I'm thankful I left my cut in my room before coming out. I grab the mower and start working on the last patch of uncut grass at the back of the club—I'm at it for at least 20 minutes in this blazing heat.

I wipe the sweat from my brow when I'm done; it's a good job the back of the clubhouse'll be shaded before the rally starts!

I look over and see Doc preparing to start the massive BBQ burner, and the thought of Sue's amazing homemade burgers makes me hungry as hell.

I stop the mower under the massive ash tree in the corner of the backyard long enough to take a huge swig of beer.

Ahh...OK, time to get back to it...

"You ready to go, Sis?"

Jade sweeps into my bedroom like a tornado, her black cotton cutoffs showing off her tanned, toned legs. She's paired them with a baby-blue shirt with flared sleeves that's tied at the bottom to show off her flat stomach, and she looks stunning.

"Nearly, hon. Can you grab my shoes?" I ask, pointing at the cream heeled espadrilles that match my flowy lace dress.

"Aw, I was hoping to wear those! Can I borrow your blue ones instead?" she asks batting her long eyelashes at me.

We'd normally argue over her stealing the contents of my closet, but since Jade found out I'm pregnant, she's been amazingly supportive. She was as shocked as me at first—so shocked I had to get her to breathe into a freaking paper bag after I told her— but now she's calmed down, she's just excited about being an aunt.

I haven't told my Momma, which I know I should've—although the first person I should have told is Bear, and he doesn't know yet either. This is not the kind of news you break over text, and I haven't gotten him alone yet...

"How ya feelin', babe?" Jade places my shoes at my feet, then drapes her arms around my neck from behind, watching me put the finishing touches to my makeup in the mirror of my vanity.

"I'm OK, just nervous as anything. I feel sick, but I don't think it's the baby...Oh God, Jade, what if he doesn't want it? I can't even deal with the stress of the bakery, let alone the thought of that..."

"Come on, deep breaths. Stop it, Sis. You only need to worry about that when *and if* the time comes, and please don't worry about the bakery. I'm going to take on more responsibility, and I'm sure Maggie would love a few extra hours. I invited her to come to the club with us, but she shut me down. She said she wants nothing to do with bikers."

"That's weird, Maggie's usually so meek and mild! I'll have to ask her why next time I see her. I get that Dagger and Bear look scary, but they aren't all like that," I reply as Jade fusses over my already pinned-up hair, messing with the strands I've left loose on purpose.

"Yeah, but some of them are man whores who think with their fuckin' dicks," she mumbles so quietly I barely hear her.

"What? What are you talking about, honey?" I wonder who has pissed off my little sis, but I know that whoever it is is one unlucky dude—my sister can get fiery when pissed off.

"Nothing Jenna, it doesn't matter. OK, are you ready to go? I'll grab the cakes, and you grab the cupcakes and pies."

She marches through my bedroom door into the kitchen, and I follow her once I have my shoes on and have applied one last coat of cherry-red lipstick, grabbing the massive cake containers before we head through the door.

On the way to the rally, Jade sings along to Miley on the radio to keep me distracted, but she starts grumbling to herself as we head down the dirt track leading to the clubhouse.

I turn to glance at her. "You OK? You seem annoyed about something."

"I don't know… I feel nervous for you, and I…just ain't keen on all the club members, that's all."

I slowly pull through the clubhouse gates, giving Tinhead a little wave as he walks past the car, but turn my attention back to the conversation as I hear Jade mutter something under her breath again. "OK…like who? Dagger? He looks scary, but I just think he's misunderstood. Besides, he's a fellow redhead, and we all gotta stick together."

"Yeah, I know. Anyway, have you thought anymore about what you are going to say to Bear?"

I haven't stopped worrying about what he might say or do, and I'm terrified he'll regret sleeping with me, but I play it cool. "I have a rough idea, I'm just nervous as hell about what he's going to say."

"Hey, are you sure you don't want me there with you? I promise I will keep my mouth shut and just be there for moral support."

I sigh, reach over the console, and squeeze her hand. "Thanks, JJ, I know you would, but it should just be us. Zara and Dani messaged me saying they will be inside when we get there, so don't worry, you can wait inside with them. You're new to the club, so they'll let the men know you're off limits."

I pull my baby-blue Beetle convertible, Vivi, up next to Zara's new Chevy, and we jump out of the car. I put Vivi's top down and carefully grab the pies and cupcakes. Jade carries a large red velvet cake and the double-layered peanut butter and chocolate one I made especially for Dani and her cravings.

I lock the car up, and we start taking a slow walk over to the clubhouse door when I hear a petrol mower behind the wall. I take a quick peek, and near enough drop the cupcakes and dozen pies in my hands into the dirt.

In the far corner of the backyard, Bear mows the lawn, stopping to slowly lift the bottom of his shirt to wipe the sweat off of his brow. The light bounces off the sweat on his gorgeous tattooed abs, glistening down the center of them and making the colors of his ink pop in the blazing heat.

Jesus, does *he have to make this harder?*

I know it's now or never, and turn back to Jade. "Sis, I'll see you inside—I'll come and find you once I've told him."

She looks around the wall at Bear and nods back to me in agreement, grabbing the container of cupcakes and balancing it on her arm like a true waitress. "OK, love you."

I slowly make my way over to the man himself. He still hasn't noticed me, so I get to really admire the stunning man I hope will be understanding. My eyes roam over his buff arms, taking in the exposed tattoos, noticing the massive red rose on the back of his left hand and the word *'Hope'* inked on his knuckles. It's like his tattoos are trying to communicate with me.

My stare flicks to the burst of color on his other arm, drinking in the gorgeous ship on his bicep. The muscle looks fit to burst out of his sleeve…

I come out of my trance as he stops the mower and sees me standing at the edge of the lawn.

"Jenna, you're here already! What time is it?" he asks as he rubs his grubby hands on his shirt, lifting it up slightly. I catch sight of the tattoo that stretches down his lower stomach, stopping just before his...

I shake my head to stop myself following that thought any further. "We came early because I need to talk to you. Can we go sit somewhere?" I ask softly, setting the cooler full of pies I'm carrying on the grass.

"Darlin', is everythin' OK?" Bear asks, coming over to stand in front of me.

I stare at his chest, trying to gather up enough strength to say what I know I need to say.

He tilts my chin up with a forefinger, forcing me to look deep into those dark brown eyes. The light bouncing off them gives the brown a honeyed golden sparkle I admire as I nibble nervously on my lip. He softly pries it out of my teeth, and his tender touch makes the dam break.

"I'm pregnant," I blurt.

Seconds pass, but he doesn't move an inch; he's frozen, unblinking.

My heart plummets.

Fuck, what if he doesn't want us?

"Bear? Are you OK? Did you hear what I said?" I ask him. I tentatively place my hand over his cheek and softly rub it with my thumb.

His eyes widen and start blinking rapidly, matching the frenzied pace of his shaky breathing.

I nervously lick my lips. "Hey big guy, did you hear what I said?"

His eyes finally look like someone turned the light back on in them, and they stare at me in shock. "*Pregnant?* But how? When? How long have you known?" he stutters.

I take his hand and start pulling him along. "Come on, let's go sit down."

We go to sit under the shade of the ash tree, and I lower myself into an old wicker chair Doc uses when he needs 'fresh air'.

"Should you be sitting in that? Hold up."

Before I can reply, Bear picks me up, one arm wrapped around my back and the other arm under the back of my legs. He sits down in the chair himself, and then places me carefully onto his lap.

OK, maybe this won't be so bad, that's one of the sweetest—and sexiest—things he's done for me.

"Are you done picking me up like a bag of flour?" I huff, grinning.

He chuckles, and his eyes never leave mine as the rapid-fire questions start again, "How? We were so careful; I don't get it."

My heart's beating faster than a fudgin' cheetah, but I hold his gaze. "You know they put on the back of the boxes, *'98% effective'*? Well it turns out we're that 2% that isn't." I let myself snuggle into his burly strong arms before I continue—I really don't want him to get upset at the next part I'm going to tell him. "To answer your other questions, I think it must have been my first time...and I've known for nearly 2 weeks. Please don't be mad at me," I wince.

The cutest little crinkle forms between his eyebrows. "2 weeks? Around the same time you were sick? Did you know then?" he asks, hurt written all over his handsome face.

"No...well, not exactly. When you came over, I did genuinely think I was sick, but after you left, Dani and Zara came to see me, and Dani started to ask all these questions..."

"And she would know what to look for, what with being pregnant and all," he murmurs, finishing my sentence.

"Exactly." I exhale, letting out a heavy sigh, and rub my sweaty palm down my dress, playing with the edges. I lean back into his hold and notice he's got his arm wrapped around my waist, possessively laying his hand on my tummy. I don't think he realizes how much hope the gesture fills me with.

"Why didn't you tell me all those times I came to see you?"

I look down guiltily, "I know I should have, but every time I tried either I clammed up scared or the bakery was too busy to step away to talk to you. I know that's no excuse, and I'm sorry I didn't tell you sooner."

"Darlin', you ain't got nothing to be sorry about. I get that you were scared, but you ain't got anything to be scared about, OK? I ain't disappearin'. You're not only the sexiest woman I ever laid eyes on, but you're carryin' my baby. I'm surprised as hell, and I don't know what the fuck to do, but I can tell you one thing—I will do everything in my power to make sure our child is loved, cared for, and safe...something I never got."

My eyes are brimming with tears that about to fall—that has to the most perfect thing he could have ever said, and it's exactly what I needed to hear.

"What the heck am I meant to say to that? That was so beautiful, Bear. I know we are still getting to know each other, but life seems to have other ideas about committing to you." I giggle softly as I wipe the tears from my wet cheeks. "To be honest, I thought you would be pissed at me."

"Babe, why would I be pissed? It's no one's fault, it's just one of those things. Like you said, we happened to be the 2%."

"W-we're OK then?" I ask, unable to keep the wariness I'm feeling from creeping into my voice.

"We are definitely more than good—I'm going to be a Daddy! If it's a girl, she ain't going out until she's at least 18!" He beams, and I don't think I have ever seen anyone smile so wide.

I lay my head back on his thick, muscular shoulder and close my eyes, filled with relief and enjoying the moment.

***

After a while, I open my eyes to see Bear staring down at my tummy, even though I know I'm not showing yet.

"What time is it, babe?" I ask, yawning my head off.

He checks his phone. "Shit, I better finish the lawn, darlin'; I still gotta get cleaned up."

"That's OK, I've gotta go put my pies inside—well, six of them. The rest are just for you," I can't stop the blush spreading over my face at the thought of his personal pies as I go to get up off the chair.

Bear pulls me back into his lap, grinning. "Oh no you don't, darlin'. I know that look; what pies have you made me?"

Damn him and damn my face!

"Nothing special; you'll just have to wait until later to try them. I'll keep them in their container and hide them in the kitchen cabinet."

"OK. I'll come catch up with you in a bit, OK? Be careful, darlin'."

I pick up the cooler of pies, and as I am walking towards the clubhouse door, Bear shouts at the top of his voice, "We can eat those in bed later!"

OH MY GOD!

I think I just might die of embarrassment as Wrench, Dagger, and Tinhead turn to stare at me and Bear.

Someone shoot me now!

~ Chapter 16 Bear ~

By around 5pm, the BBQ is in full swing. The drinks are flowing freely, and empty bottles are overflowing the garbage can by the temporary bar set up outside. Tin and Jewel are busy serving—and drinking, but I ain't gonna rat the prospect out, it's a rally for everyone.

I'm standing chatting to Dagger about bikes and wondering when the Georgia chapter are gonna turn up. As we sip on our beers, I can't help glancing over to the other side of the bar and watching Jenna drink a Coke. I'm trying not to overcrowd her, but I can't help it; it's like an invisible line tugs me across to her.

Right on cue, she turns around to catch me staring at her in that fuckin' gorgeous floaty dress that exposes her creamy, smooth shoulders. She looks like a princess. Nah, scrap that, she's more beautiful than a princess—she looks like a queen, and I'm sure as hell gonna treat her like one. I raise my eyebrows and give her my cockiest smile and a wink for good measure. She returns my smile with a coy one, making my damn heart miss a freakin' beat.

"Are ya hearing me, Bear? Do ya want another Bud?" Dagger slurs. He's had quite a few already; he may be slimmer than me, but he has me beat on holding his beer—he's pushin' 40.

I drain my bottle and shake my head. "Nah brother, I'm all good. Just gonna go check in with the Prez."

I decide I have left my little Cupcake on her own with her girls for too long, so I take off to get me some of that sugar. As I walk over, I overhear some of their conversation.

"So, he's happy?" Zara asks her.

"Of course he is, Zar'! what do you take Bear for? If I know him, he will be just like Axe," Dani replies before Jenna can answer.

"I guess, but I don't exactly what that means for *us*," Jenna admits.

I quicken my pace and interrupt her before she starts getting any fucked-up ideas in her head. "I'll tell you exactly what that means for us, Jenna Smith; it means I will be by your side every step of the way. I ain't going anywhere baby—wild horses would have to drag my ass away, and even then, I would claw my way back to you. You best stop thinkin' I ain't gonna be around," I try to swallow the lump in my throat, my arms crossed defensively as I look her straight in the eye.

"Bear...I was just saying I didn't know, neither of us do. What if we don't work out?"

"Jenna, you know I ain't into repeating myself, but I ain't going anywhere, OK? You know you can rely on me. I'm gonna support and care for both of you."

I hold Jenna's gaze, but hear sniffling to my right. Zara claps me on the back. "Shiiit, Pooh Bear, you're gonna make us *all* cry, not just Dani."

Neither Jenna nor I say anything at first, but then she wraps her arms around my neck, pulling my head down to rest against hers. When she speaks, it's in a whisper so soft that her breath tickles my face, "Now you listen here, Bear Jameson. If you mean all those amazing things you just said, our child and I are going to be so lucky to have you in our lives. I'm sorry if I made you think I wouldn't have any faith in us. I can't help having walls around my heart, but I hope you know that they are slowly coming down... just for you."

Her lips are so painfully close to mine that electricity crackles between our bodies as I lean in and capture them, pulling her luscious body into mine.

Mmm, fuckin' perfection.

As our tongues wrap together, the taste of my Cupcake takes over my mouth, sinking into my taste buds as she relaxes into my arms.

Like fuckin' hell I'm goin' elsewhere. We may have only slept together a handful of times, but I already know there's nowhere else I would rather be. This woman, our child, and my club are all I need.

"Bear, you haven't told anyone about me being pregnant yet, have ya?" Jenna asks into my chest as I hold her close to my heart.

"Nah, darlin', and I ain't gonna say anythin' until we decide to tell everyone together. Are the girls gonna keep quiet to Axe and Flex too?"

"I think so, I did say that I wanted to wait until the first scan to tell people."

"Good. I think you should tell your Ma that she's gonna be a Gam-Gam, though," I chuckle, making her grumble into my shirt.

"I know you're right, big guy, but you haven't met my Momma."

***

After checking in with Axe and letting him know there's still no sign of the Georgia chapter, I'm chatting to Doc at the BBQ burner, practically drooling over the smokiness of Sue's burgers as they cook. My whole mouth fills with saliva, but it's not just the meat making me hungry. Every time I look back at Jenna in that white dress, the light breeze lifts the edges, giving me a glimpse of her thick thighs. I quickly shake off the thought of running my large hands up the back of his thighs and letting my tongue delve back into that sweet-as-honey pussy.

"I'll catch you in a bit, Doc. You better save me 2 double cheeseburgers, and throw in a hot dog too," I say, slapping him on the back.

"Sure thang, son. I'll keep 'em warm for ya," he replies, not looking up from flippin' burgers.

I stride over to where Axe and Flex talk to Red, the VP of the Missouri chapter. He's half Native American, so his name's ironic but he loves it. A red bandana covers the front of the ink black hair hanging down his back.

As I reach them, I hear the roar of bikes in the distance. Catching Axe's eye, I nod to the gates out front.

He clocks my movement, excuses himself, and meets me as I go. We walk around the corner to the front together.

"I was just about to come over and ask you if you'd heard from the Georgia chapter yet, but it sounds like they're already here," I say.

Axe flanks me, and Flex falls into step on the other side. I pull back a notch to let Axe take the lead.

"Yeah, I was wonderin' if they were ever going to turn the fuck up. Tin!" Axe yells, turning to face him, "Get Wrench!"

As the bikes come rumbling down the dusty dirt track towards the clubhouse, I'm hoping to hell they have brought a van, or a cage at least.

We see Grinder roll through the gates as Wrench and Tin come and meet us. Next is Hound, followed by Beef, the Enforcer—he's so fuckin' huge he rides a trike, because the last bike he had, he left a huge dent on the tank. Bullet, the Sergeant at Arms, rides next to him on his matte Fat Boy. Spud follows them in—he's gotta be older than Doc, I swear that guy is like freakin' Santa! He's never gonna die, but if he does, he always says it will be on his 'baby'; his vintage black 1960s Harley. Killian pulls up behind him on his 1988 Softail, along with an oldish dude who also rides a vintage Harley. It's not as old as Spud's, but still in mint condition. The spray job is beautiful—a dark scarlet. The rider has a lid and shades on, but I can see he has a long ginger beard that's graying.

I wonder if this is Hound's old man?

He hasn't got a cut, but the old club members who are loyal still get to come to the rally.

The next thing we see pull through is a blacked-out van with dirt and dust sprayed all over it that parks up next to Grinder's bike.

"Thank fuck, looks like they listened," I grumble to Axe and Flex, who are standing in front of me now.

"*Hermano*, it looks like the party is in full swing already." Grinder announces as he jumps off his bike, striding towards us with Hound following suit and the rest of the club following close behind.

"We couldn't wait for you to turn up, Grinder. I see you listened to my request—come and join the party, and Wrench will check over the merch with Dagger,"

Axe flicks his head, and I follow him, Grinder, Hound and Flex with Tin and Brains next to me and the rest of the chapter behind us.

"The other chapters are here already. Follow me and I'll introduce you to my Ol' Lady," Axe can't help boasting.

Seeing the pride on his face, I can't wait until I can tell people we are expecting. I follow them into the backyard and go straight up to Jenna, wrapping my arm around her waist and pulling her back flush up against my front. As I lightly place the softest of kisses on the back of her neck, her sweet smell washes over me in waves. It relaxes me as instantly as ocean spray cools hot skin on a summer's day, and I drink it in.

"Mmm, Cupcake, did I ever tell you how much I fuckin' love your perfume?" I whisper, my breath tickling her skin and sending goosebumps down her neck and the back of her arms.

She leans into my body, knowing I've got her. "I'm not wearing any perfume," she sighs against me, and I look up over her shoulder and see the other girls and Jade looking over at us.

"Well that would figure, I already know you smell fuckin' divine all on your own. You're so soft and smooth and flawless, it's like you have virgin skin. Well, I guess you do; you haven't got any ink." I place a kiss against the side of her neck, which she instantly reacts to by tilting her head more so I can get at it better.

"Hmm...I may have 'virgin skin' when it comes to ink for now, but it's not flawless—I've burnt and cut myself while baking more times than I can count," she says softly, moving her head to rest as close as she can to my shoulder. The soft glow of the sun illuminates her as she does, making all the different shades of red in her hair shimmer.

I rub up and down her forearm with my free hand and link our fingers. "Darlin', ink would look hot as hell on you, but you gotta wait 9 months. Plenty of time to decide what you want," I whisper into her ear, making her shiver.

Sexy minx…

My eyes drift over to Doc, who's standing at the burner with his spatula in midair, about to flip the burger that's on it, but frozen like he just saw a ghost. His eyes are practically poppin' outta his head as he locks eyes with me, then looks back around the corner of the clubhouse. As the figure steps into the yard, it's like my whole world tilts, and my arms fall away from Jenna.

Standing in front of me is an older guy, but that's not what has my stomach falling out, and nor is the long as fuck graying beard. No, it's the fact I feel like I'm looking into the fucking mirror 30 years from now!

The man in front of me is a dead ringer for me…and I have never seen him in my life.

"Bear, who's that?" I ask warily. The man in front of me looks exactly like Bear, but he never mentioned any family beyond the club. The man has Bear's eyes—and love of tattoos, going by his highly-decorated hands.

Bear is as stiff as a board against me, and his usually tight hold of me has gone—his arms are flopped down by his sides. "Darlin', I don't know, but I intend to find out. Are you OK if I go and see what the fuck is going on? This better not be someone's idea of a sick joke," he grumbles, his nostrils flared angrily.

"Yeah, go. Just come find me after, OK? I won't leave until I've seen you."

He looks reluctant to leave as he unlinks our fingers.

I look him dead in the eye, needing the conviction in my voice as much as he does. "I promise, OK?"

He waits, his huge brown eyes searching mine for uncertainty. Finding none, he nods and walks off in the direction of his older doppelganger. Despite my worry, I admire his wide, strong back and gorgeous taut butt as he walks away to confront the man. Within a minute or two, I can tell by Doc's face that things may be getting heated already. I see Sue elbow him to go over and help Bear, then she walks over to me.

Oh God, I wish I could give him the support he needs, but this is for him to deal with—something tells me he isn't going to like the man's answers, though.

"Sweetheart, try not to worry about them. One thing about these biker men of ours is that when they're pissed and need to sort shit out, they get straight to it; usually with their fists. Come on, let's get ya something to eat and a fresh drink." Sue says, wrapping her arms around my shoulders and guiding me to Doc's burner, where she serves me a big well-done burger, some corn, a hunk of cornbread, and her homemade mac 'n cheese—it's like a big hug on a plate.

"Here ya go, darlin'. You can sit down in my chair next to the girls, seeing as I've taken over Doc's duties."

"Aw, thanks Sue. This all looks delicious!" I call over my shoulder as I walk off to sit next to Zara. Settling into my seat, I look around the rest of the backyard.

Everyone's spaced out, mixing with different chapters. The club members and their families are a mix of different races, sizes, and ages—the youngest being 4-year-old Trixie, who is the daughter of Red, the VP to the Missouri chapter. She's cute, and gorgeous, with cocoa skin and the thickest black hair you ever saw. Then there's Cole, Tank's youngest, who is busy trying to steal some of his Pops' beer—a typical teenager. Even though the members are diverse, it's like a big family gathering, everyone connected by their love of their club.

"You OK, Jen? You look like you're off in your own world again," Dani says, sitting opposite me and rubbing her growing baby bump.

"Yeah hon, just people-watching."

"Yeah, there's a lot to take in, isn't there? It's mine and Zara's first rally too. Like I said earlier, Axe did warn me it can get rowdy once the little'uns are put to bed."

I turn to ask Sue what exactly 'rowdy' might mean, but before I can, Trixie comes running up to her, wrapping her little arms around her legs.

"Hey S-sue, can I have a booger? Wit' lots-s of sauc-ce?" she says in the cutest little lisp.

"Trixie, what do we say when we ask for something?" Sue asks gently, stooping to Trixie's height.

"Umm…can I have a booger? Wit' lots-s of sauc-ce, now?"

Sue tries to hide her smirk by pursing her lips, and me and Dani look at each other and mouth, '*so cute!'*

"No, we say please, you know that. If you say please, I will get you a burger with lots of sauce and maybe some fries to go with it."

"Umm, 'kay. S-sue, can I have a booger, pwease?"

"Of course you can, darlin'! Now, you go sit over there with Dani—she's real nice, you met her earlier. I'll bring it over, OK?"

Trixie practically sprints over to Dani's side and climbs up beside her in the spot Dani has shuffled over to give her. "Hi Dani, my name's Trixie! My Daddy is over there. Where's your Daddy?"

Dani shoots me a pained look, and I shake my head and chuckle softly—only kids can get away with such things.

"Hi Trixie, you have a lovely name! My Daddy isn't here," Dani says, her voice dropping to a dramatic whisper, "but can I tell you something?"

"Yeahh! Sure fang, Dani," Trixie replies. Her eyes are wide as she waits on tenterhooks for Dani to divulge.

"I'm having a baby! Your Uncle Axe is going to be a Daddy too."

Trixie's face lights up like a Christmas tree. "WOW! That's so cool! When is your baby coming?"

"Oh, not for a little while yet sweetie."

"Ohh, OK," she nods slowly.

"What about you? Are you havin' a baby with Unky Axe?" she asks, pointing her little forefinger at me.

"No sweetie, I'm not."

"What about you?" she asks Zara, who practically chokes on her double JD and coke. She coughs and splutters, her face screwed up in disgust.

"*Hell* no, I'm not! I'm with your Uncle Flex."

"Oh, OK...s-s-so are you having Unky Flex's baby?"

Zara's face is a picture of pure shock. "Um, no Trixie. I'm not," she responds, flustered.

"Why not? You not like him? I think he's bery pwetty."

The four of us burst into giggles at her confused expression—Trixie is definitely a little cutie.

"Hey Trix, what's that you got in your pocket?" Jade pipes up. She's been quiet since we arrived, which is completely not like her.

"W-what do ya mean, in my pocket?" Trixie starts feeling around in her dress pockets and pulls out a little bar of candy Jade snuck in there when she was talking to Zara. She beams from ear to ear, and so do we—it's totally infectious.

"Fanks...what's your name?"

"It's Jade. Guess what, Trix?" Jade grins, pointing at me. "You see that girl there? Her name is Jenna, and she bakes cakes, cookies, pies...everything yummy you can think of."

Trixie's eyes grow as big as the cookies I make, and she swivels her head around to face me like a cute little owl. "Wow, that's-s cool! Have ya got any cookies-s now? I love cookies-s, they are my fav...fav...my bestest."

I instantly beam at this gorgeous little biker princess, suddenly filled with love for the baby growing inside me who could be our own. "No, Trixie, I don't, but if your Momma or Daddy says it's OK, we can go get you a little somethin' from inside. What d'ya think to that?"

"I don't have a Momma, but my Daddy is all I need! I'll just go ask him."

Before I can ask what she means by not having a Momma, she climbs down and takes off running as fast as her little legs will carry her in the opposite direction.

"What a little cutie she is! Probably a handful, but definitely cute as hell," Dani says with a gooey smile on her face.

***

Later on, around 9:45pm...

I get up from my seat and stretch and yawn loudly. "Ohh, God I'm tired. Have you heard from Flex or Axe?" I ask the girls, suddenly feeling slightly nauseous at the smell of the cooked meat, I decide to stand on the opposite side of the circle.

"No, not yet hon. Why don't we go get your cakes and offer them to everyone? We might see Bear around," Zara suggests, reading my thoughts.

"OK babe, that sounds like a good Idea. I'll go cut them; can you help Tin set up the table for the cake? It's inside on the bar. Once the table is set up, we can go around telling everyone, but if I don't do anything soon, I may fall asleep on my feet," I joke.

I look over and see that Dani's nearly there, snuggled up against Sue's arm.

***

Once I've finished cutting the cakes up, I head out to Zara to find she's set the table up with silverware, plates, and napkins at one end, leaving me plenty of space to put all the cakes, pies and cupcakes at the other.

"Come on then hon, let's go see if we can find one of our men," Zara announces loudly—I think she's had a bit too much to drink.

We're heading towards Axe's office when we hear an animalistic roar followed by the sound of something smashing—a chair, I think.

"SO, LET ME GET THIS RIGHT, ARE YOU STILL TRYING TO TELL ME THAT YOU DIDN'T KNOW I FUCKING EXISTED?!" a familiar voice roars from the other side of the office door so loud I swear the walls just shook.

The realization of who it is makes my breath stick in the back of my throat.

"Oh my God, Zar', that's Bear! Whoever that man is, he must be bad news; I have *never ever* heard Bear yell like that!" My heart pounds, and I hope to God he's OK.

Zara gives me a quick nod, knowing I'm right. Bear may look scary, but he's a big softie and she knows it. "I'm gonna go and tell them I think they all need a break; they've been at it for hours. Come with me; I think seeing you will help ground Bear. It always helped Flex."

Before I can object, she grabs my hand and marches me up to the office door, banging on it loudly to interrupt the shouting.

"Who is it?" Flex yells, annoyed.

A second later, he swings the door open, and the frown and hard lines on his face soon dissipate.

"Sugar, what's up? Is everything OK?" he says softly, looking at Zara like she's the most precious thing ever.

"I'm OK, babe. Me and Jenna just came to tell you all we're serving up Jenna's cake and cupcakes. We thought you could all do with a bit of a break." She says the last part softly so the men in the office don't hear, but she made sure to say my name extra loud.

Flex gives her a wink and a smile as the door swings open wider.

Bear stands on the other side, his jaw clenched so hard it's looking like it's about to break. He seems to relax as his eyes finally meet mine. "I'm getting some cake and that's me done for the night," he hollers over his shoulder to all in the room.

"Cupcake...I don't think I have ever been happier to see your beautiful face. I need some of your cake." He wraps his arm around me, and I instantly melt into his side, feeling safe in his arms.

As we walk back towards the bar area and leave Zara and Flex to it, I stop. "Oh, did you forget you have your very own pies to enjoy instead? How about we take them back to your room and we can talk?"

I start pulling his hand towards the kitchen to grab them, and he chuckles. "Darlin', like hell I was gonna forget about those pies—I need to find out why you went as red as the cherries you put in them girly drinks you like so damn much mentionin' 'em."

We collect the pies, and Bear guides me down the corridor to his room. I feel like a naughty schoolgirl going into the boys' dorm, but he has his hand placed at the base of my spine in a possessive gesture that makes me feel all warm and fuzzy inside.

"Here we go darlin'," he murmurs as he unlocks his door and pushes it open, revealing a warm, clean room.

The pine green bed sheets seem fresh and inviting, and the comforting smell of Bear's aftershave still lingers in the air, smelling like comfort and smiles. I step over the threshold into his domain for the first time, and he slams the door shut, making me jump a little.

Bear rests his chin on my shoulder, wrapping his arms around me gently and strategically placing his big hands over my stomach. "What a fucked-up day, babe. It's all kind of fuckin' with my brain to be honest with you," he whispers against my neck.

I stand deathly still as a wave of fear rolls over my body.

Oh God, is he talking about the baby? Did that man change his mind? Please, God, don't say he's gonna leave me.

He moves from behind me and goes to sit over on a chair next to a small table in the corner of the room. Once he's sat down, he leans over and exhales a gust of air.

"Fuck! My head's fucked up. I need you, Jenna," he chokes out, his head bowed.

Stupid Jenna, it's not about you or the baby right now—whatever happened in that room is big!

I walk purposefully over to where he's sitting and kneel down in front of him, placing my hands softly onto his knees. "Do you want to talk about it, babe?" I ask carefully.

"Not right now, darlin', but there is something you could do for me," he growls in reply, his head still drooping between his arms.

"Anything, but first can I show you your pies? I think you'll find them delicious…and amusing," I giggle.

He tosses his head back, revealing the stormy look in his eyes—not only angry, but lost.

I take my time to analyze him, but decide he will like my little surprise and grab the container with the pies in it, placing it on the table in front of him. As I slowly start to peel the lid off, I step to the other side of Bear so he can see exactly what pies I made him.

"FUCKIN' HELL!"

He roars with laughter, near enough falling off his seat, and I breathe a sigh of relief—that's the response I was hoping he would give me.

"Darlin', these are fuckin' amazing! This is just what I needed to see," he says, staring down at his very own 'muff pies'. One is an open-top cherry pie with a pastry 'M' on top, but I got a little more creative with the second. I made a 'muffie' — a muff pie selfie in pie form—the pastry has a 2-inch slit on the top that I sprayed pink and orange edible glitter above, and the filling is stewed strawberries with white chocolate. I have a filthy mind now Bear's popped my cherry.

"Jesus, Jenna! You trying to give me a goddamn heart attack?" Bear asks, staring wide-eyed at me from his chair.

"Well, I was thinking you could eat them after...you eat me..."

His nostrils flare like he can smell my arousal from where he's sitting, and I see his eyes grow dark and passionate with a hint of playfulness. "Jenna... fuck, darlin... take your dress off."

I just stand unmoving, unable to utter a single word in response. He looks like a man determined, and I know he'll stop at nothing to get what he wants. Just because Bear is a big softie doesn't mean he's not still a typical alpha biker.

Mmm...

The look he's giving me makes me squirm and my ivory lace panties wet.

"Jenna...I said take your dress off. Now!" he growls between gritted teeth, trying to control his lust. He sits with his legs spread wide, staring, every inch the pure alpha male commanding the room.

Jesus, I feel like I'm a submissive and he's my dominant.

In response to that little thought, a small shiver runs up and down my spine. It's like his legs are calling me to him, so I go to stride over to him on shaky legs, still wearing my heels and dress. I already feel too dirty to be in the virginal white dress, especially after all the stuff we've done.

Yeah, I may go to hell, but I'm going to have some hot sex getting there.

I saunter closer and closer to his legs until I'm pretty much standing in front of him. "Like this?" I say in a soft, husky voice, casually lifting the bottom of my dress up my thick thighs.

"Yesss, that's it gorgeous. Now the rest of it...let me see all of you," Bear commands.

How can I refuse him when his eyes are so wild with lust? He's devouring me with his signature intense stare through hooded eyes, licking his lips painfully slowly.

In the warm, soft glow of the lamp on his nightstand, I carry on lifting my dress higher, the fabric gliding over my stomach and breasts—I had to leave a bra off today as my boobs are too sensitive to stand one, but you'd never tell from the support sewn into the dress.

My boobs pop out easily, and I have to bite back a moan from the relief. I tug the dress over my head and let it drift gently to the floor in a whisper. My heart is beating as hard a drum in my ears.

I risk a look down at him through my eyelashes, and his heated gaze makes electricity crackle between us. "Jenna, fuck baby... you are breathtaking," he rasps.

Before I can catch my breath, Bear is unbuckling his pants and yanking them down. His marvelous cock bobs free, a teardrop of cum spilling out of it already. I admire his thick thighs and the deep green octopus that wraps around his leg, and the need becomes too much.

"Bear...touch me. Please," I plead with him.

"My fuckin' pleasure, darlin'!" He yanks my hand, pulling me so close to him that my shins are close to skimming his balls. His callused hands stroke their way up the inside of my thigh carefully, intent on reaching their destination—the frilly edge of my lacy panties, "Hmm...Jenna, did you wear these especially for me?"

"Maybe..." I say breathlessly. "Ahh, Bear!" I gasp as he moves my panties to one side and slips one of his fingers deep inside me.

"Mmm, and your pussy is dripping for me too, Fuck, babe, you're soaked. I've been thinking about being back inside of you since I laid my eyes on you this afternoon," he murmurs, pressing his thumb on my bud through my panties.

"Ahhhh…" My legs start to buckle, and I automatically grab the back of Bear's hair, holding onto him for dear life as his fingers stroke me painfully slowly and steadily.

Damn him, he's trying to torture us both…

"Ahhh! God, Bear...You have too many clothes on. I need to see all of you too! Ahhhhh!"

I pull this gorgeous woman's lacy panties off. She's a fuckin' temptress, especially when her magical pussy is sucking my fingers deep inside that tightness.

She steps out of them, holding onto my biceps. Her nails bite into my skin, and I grab ahold of her juicy ass and position her over the throbbing head of my dick.

"Babe, I need to be inside of you...Now!" I instinctively go to grab my wallet for a condom, then realize what I'm doing. "Darlin', you OK with me going in without a condom?" I ask quickly. I'm dying to be inside her.

"Yes, Bear. I need to feel all of you..."

"Darlin', that's all I need to hear," I grip her tighter and pull out my fingers, fully seating her on top of me and making her hiss.

"Ahhh, fuck! Bear..." As her breath catches, I give her time to readjust to my size and thickness.

"Darlin', take it easy. Mmmhmm...that's it," I groan as she starts wiggling her juicy ass against my lap, easing my cock deeper inside of her until I'm all the way in.

"You feel so good...I feel so full." She tugs at my shirt. "Babe, take this off. I want to feel your skin on mine," she pants.

I hold the soft, supple skin of her waist tighter, pull off my shirt and throw it aside, not giving a shit where it lands. Sweet mother of God, as soon as she lays her petite hand back on my skin, it feels like perfection. She shifts on my lap, and her pussy clamps down so hard I can't help the groan that escapes me.

"Jenna, you're gonna have to move, baby. I don't want to hurt you."

Next thing I know, my sexy, voluptuous woman starts wiggling up and down on my dick. "Oh, sweet Lord," she moans.

"Fuck, baby, if you keep clamping down on me like that, I'm gonna blow before I can get you off." I grit out. She tries to lessen the grip, but it's still as tight as a fucking fist. "Feed me your tits, babe. I need them in my mouth."

She plucks her nipple, making it hard, and then she gives me exactly what I want. As soon as my lips lock around it, she gasps and starts riding me like a fuckin' pro.

"Mmmm, just like that...Oh God Bear, you feel so good. I can feel all of you," she whispers breathlessly as she carries on riding my cock. It feels like fuckin' perfection. "Bear, I need...I need more."

I groan at the feeling of her choking my dick and start to move my hips, driving my nails into the skin of hers.

She quivers violently as I drive myself even deeper. Our thrusts are perfectly in sync, and she's riding me like a bucking bronco. I can feel myself scraping her cervix—fuck, if she wasn't already pregnant, I'd plant my seed deep within in her just to tie her to me in every way possible.

"Jesus, Jenna...I'm not gonna last..."

With that, the sexy woman clamps down harder on my dick, places her forefinger right on her bud and flicks herself; one, two, three, four, five times.

She throws her head back in bliss, shaking and trembling as her orgasm hits at the same time as mine starts to overtake me. "Fuuuck! I'm going to…ahhhh!" she cries, nearly deafening me. She's a beautiful, panting, sweaty mess, her sweet-as-honey cream running down her thighs as she collapses onto my shoulders, still pulsating around me.

I grab her thighs tightly and grind my cock deep inside her over and over until I join her, bathing her in my cum. "Fuckin hell baby, that was…that was…"

"Amazing!" she mumbles against my neck. Just then, she sneaks out her tongue and gently licks the sweat off of my skin.

"Babe, I don't want to spoil the moment, but did you just lick my neck?" I chuckle. This girl is all the right kinds of wacky and kinky, and she is constantly surprising me.

"Umm…maybe. You just smell so delicious, and seeing you sweat is sexy—it makes you seem even more manly."

***

A while later, we are laying in my bed, Jenna snuggled up next to my heart with her arm wrapped around my waist. One of my arms is tucked under my head, and my other hand is running through her soft hair. I feel so relaxed with Jenna, we just get each other. I want to bask in the after-sex closeness, but my head isn't in this room; it's on the information bomb that went off earlier this evenin'. A fuckin' minefield is an understatement—everything I thought I knew was blown open wide!

"Bear?" Jenna whispers sleepily into the darkness of my room.

Fuck, I thought she fell asleep! All I've been able to do is go over things in my head again and again. I look over at my phone to check the time. Shit, it's just after 2 in the mornin'.

"Yeah, darlin'? You OK?" I croak. My voice sounds like sandpaper.

"Yeah. What's up? You've been deep in your own thoughts since we got into bed, and you haven't even touched the pies I made you. I know there has to be something on your mind, so come on, talk to me," she demands, still wrapped around me like a spider monkey.

"You know me too well, babe. Some fucked-up shit happened tonight. Did I ever tell ya about my childhood?"

Jenna shakes her head.

"Well, it ain't pretty, baby. Ya sure you wanna hear it?"

I place a gentle kiss at the back of her head, and she eases herself out of my arms and props herself up on her elbows, the bed sheet falling to rest on her plump boobs, those ruby red nipples poking through.

"Yeah, I want to know everything. Tell me," she implores, cupping her little hand against my face and rubbing my thick beard. The light from the main room of the club where the party is winding down casts a soft, warm glow over her beautiful body and makes her eyes sparkle in the darkness.

"I'm still trying to get my head around it all, but I think I met my Dad today, after 35 years."

"What? What do you mean, babe?" Jenna whispers, her eyes widening in pure shock.

"That man we saw outside is Striker, the former president of the Georgia chapter, and he apparently didn't know I existed. My Mom—if you can call her that—didn't want me and put me up for adoption at 3 years old. Apparently, I was 'too much for her to deal with'", I scoff, putting her crappy excuse in air quotes. "Growing up, I was angry all the time, so I was never adopted and got passed from children's home to children's home until I was 17. At that point, I started livin' on the streets; I was a dirty, skinny fucker eating scraps, dealing drugs, doing anything to get a bit of money to put food in my belly. I used to fight and steal, but you gotta know, darlin', I didn't have a choice..."

"Sweetheart, you don't have to explain anything to me, OK? You had to do what you could to survive, but you should have been loved and taken care of."

"'Sweetheart', I like that...Well, as I was sayin', apparently Striker didn't know my Mom was even fuckin' pregnant. Only thing I know about my Mom is that she was a club girl in the Georgia chapter—that's how he met her. She fucked anything that moved. I guess I got in her way and she didn't want a 3-year-old cramping her *fuckin'* style. I was always told that my Mom didn't know who my Dad was, but when I saw Striker earlier...well you saw. I look exactly like a younger version of him."

Jenna's looking at me in awe, like I'm goddamn Superman or something. Her beautiful mouth is slack for a second before she grabs the side of my head and slides a finger down my cheek. "Babe, I don't even know what to say to all of that, but you are absolutely amazing to have gotten through all that. You are incredibly strong, as strong as…well, a Bear. So, is he definitely your Dad?" Her eyes are curious, wet, and filled with pain rather than pity.

"Darlin', it's OK, I survived. If I think too much about it, it will fuck up my head. I'm pretty sure Striker is my dad—it all makes sense now."

"What does, babe?"

"I always thought I looked similar to Hound— Grinder's VP. Well, it turns out there's a reason for that; we're brothers. That makes Grinder my cousin too. I've gone from not having any family except the club to having a Dad, a half-brother and a cousin in one night."

~ Chapter 19 Jenna ~

I think Bear is taking everything really well after his night of revelations. I don't know what I'd do if I were him; I thought finding out I was pregnant was shock enough. His solution is apparently to find solace in me...literally. He's been eating me out since I woke up to find him staring between my legs. Yeah, his response to finding out I had gotten everything waxed off of my 'muff pie' might be the reason why he's licked me out twice already...he was clearly too overwhelmed to notice last night.

***

6am...

"Baby, stupid question, but where's all your hair gone?" Bear growls.

I peel my eyes open, and what I can see has to be the most gorgeous view in this world. I may be slightly delirious from lack of sleep and all the fucking we've been doing, but who doesn't love waking up with a beautiful god of a man between their legs?

My legs have been thrown over his shoulders, and that's no mean feat. His shoulders are as broad as he is tall, so I'm left spread-eagled, and Bear's eyes are dark with desire and need.

"W-what did you say, Bear?" I ask him through a yawn.

"Cupcake, where has all your hair gone?" he asks, his gaze flicking down to my pussy.

I can feel my face heating up under his stare, but I decide to gather up my courage and tell him the truth; fuck it. "Well, I decided the only hair I want in between my legs is your beard...if you're missing it too much, that's when you can eat the pies I made ya. That's why I made you one with glitter for my hair."

I just stare at him, neither of us breaking eye contact. After a few seconds, he raises his eyebrow, and then the biggest, dirtiest grin spreads across his face. His eyes momentarily flick down to my bare pussy, and then in slow motion he bends his head down and swipes his tongue against my dripping opening...

***

Even now, he still hasn't let up.

"Ahhhh! Fuck!" My clit is so sensitive that I can't hold back any longer. "Beeeeaaaar!" I shiver and shudder under his mouth, fisting his hair and grinding my pussy into has face as I ride out my orgasm.
"No more, Bear, I don't think I could take it," I exhale in exhaustion, flopping back on his pillow. A gust of his aftershave washes over me as I do.

"Darlin', I just can't help it. Each time I taste you is better than the last. When you said you wanted the only hair on this pretty little pussy to be mine...Well, who the hell am I to refuse you?"

I look down between my legs to see Bear looking up at me, his lips and beard glistening from my cum. He's pulled God knows how many orgasms from me since last night, but seeing him with his hair ruffled from me grabbing at it, my cum over his face, and sweat glistening on his chest, I could jump his bones all over again.

I know we probably haven't got time for that, though; I need to make an appointment at the doctors' office and then go help Maggie open up. I think she's loving the extra responsibility—she's definitely been holding back on us for a while now.

"Bear, I gotta get goin', I've got to help Maggie open and set up. Have you thought about what you're going to do with all the new information from last night yet?"

Bear sighs, placing my legs back on the bed gently and positioning himself at my side so that one of his huge hands engulfs my muffin top. "Jenna, I haven't got a clue, but I do know one thing; you, our baby and my club are all I need. The rest of that shit will sort itself out. OK, darlin'?" His eyes shine with sincerity as I melt into his hold, and he rolls me over.

I can't help wondering if he's going to wake up and realize this isn't what he wants at all, and I'm filled with dread. My walls are slipping down, but I hope that whatever happens between us he will do whatever he can to take care of his baby.

Bear plays with my hair, flicking it back and forth between his fingers from root to tip, making me relax, and then he lays the softest kiss on the top of my head. I sigh, feeling small and cherished in his arms.

I leave the clubhouse around 9.30am, fighting waves of morning sickness as I drive home. Jade is fast asleep in the passenger's seat next to me, so she's no help. From the looks of her, she was comatose last night; there's mascara crumbling underneath her eyes, the smudges making her look like Kung Fu Panda.

I drive to the bakery as swiftly and carefully as I can, hoping that a big cup of coffee and some triple chocolate brownies will be enough to wake Jade up. When I pull up to the bakery, I notice Maggie's already inside, busying herself with setting up the coffee machines and turning the lights on.

"Come on, sleepy head, wake up! We're home; and we both need to freshen up."

I elbow Jade in the ribs, jolting her awake, and she sits up, wiping a little bit of drool from her lips. "Oh God. Sis, do you have to be so loud? My fuckin' head is pounding. I know I can drink, but fuck, those bikers are big drinkers, not to mention the women! Did I tell you Sue drank Doc under the table? He almost collapsed outside."

"Jade, quit your yapping! Let's get movin'," I tell her, rolling my eyes as I get out of the car and start letting myself into the bakery.

The door chimes, and Maggie swivels around so quickly she nearly knocks over the cartons of milk behind the counter. "Oh my Gawd, Jenna! Ya scared the life outta me!" she drawls.

I can't help but love her deep Tennessee accent, and it's infectious—Jade and I have much stronger accents ourselves when we've been around her. She seems more jumpy than normal; her peachy glow is pale from shock, making the freckles scattered across the bridge of her nose stand out. Her blue-gray eyes jump around all over the place.

"Sorry, hon, didn't mean to make you jump. Are you OK?" I ask, worried.

Maggie waves a dismissive hand. "Yeah, you know me, I wasn't paying attention...How was last night?"

I frown. I've never seen her like this; usually she's very attentive when at work. She may be my intern for now, but I'll be offering her a full-time position in a couple of months when she's done with school and I can't stay on my feet for too long. She's been amazing since she started; I only have to tell her something once or twice and she's got it. Yeah, she sometimes checks with me or Jade to make sure things are correct, but other than that, she could run this place on her own. She's usually so meticulous that I know my bakery is in safe hands with her.

"OK. It's all right, honey. It was great, thank you…although someone is still feeling a bit worse for wear," I nod to the door, where we can see a very slow and unsteady Jade walking across the street where I park my Vivi, complete with my shades she's picked up from the car.

Maggie and I try to hold in a snigger at Jade's state as she staggers through the bakery door.

"Euuurrgghhh. I need caffeine like now, Maggs. One extra-large black coffee and some cake or brownies if we have any left over," Jade orders, flopping onto one of the seats nearest to the door.

She's going to be fun for the rest of the day…

***

Around 2.30ish, I get a wave of nausea, so quickly grab a bag of plain chips and a weak tea to sip on and sit in the back office. I put my feet up on a box and try and rest for a while, tiredness washing over me.

Maybe I shouldn't have sat down, I'm really sleepy all of a sudden…

***

"Jenna? Are you in here?"

I crack an eye open and see Jade standing by the office door with a worried look on her face.

"Is everything OK out there? Do you need me? I was only in here for a break," I tell Jade, yawning.

"Jen, you've been here nearly an hour and a half. I thought you'd gone upstairs, but you weren't there. Are you OK?"

"An hour and a half? God, I thought I'd only just closed my eyes. I'm OK, just a little tired and feeling sick. Oh shit, are you OK for another 5 minutes? I forgot I need to call the doctor and book an appointment."

"Of course, as long as you're OK."

***

I'm back in the bakery after my little break, nibbling on a stem ginger and brown sugar cookie. They seem to going down a treat, both in the shop *and* with my cub.

As it's started to get a lot quieter near closing time, I go over and give Maggie a hug. "Maggie, thank you so much for opening up and setting up, but you can go home. Don't forget to take the leftover subs and brownies home for you and your Dad, OK?"

"Thanks, Jenna. I honestly don't mind, I'll always help any way I can."

"I know you will, sweetie. You go grab your purse, and we'll see you in the mornin'."

My now more alive sister comes over to help me wipe down tables, and we watch as Maggie leaves and crosses the street to catch the bus home. "How ya feeling now, Sis?"

"I'm OK. Would you mind locking up? I wanna shower, wash my hair, and jump into bed."

"Yeah, sure thang, babe, I got ya. Head up, I won't be long; I feel dead on my feet."

***

Feeling relaxed, I eventually slide between my cool bed sheets, and bite back a contented sigh as I get comfortable. I grab my phone, realizing I haven't looked at it since I called the doctor, and see Bear has texted and called me. I decide to call him, and he answers on the second ring.

"Darlin'," he greets me in that gruff, sexy-as-sin voice.

"Hey big guy, how are you? I miss you, I've just got into bed," I sigh.

He chuckles. "Aw, darlin'. You want me to come over and give you a massage? You can give me one."

"I'm fine, Bear," I laugh. "Just wanted to check you were OK."

"Darlin', if you want me there, I'm there. You want me to snuggle up to? I'm there. You want me to give you a foot rub? I am *there,* baby."

"With whistles on your balls?" I giggle down the phone. I've never been like this with a man before; there's definitely something about Bear that draws the sassiness out of me and makes me drop my barriers.

"Jenna, now you've seen what I'm working with, you should know they would have to be some pretty big whistles. I'm all good, babe, not long got into bed myself. How was work?"

I shake my head at his crude comment, a smile spreading across my face as a warm fuzzy feeling blooms in my tummy. "Busy. Oh, I made a doctor's appointment for next week, so if you would like to…umm…I mean, you don't have to come if you don't want…"

Bear interrupts my nervous panic, his deep voice calming me. "Jenna, I would fuckin' love to come to the appointment. What exactly happens? Do they scan ya or what?"

The knot in my tummy eases off at his words. "OK. No, it's just a talk. The scan should be between 6 and 8 weeks in, but I would really appreciate the support if you came anyway."

"Cupcake, you ain't gotta ask, OK? I will be there, I promise ya."

I fight back tears at the rush of love I feel, my throat suddenly so thick I'm struggling to swallow. "'Kay Bear. I'm gonna get some sleep, babe. Night."

"Cupcake? Are ya OK?" he asks, concern lacing his tone.

"Yeah, I'm OK. It's…It's just that you said exactly what I needed to hear. Ignore me, I'm just over tired."

"Darlin', listen to what I'm about to say. I ain't into tellin' you what you want to hear; it's the truth. I want to be there every step of the way—we're gonna figure it out together."

"OK big guy, I get ya. Thank you for being you."

"Darlin', I would do anything to make sure that sexy-as-fuck smile stays on your face for good. I'll let you get some shut-eye, baby."

"OK. Night, Bear."

"Night, darlin'."

As we hang up, I grin and sigh in contentment.

Maybe, just maybe, I can actually start to let the walls around my heart down. The more time I'm around him, the more I miss the big guy when he's not around.

I snuggle under my bed sheets—even though the air-con is blasting through my room, I love how safe it makes me feel. My eyes soon get heavy, and I start to drift off, thinking of my gorgeous man with all those tattoos and piercings.

As I place my palm against my stomach, I realize I hold a part of him with me.

A week later...

I only got out of bed and had a shower a few minutes ago, but my mind won't stop racing already. I still can't believe I'm gonna be a Dad, or that I've met mine after 35 years...on the same day! How fucked-up is that?

I have so many unanswered questions, but Striker told me my Mom stayed in the Georgia chapter for a while before she got pregnant, and then once she'd had enough of me, she put me up for adoption. Striker remembers her bein' pregnant, but because he suited up—like father like son—he assumed someone else had knocked her up. He said she went away for about a month, and when she came back, it was like nothing had happened.

I may be 35, but that last part cut like a motherfucker. Even though I never met her, it hurt to know I was nothing but an inconvenience to the woman who carried me. My baby might have been a surprise, but of the best kind—never a mistake. Nope, this baby will not end up like me—no child deserves that. They are going to be my second chance, and I am sure as hell going to make sure my child knows that they are loved and wanted. Whatever happens between me and Jenna, I will always be there for them—my child will know its Momma *and* its Daddy, that's for damn fuckin' sure.

I stroll through the main room with my head held high, looking forward to seeing Jenna later.

Who woulda thought I'd be so excited about seeing the doctor?

"Yo Tin, where are Flex and Axe at?" I bellow at him, scaring the shit outta of him from where he stands behind the bar.

He swivels round fast. "Fuckin' hell, Bear, you trying to make me shit myself? Jeez..."

I can't help the laugh that erupts from me. "Sorry, man, but that was fuckin' funny. Anyway, you seen the Prez today, or is he still in bed with the missus?"

"Nah, he and Dani were in the kitchen getting breakfast last time I checked."

"Thanks bro, I'll catch up with you after."

As I'm just about to turn around the corner, Tin hollers, "Bear, how are things with Little Miss Sweetcakes?"

I chuckle and yell back over my shoulder at him, "Sweet as fuckin' honey, ya cheeky shit! You need to get laid already brother!"

I leave him guffawing to himself and head off to the kitchen when I see Axe walking up to his and Dani's room. I drop back—I don't want to overhear anythin' I shouldn't. Normally he wouldn't give a flyin' fuck if I walked into his room, but now he's got an Ol' Lady we have to show more respect than that. I briskly knock on their door and step way back against the opposite wall. The next thing I hear is Dani gigglin'.

"Yeah?" Axe yells through the door.

"Prez, it's Bear. Can I have a quick word?"

After a minute, the door creaks open a sliver and I see Axe's confused face come into view. He's shirtless, which I've seen a million times, but I think he's trying to hide Dani, who's probably still in bed.

"Everything OK, Bear?"

"It's nothing urgent, just wanted to talk to you about somethin' when you're free."

"OK brother, I'll be out in thirty tops."

"Axe, it's OK!" I hear Dani yell from behind the door. "I need to get up for work anyway; I have the start of a sleeve I designed booked at ten. I can't freakin' wait, baby."

Axe turns to look over his shoulder. "Sweetness, are ya sure? Your ass is mine later, woman."

"Love you, Mr. President," I hear Dani say in breathy voice. There are more giggles, followed by the sound of a door slamming.

Axe frowns at the grin covering my face. "Don't say a fucking word! I'll meet you in my office in 5, OK?"

"Sure thang...Mr. President!" I yell, making quick work of eating up the distance between me and Axe's office.

Fuckin' hell! I shake my head, chuckling to myself.

***

I stand just inside of Axe's office waiting for him, but I'm not there long before I hear the slapping of his chains against his boots coming down the hallway that leads to his office. The door handle turns, and in walks one of my oldest and best friends—fully dressed this time, wearing a Devil's T-shirt and his cut proudly.

He slams the door with the heel of his boot and gets right down to business. "All right, brother, what's this all about? It's not like you to come and see me early in the mornin'," Axe inquires, a puzzled look covering his face.

"Sorry about that, Axe," I say, scratching the back of my neck nervously. "Uh…the thing is…I need to know, uh…about Striker. Did your Pops know? I just can't see how no one guessed…I look just like him." I exhale a huge breath and start rubbing my chin and tugging on my beard.

"Brother, sit down." I drop into one of the chairs at the table, and Axe does the same, still talking. "Look, Bear. I swear to you, the first I knew about it was when Striker met you. I don't know why I didn't notice at first, but as soon as you stood next to him, even a fuckin' blind man could see you were his son. I don't think my Pops knew jack about Striker, but if it makes you feel better, I can ask him. I know you've probably got a million fuckin' thoughts running through your head—hell, I'm still shocked by it too—but either way, it's clear as day that you were born to be a member of this club."

He tells me exactly what I need to hear, and he's right—I was born to be in this club, however I got here. It saved me when I was 20, and I found out I was gonna be a Dad and found my own Dad all because of the brotherhood.

"Yeah, you're right. It's just all fucked up. Thanks, man."

"You good now?" Axe inquires, slapping my knee.

"Yeah. I guess the only way to find out what happened is to talk to him again—but with less yellin' this time. Oh, if you need me later, I'll be with Jenna around 1."

In response, Axe does a double take, his eyes widening slightly. "No, not you too? What's the story?

Come on, I know *you* ain't grieving a wife and can't pull your head outta your ass to go after the girl, but I also know you've never worried about telling me you're gonna be with a woman before. This has gotta be big."

I wet my lips and swallow before I can speak. "Shit, Axe, the hesitation ain't on my part! *Trust* me, I've told her I want her, but a dude fucked up her head in college by fat-shaming her in front of the whole school at a dance. He gave her major trust issues, so she didn't want any more than a one-time deal, but I kept tryin', and we turned into 'friends with bens'."

"Fuck, man, these motherfuckers who abused our women need teaching a lesson! If I could bring back Spider, I would happily take my time ending him for what he did to Dani. Maybe that's your answer..."

***

"Finally, you're here! I thought I was going to have to go without you, big guy. Everything OK at the club?" Jenna greets me as she jumps into the club's cage. I'm fuckin' bummed she can't go on the back of my bike until the baby's here, but at least that's somethin' else to look forward to.

She takes my breath away—her personal perfume, aroma, or whatever ya wanna call it, washing over me like a calming balm. She's wearing a yellow summer dress similar to the white one she wore last week, and the flash of her bare thigh as she adjusts her seatbelt gets me hot.

"All right big guy, my face is up here. Keep staring at them and you'll have them wrapped around your stupid head," she chuckles, making my head snap up in response.

In that moment, the cage's atmosphere grows heavy with lust, my dick aches, and I can almost taste her. "Darlin, how the hell is an offer like that gonna stop me from starin'? I would happily stare at your thighs all night long." My eyes snap back to them, and I watch her squeeze her legs together.

Yeah, I got ya, darlin'.

I can't help but slide my hand across the console; my big tanned hand reaching her creamy thighs that feel like fuckin' velvet. I feel her body's reaction to me and flick my eyes back to Jenna's, staring deeply into them. My other hand trails a finger down her cleavage, skimming deliberately over her breasts with feather-like touches—I know they are 'tender as a castrated cat', as Jenna put it over the phone last night.

"Mmm, darlin', I fuckin' missed you," I whisper into her ear. She automatically responds by tilting her head to one side. "I bet if I dip my finger in…"

I admire this breathy, horny-as-fuck minx. I was her first, so I know exactly when she's turned on to fuckin' hell. I am gonna make damn sure I am her last, too, especially with my child growing in her belly.

"Bear?" she breathes. "We're gonna be late."

***

"Calm the fudge down, Jade! I *told* you I wanted Bear with me. Jeez, stop being such a big worrywart. Yes, I understand you wanted to come with us, but this is mine and Bear's baby. Don't get upset, Sis. I know. Don't worry, OK? We'll see you soon."

"Is she pissed at ya, babe?" I ask across the cab as we are driving back from the doctor's appointment.

Jenna sighs heavily. "Oh, she wanted to come with us. I *told* her that I wanted you there with me! I don't know what planet that girl's on at the moment, but for some reason she's on a mission to find anything to get angry at. It's not like her at all. I can't deal with her as well as concentrate on our lil' bear cub." She says the last three words with such happiness in her voice that I'm filled with pride. I glance over to see my woman smiling a small, shy smile with the cutest little sparkle in her eyes.

"Bear cub, huh? I fuckin' love that, Cupcake—it's as cute as its momma. Do you want me to talk to her? You definitely don't need the stress from her acting out, and it sure does sound as though something else is going on. It's not her...ya know...her monthlies?" I say, embarrassed to be saying things like that about my child's aunt.

"No, I don't think it's that, babe. Anyway, let's not talk about that...so, are you excited for our first scan in a couple of weeks? I don't know if I can hold in our news until then, and I *definitely* hope my morning sickness will have subsided by then..."

"How about we stop at the drugstore and grab your prenatal vitamins and the ginger and lemon tea the Doc suggested? I will promise I will try and keep quiet about our news, but you know I can't help it. I'm gonna be a fuckin' Daddy! I'm fuckin' buzzing!"

As we stop at a red light, I grab ahold of the back of her neck and tug her toward me so her lips meet mine. I dart my tongue between them, and her taste erupts on my tongue, filling my mouth with the flavor of honey, sunshine, and the woman of my dreams.

I pull away from her beautiful full lips and hear cars honking at me, but ignore them. "Mmm...perfect, darlin'."

She blushes from the apples of her cheeks to her little earlobes as I absent-mindedly stroke her jaw, looking deep into her eyes. We are in our own little bubble, just the three of us...

The bubble is exploded by the roar of an engine pulling up right beside the cage.

"You fuckin' dick..."

I swivel in my seat to look at the red-faced puny lookin' douche with a receding hairline sitting in his white soft-top E-class Mercedes-Benz. As we make eye contact, he instantly turns from ruby red to a pale shade of gray, only getting paler as he takes in my size, my cut, and the angry look on my face. He stares wide-eyed, a shit-scared look covering his own face.

"You were saying? Dick what?" I growl out of the open window on my side, leaning my thick, wide arm on the window frame. I can't help but grind my back teeth at the little shit.

He splutters and stutters for a second, then clears his throat whilst rapidly blinking like he's tryin' to bat his eyelashes at me. "Uh, nothing. Did you realize the red light turned green a while back?" he says, scraping his hands through his nearly non-existent hair.

Who the hell does this bastard think he is?

"As ya can see, *dickwad*, I was kissin' my woman. If you were in such a motherfuckin' hurry, you could have gone around us." I growl.

Jenna snaps me out of my anger by caressing my thigh, whispering into my ear softly, "Big guy, ignore this douchebag, he's just jealous. He probably ain't getting any...unlike you, *Jam Jar*..."

Her hand trails deliberately up my thigh, her little pinkie brushing my package through my jeans. Instantly, the beast is awake.

Without looking back at the punk next to me, I pull off so I can sink my *'jam jar'* into this gorgeous woman somewhere a little more private...

The day we finally get to see our lil' bear cub...

"Jenna, are you OK, babe? Let me in, Bear's here to collect ya," Jade calls. She's been hanging around outside my motherfudgin' bathroom all morning.

My morning sickness has been terrible for the past couple of weeks—I can hardly keep anything down beyond sips of tea. Definitely no coffee; even the smell makes me heave. I've been no help whatsoever to the girls, and I had to tell Maggie—she was seriously worried about me, but now she knows, she's so excited for us. She swears it's a girl, but Bear insists our lil' bear cub is a boy, being a typical alpha male and all.

We haven't told anyone else yet, but we're hoping to tell everyone after this scan—including my Momma, which is going to be fun. Thankfully, she lives a 2-hour drive away in Cooksville, and she works the night shift at the local hospital. She's probably going to give me a lecture about it, though—although we aren't really practicing, she classes us as a 'God-fearin' family'—so it's best I do it over the phone.

As well as my horrible morning sickness, I've had to take antibiotics to fight my on-and-off water infections. It's been fun trying to swallow the antibiotics when I can actually keep any food down me and want something to eat...not.

"Stop worrying, I'm OK! I'll be out in a minute, just freshening up!" I shout through the bathroom door.

I hear Jade huff and walk out of my bedroom, followed by the loud stomping of biker boots that sets my lady parts a-tingling.

"Darlin'? You ready to go? Is our lil' bear cub giving you trouble again?" Bear chuckles, trying to break the tension—he knows I'm anxious about the scan.

I honestly can't fault Bear, he's been great. We may not be official, but when he called me his woman after seeing the doctor for the first time, I didn't freak out or feel like he was pushing too soon. It felt...well, I guess it just felt right.

"Stop ya bellyaching, I'm coming, I'm coming. I'm just putting a bit of blush on." Once I'm done, I swing the door open to reveal the sexiest man that ever lived. Well, maybe after Aquaman and Batman, but they ain't going to barrel their sexy asses into my bed anytime soon, and I don't think they have a fuckin' *jam jar* hanging between their fudgin' thighs.

Bear's sitting on my ottoman, head propped on the foot of my bed and one ankle crossed over his knee, the denim tightening near his crotch—it's like I'm being called to it.

Sweet God, I've gone from puking my guts up to horny as a she-cat.

"Cupcake...if you keep staring at my dick like that, you're going to be bent over your goddamn bed, screaming my name and holding onto the bedpost as I fuck your tight cunt so hard I'll put another bear cub inside of ya," he growls.

My eyes widen and my mouth hangs open in pure shock, but tingles run up and down my body, reaching my core. I clench my legs together as his big dark eyes scrutinize me. His nostrils are flared, and he readjusts his thick, juicy...

"All right, are we ready? I feel tons better," I say rapidly. If we stare at each other any longer, I know Bear will be true to his word.

I walk through my bedroom and have nearly made it out to the living room when a strong hold on my arm tugs me back. I twist and fall into Bear's big arms, my face planted into his chest, I grip ahold of the front of the ebony t-shirt underneath his cut, and he cups the back of my head.

"Darlin'..." he says gruffly.

I decide to take a quick peek underneath my eyelashes and see the big guy staring at me like I hold the moon. "Yeah?"

"Gimme your lips."

There's no way I'm going to refuse him. Whether he knows it or not, this man is fast becoming my whole world. I stand up on my tiptoes and tug on his thick beard, which I know he loves, then place my lips gently on his in a delicate butterfly kiss.

Bear has other ideas, and I'm glad—I need more as much as he does. He licks the seam of my lips, and I instantly open my mouth to him, tasting him on my tongue. Our tongues spear each other's mouths frantically like they're marking their territory, and I'm not sure how long it lasts, but when we eventually pull apart, we pant heavily like we've been underwater for a half hour.

There is barely an inch between us—if that—and my forehead rests on his. My hair was in a loose ponytail, but now I bet I looks like I've been dragged through a big-ass hedge backwards.

"I bet my hair looks a mess," I mumble breathlessly against his chest, taking in lungfuls of his scent.

"Fuck, darlin', you could never look a mess! You would never think you've been throwing up most of the morning—you're beautiful as ever, sweetheart."

In response, I snuggle into him, knowing more of those walls are crumbling down...

***

"Miss Jenna Smith!" the sonographer shouts into a room filled with women, their partners, and their family members. We're all here for the same reason—to see our babies, whether it's the first time or the tenth.

I grab hold of Bear's hand and give it a squeeze as we walk towards the woman shouting my name out. She's wearing deep green scrubs with a badge hanging from her hip. I can barely make out the name on it, but I think it says Lynda.

"Are you Miss Smith?" she says a little more softly.

"Yes, that's me. Is it OK if I bring...the dad...with me?" I ask, bracing for the judgmental look Bear always gets.

She looks over at Bear, seemingly unfazed by his tough exterior—I think I'm gonna like her—then escorts us to the scan room and pushes the soft-closing door shut. "All right, hon, I need you to get comfy on the bed, pull your dress up underneath your breasts, and wiggle your panties down slightly. At this stage, they have so much space they could be anywhere."

I do as she says and wiggle down the bed to get comfortable.

"Is this your first, hon? I'm just going to squirt some of this gel onto your little bump. It may be a little cold, but I've tried to warm it up for you."

"Yeah, this is my first. Ooh, that is a little chilly." I try not to tense up, but the gel is practically freezing on my skin.

"I may go a little quiet once I've found baby, but I'm just checking everything's OK." She presses down hard onto my full bladder, wiggling and jiggling the handheld wand over my stomach.

I stare up at the ceiling in a kind of trance, waiting and hoping for her to tell us everything's fine.

I'm not doing it for long before a warm hand grasps and squeezes mine. "You OK, babe?" Bear whispers.

"Yeah—"

"Here you go, Mom and Dad," Lovely Lynda announces, cutting my response short, "say hello to your little baby."

Both me and Bear whip our heads around, and there on the screen is a white bean shape.

"You only have one baby in there. I know it looks like a blob of white, but this is the heartbeat fluttering away," Lynda explains, pointing to the screen, "and they're the start of its limbs."

I can't tear my eyes off the screen, reluctant to even blink. Our lil' bear cub is curled up onto one side, so the picture we get isn't the best, but we couldn't care less— we're just ecstatic that we got to see our little baby. As Lynda finishes up checking my ovaries and Fallopian tubes to rule out any other problems that could occur, we're just in a silent daze.

Once I'm cleaned up and we're in the hospital coffee shop, Bear grabs me and pulls me into his lap, stroking my bump as I hold the little black-and-white picture of our future. "Jenna, God...I don't think I actually have words right now," he chokes out, making a lump form in my throat.

"I know babe, I know. Bear, can I say somethin'?"

I'm nervous as hell, but I need to ask. My hands are so sweaty I can't help rubbing my palms up and down my thighs.

Bear doesn't say a word, a curious look covering his handsome face.

"Bear...what are we? *Are we* just friends with benefits? I know our situation isn't ideal, but I gotta know the truth," I ask, trying not to stutter or stumble over my words.

Bear grabs hold of my chin between his forefinger and thumb, making me lift my head to meet his eyes. "Darlin', let's get one thing straight. There is no way I want to be just friends with benefits, you got me? You have my baby inside you, so I won't accept anything less than you bein' my woman, Jenna," he says in a low growl. His eyes are as serious as they were the night I told him I was pregnant, and the effect is instant.

I squeeze my thighs together tightly and raise my eyebrows in defiance, trying to hide how turned on I am by him getting all alpha male. "Like that is it, big guy?" I say, pursing my lips in an attempt not to give anything away.

"Damn straight, that's exactly the way it's going down. You're *my* woman, and you're pregnant with *our* child. End. Of. Story."

Just like that, the last of my walls come crashing down.

I nestle up into Bear's neck, and he wraps his thick arm around my waist, pulling me closer to him, then whispers into my ear so quietly that only I can hear, "Cupcake, can we go back to your place?"

"Why's that, big guy?" I ask just as quietly—I know what he's about to say, and I don't want anyone overhearing.

"Because I have been dying to get back inside you since earlier, darlin'. I wake up hard as steel every morning thinking of that magic pussy of yours and how I molded it to fit just me."

His words send vibrations through my every fiber, making my nipples pebble instantly underneath my dress, my clit hard, and me wet as hell for him. "OK babe, but only because you asked so nicely," I giggle softly in his ear.

***

That night at the club...

"Oh. My. God! I'm so freaking excited that I can let out the secret now! It's been *so* hard to keep quiet that you're pregnant with your *bambino* at the same time as me!" Dani squeals in my ear, hugging me tight.

"Dani, get off my woman! You're gonna squeeze all the air out of her," Bear chuckles off to the side.

Dani lets go of me, and she and Sue turn toward Bear at the same time. "*Your woman?!*" they yell in unison with matching Cheshire Cat grins.

Bear glances over to me with a twinkle in his eye, knowing as well as I do that I am *his* after we took a detour back to my apartment and he ate me out on my kitchen counter, then bent me over the table and fucked me raw. God, I can still feel the hard wood rubbing against the tops of my thighs and the pulsation in between my legs.

Without breaking eye contact with me, he yells, "Yeah, you heard me right, *my* woman."

"Aww, I'm so happy for you both! Woohoo!" Zara says as she comes waltzing into the room with Flex. Both of them look flushed, and Flex especially looks thoroughly fucked, his hair ruffled like Zara has been pulling and yanking at it and running her fingers through it.

"Bear, son, have you told your Dad the good news?" Sue asks as she walks over to him. She stands next to Doc on one side of the bar, and he and Axe are on the other, both drinking in celebration of the fact they are both going to be Daddies soon. Dani is due in roughly a month and a half…I think. It's hard enough to work out how far along I am in my pregnancy, let alone where anyone else's is at.

Bear's face drops slightly at Sue's words, his eyes losing some of their sparkle, "Nah, I ain't. I will probably arrange to meet him soon, but I'm still trying to get my head around it. I'm over the goddamn moon that I'm going to be a Daddy, though."

I walk over, wrap my arm around his waist, and put my hand in his back pocket. "Correction, big guy, you're going to be a Papa Bear."

~ Chapter 22 ~

Bear

7 weeks later...

"Cupcake, I fuckin' hate leavin' ya too, but I should only be gone half a day at most. I'm meeting Daddy dearest at some burger joint between us both to talk."

"Bear, it will all be fine. Just go and ask him what you need to—don't worry if you're not ready to have a relationship with him. Let me know before you leave there, OK?"

"Sure thang, darlin'. Come here, give your man a kiss before I leave."

She does willingly, softly placing her full, juicy lips against mine. She tastes of the apple she nibbled on for breakfast mixed with honey from her oatmeal.

"Mmm, remind me why I need to go again?" I mumble against those warm soft lips of hers, putting a hand on her stomach—which is now slightly rounded thanks to our growing bear cub.

She rests her forehead onto mine, her hair falling around us like a curtain. It's got so thick that no hair tie can hold it up. Little wisps of strawberry-blond with gold flecks shine in the sun blazing down on us. "Because, babe, you need to go talk to Striker. I'll be here when ya get back, and I'll make you your favorite pie if you're lucky," she replies with a smile, her eyes still closed.

"Fuck yeah, cherry poppin' pie! Mmm, let's go straight upstairs and relive that when I get back, shall we?" I chuckle, nipping her plump bottom lip.

Jenna gives me a little shove and a playful swat on my forearm. "Bear, shush! I don't want everyone hearing about that, especially not my customers! You know the gossips will be eating it up."

I wrap my arm around her waist and pull her close to where I'm sitting on my bike, "Darlin', I couldn't give flyin' fuck if anyone hears me—they all know we're together, I put a baby in you! I can't help it, you wearing those dresses makes me hard as fuck," I grumble into her lips as I capture them one last time.

"Mmm, hurry back, won't ya?" Jenna asks.

"Of course, babe. I'll let ya know when I get there, and when I leave, OK? Right, I'd better go; the sooner I leave, the sooner I can get back. I love ya."

"Love you too, big guy. Ride safe."

Every time she's said those words, it's made me swell with pride. In a way, I guess Jenna's my first too— my first time actually being in love with somebody. Sue told me she loved me when I first came into the club, and I love her, Doc, and my brothers like family, but to know I actually can love someone else like this is huge for me, fuckin' monumental.

I shove my lid on and pull off as I wave to the kinky little goddess who is the mother of my child. She may have acted all innocent at first, but when she gave me one of those cherry pies the other night, I turned her on by fingering it. She put it down to pregnancy hormones, but I know that it's BS.

***

I've been riding for near enough 3 hours in the blazing heat—my arms and face are gonna be darker than my beard by the time I get back to Tennessee. I pull off the I-75 onto the 386-510 Old River Road in Cartersville, ending up near the Etowah River, then park my bike under one of the trees, pull off my lid, kick up the stand, and lean back, waiting for my—well, Striker—to turn up.

As I'm waiting, I take a good look around. This might be a long-ass dirt road at the back end of fuckin' hell, but all I can hear is the river I saw the bank to a while ago, the water burbling as it travels over the rocks. The smell of soil and freshly cut grass fills my nose, and I bet Jenna would love it here.

My appreciation of nature is cut short by the roar of an approaching engine.

That must be Striker coming around the bend—he's still about a 5-minute ride away.

Sure enough, he rolls up 5 minutes later.

"Ya all right, son? You been here long?" Striker drawls huskily, his 30-a-day-for-30-years habit making him croak.

I shudder, though I'm not sure if it's because he called me 'son' or at the sound of his voice. I'm so fuckin' glad I gave that shit up once I got into the club, although I never had much of a choice—it was either that or feel the wrath of Doc and Sue for the next 15 years.

He slaps me on the back as he parks his bike behind mine, sending my hackles up.

"Hey, *Striker.* Nah, not long; your ride all good?"

He rubs the back of his neck, his eyes shifting between me and the floor and then back again.

Fuck, I can't help shifting awkwardly myself. "Look, Striker. I know this is awkward for you. Hell, it's awkward for me too, but I've had time to think about everything and talk to Axe since I last saw you, and I gotta admit it seems like one big fucked-up coincidence. I don't know where we go from here, but I need to know something; do ya know where *she* is?" I say, instantly feeling lighter.

"She? You mean your Momma? Nah, I aint seen her in years. Why, did ya want me to find out where she is and reach out to her?"

I shake my head quickly as we walk toward the river. "No. I want nothing to do with her, she gave me up and never looked back. At least you have a decent excuse, ya didn't even know I fuckin' existed."

Striker's face softens. "She wasn't that bad, just young and wantin' an easy life. I'm not excusing what she did, but if she'd have told me, I would have helped her out and made sure you didn't get put into the system. It's just fucked up; she knew I had Hound by then, so you would have grown up with a brother. I split with Hound's Momma after she found I had slept with your Momma, but I raised him all right."

I can't stop my blood boiling at the mention of that word, which has a very different meaning now to what it did all those years ago. "She ain't my Momma, all right? I didn't have one back then, and I sure as fuckin' hell don't have one now. My Jenna is more of a Momma to my unborn..." I trail off, seeing the shock etched on Striker's face.

"Your woman? She's pregnant? Oh fuck, does that mean I'm gonna be a Grandaddy?!"

We've walked closer to the riverbank now, and I can see the water splashing against the side. The current looks strong enough to take a man of my size off their feet without a second thought.

I'm considering my reply and watching the sunbeams bouncing off the water when I'm interrupted by my personal phone vibrating. "Hold up, I need to get this. It may be Axe."

I answer it, and even though the line is crackly and broken up, I hear Jade's words loud and clear.

"BEAR! You need to come. It's Jenna!"

Jenna

"How much longer on my coffee, Ma'am? My cinnamon swirl has started to get cold."

"I'm so sorry; let me get you a fresh one on the house and bring it with your coffee, sir. Please bear with us, it seems everyone in town wanted to try my new cake recipe," I say with a smile before heading off to grab his black coffee and a warm cinnamon swirl.

I should be grateful for the custom, but the bakery is so packed I've had to use the walkway outside as a makeshift sitting area, and I'm exhausted already. Maggie and Jade are equally rushed off their poor feet—at this rate, I'm gonna have to call Bear to ask him to come back and help!

I can't help the smile that spreads across my face and the flip flop of butterflies filling my tummy at the thought of my man. If someone had told me this time last year that I was going to lose my virginity and as a result be madly in love, pregnant, and trust a biker with all my heart, I would have called them crazy.

***

After a while, the brunch rush seems to have calmed down, and the exhaustion crashes over me like a wave.

"Sis, you haven't stopped! Go sit down over there, and I'll bring you an herbal tea and some of your ginger cookies," Jade says, giving my shoulders a little squeeze.

I ain't even gonna fight her on this; I'm pooped and it's only 2:15pm.

I sit over in the corner booth reserved for our breaks or when the girls come in, propping my feet up. The cool cherry leather soothes the back of my calves.

Ahhh...

Jade sidles over carrying my herbal tea and a cookie, then sits down next to my legs, moving them to rest on hers. Next thing I know, a flash of heat passes over me, rising over my face and neck. I try not to panic—the doctor did mention you can get hot flashes, but I've started to sweat profusely too.

"Is it just my hormones, or is it hot in here? I'm sweating like a dirty pig! Pass that napkin, will ya?"

Jade hands it to me, and I use it to start fanning myself speedily in an attempt to cool me down. I glance back at Jade, who hasn't said a word, but has a confused look on her face, a concerned frown forming a little crinkle between her eyebrows.

"What's up, honey? It's nothing to worry about, it's just called being pregnant."

Jade shakes her head. "Sis, you don't look too good. You're as red as these booths! I think we should get you to the hospital to get checked out."

"Jade, don't be silly! We've been super busy, that's all. I'll call the doctor to come and check my blood pressure, but I'm sure it's just a combination of rushing around and being pregnant." My words come out a little more firmly than I wanted them to, but I don't want all the fuss of the hospital.

"No, let's go to the maternity unit for a check-up. I won't take no for an answer," she insists. As she leans in close to my face, I see hers is full of worry. That crinkle between her eyebrows is back, but a lot deeper this time.

***

It all seems a blur as I walk into the maternity unit with Jade right by my side. Maggie is back in the bakery; I felt awful leaving her, but Jade told me she'd be fine.

Was Jade right? Should I be worried about how I'm feeling?

The hot flash has subsided, but I still feel terrible; like there's a bug hangin' over me or something.

Once I'm checked in, a nurse called Andrea finds me a cubicle and asks me to undress and pop on my hospital gown, which is a pale seaweed green color with hundreds of tiny little white squares on.

Everything smells so sterile—of bleach mixed with that signature 'hospital smell' everyone knows. The walls of my cubicle look like they were once a cream color, but have long faded to a pale gray, and sun-bleached posters and decals cover the walls. Even though the walls are busy with helpful information and the buzzing and beeping of monitors fills the air, all I can do is keep staring at the pattern on my gown. I can hear all sorts of conversations, but all I am focused on is whether our cub is OK.

"Can I come in, hon?" Nurse Andrea asks from behind the blue paper curtain.

"Yeah. Is my sister out there?" I don't want to be alone, but truth be told, I would much prefer to have Bear here.

Andrea slides through the gap she's created. "She told me to tell you she's trying to call Bear, but the call keeps dropping off. She'll be back soon. All right, sweetheart, the doctors are just doing their rounds; you'll be seen as soon as possible. Are you able to do a urine sample for me?"

I just stare at her, completely bewildered.

Urine sample? Doctors?

Eventually, I stutter out a reply. "Uh...s-sure, I can try. Why do the doctors need to see me? I only came in because I feel a little warmer than usual."

I just want to go home; I don't understand all this fuss!

"It's just protocol, honey," Andrea says, putting a hand on my arm.

I inwardly roll my eyes, but take the paper cup and head off in the direction of the bathrooms. On the way, I see Jade walking back, and she rushes over, grabbing me by the biceps.

"Hey honey, what are you doing up and about? Has the nurse seen you yet?"

"Calm down, Jade, I'm fine! I have to give the nurse a sample, and apparently, I have to see a doctor too. Have you been able to reach Bear?" I ask, trying and failing to keep the nervousness out of my voice.

Jade's eyes soften a touch and she rubs the back of my arm, "I've tried several times, honey. Let's wait for the doctor first, then worry about Bear."

After a lot of waiting around and a lot of Jade toing and froing trying to contact Bear, the doctors come into my cubicle. Jade's just gone to call him again, but otherwise she's been here holding my hand and reassuring me. She's done everything I needed her to, but I just want Bear to wrap his arms around me and tell me everything is going to be OK.

As they leave, I look down at my arm, where they have poked and prodded to find a vein and check my blood—I look like a pin cushion. My head snaps up in hope as Jade rushes back through the curtain.

"I got through to him! I didn't hear his response because the signal was crappy, but he could hear me, I'm sure of it!" she screeches, almost knocking over the nurse who's checking my vitals.

I let out a big breath I didn't know I was holding in, my shoulders slump, and I flop back onto the bed, instantly relaxed now I know he will be on his way back.

***

Time seems to stop in this cubicle—it feels like I've been here for days. Jade busies herself with getting us both drinks and me something to eat—I requested a chocolate muffin, mostly to give her something to do while we wait around.

As I'm clearly going to be here for a while, I decide to rest my head on the scratchy, starchy pillowcase. As soon as my head touches the pillow, my eyes grow heavy, and I start to drift off slightly, but it's quickly interrupted when I hear a monitor in the next cubicle go off. I sigh and sit back up, and Andrea comes back to take my blood pressure, checking and rechecking it.

"Sweetie, you need to start taking it easier. You can't work as much as you're used to, especially because you said you're on your feet 90% of the day. Your BP is very high, and we can give you a prescription to control it, but due to bed shortages, the specialists here are referring you back to your family doctor for daily check-ups."

I will Jade to hurry back, and am seconds away from crying in frustration at the thought of daily check-ups when I hear a familiar loud, confident gait walking down the hall, followed by the deep rumble I've been longing to hear.

"Jenna Smith? I'm looking for Jenna Smith."

"Bear! I'm in here, babe!" I yell at the top of my lungs.

The curtain whips open to reveal my very own big beast. His eyes look wild with fear, and he scans my body, his face falling slightly when he sees the Band-Aids over my inner arms from the blood tests.

"Jenna..."

The last of my strength crumbles away, and I can't help my bottom lip from wobbling. I try to bite down on it to stop it moving, but that only makes the tears that are already filling up my eyes slowly cascade down my face. I love the bones of this man.

"Jenna...baby," he rasps.

My vision is all blurry, but I watch as Bear eats up the space between us in one stride. He wraps his thick arms around me, and I instantly nestle my face into his neck, inhaling his special 'Bear' smell—bergamot, leather and mint. The tears fall freely as it takes over the hospital smell and I cling to him tightly. In that moment, we're in our own little bubble.

"Knock knock! It's just me, Sis. Can I come in?" Jade whispers through the curtain.

Bear reluctantly pulls away, letting my arms drop to my side. He gazes down into my eyes, searching them. My tears have stopped, but he reaches down and gently swipes away the remnants, then leans down around gives me a soft, tender kiss.

"Ya can come in, Jade," he replies gruffly.

She comes waltzing in, swinging a little paper bag and carrying the drinks in her other hand.

"You OK, Sis? I bet you're happy to see Bear!"

She elbows Bear in the ribs, and I smile. They've grown close since I found out I was pregnant, almost like a brother and sister, and I'm so grateful they're here to support me.

"Y-yeah I am," I stutter. "Before you both got here, the nurse advised me that because of bed shortages, I should see my own doctor for daily checkups—although they did give me a prescription to help reduce my high BP."

I haven't let go of Bear's hand, and he gives it a squeeze as he sits by my side. "High BP as in blood pressure? Do they know why?" he asks with unease in his voice as he traces the back of my hand with his thumb, making me meet his eyes.

I stare deep into those chocolate pools full of worry. "It's OK, they just want the doctor to keep an eye on it. I've been passed from nurses to doctors to specialists all day who don't even know my head from my fat ass. All I really want to do is go home, have a bath, wash my hair, and get into bed," I sigh, leaning against Bear's shoulder.

He wraps a strong arm around me, and I feel the tension melt away. "Well, that's exactly what we're going to do, okay? You're safe now, darlin'."

"Darlin'! I've run you a nice warm bath. Come and get in it before I grab your sexy ass and dunk ya in this tub myself!" Bear hollers from my bathroom.

Ever since we got back from the hospital, he has been fussing over me, even fluffing my pillows when I sat down on the couch. In the end, I had to ask him to draw me a bath just to give him something to do to help.

I walk back into my bedroom, but stop just inside the doorway, shocked by what I see. Every surface Bear could find is covered with candles of all kinds—small, large, battery powered, and all the colors of the rainbow. God knows where he dug all these out from!

I walk over to my bathroom, mesmerized, my eyes darting around the whole bedroom. When I get there, I see a sea of tealights and my gorgeous, loving boyfriend—although he is *definitely* all man.

His beautiful face is illuminated by the glow of the flickering lights, revealing a slight golden shimmer to his beard I've never noticed before.

"Bear...y-you did all this? This is amazing! You didn't need to do all this for me." I try and choke back the emotions threatening to burst out of my chest as he steps in front of me and drops to his knees with a thud, lifting my dress up over my bump to talk to it.

"I did this to take care of you, and I will continue to do so. You and our child are my main priorities, OK? I love you both so much, and I am more grateful for you than you know. I can't wait to be a Daddy."

He places a soft, lingering kiss on my belly, tickling me with his beard. I can't help but start to burst into giggles like a little girl at first, pushing through them to reply, "You are the sweetest man I have ever known. Did you know that, my loveable teddy Bear? I love you both more than words." I run my fingernails through his hair and against his scalp, and can't resist giving his thick hair a sharp tug.

He stands up straight, then bends down and places a soft kiss on my lips whilst caressing my bump. "Come on, Cupcake, get in the bath and relax before I show you exactly how sweet I can be when I bend you over that bathtub and fuck you red raw," he growls with a devilish grin. "Listen to your man and get your sexy ass in the tub, OK? I'll be outside if you need me."

Bear takes hold of my head, cradling it like I might break, and places a big kiss on my forehead, then my nose, and then my lips, before leaving me to get into the bath.

Once he's gone, I take off my dress and toss my panties into a heap near the open door before testing the water with my big toe. It's just right, so I step into the tub and let myself sink into it with a big sigh as the scents of jasmine and ylang-ylang hit my nose, instantly making me feel all warm and relaxed. Muscles that I didn't realize were tense start to unwind as I lean back in the tub and watch all the candles flickering and casting shadows on my bathroom walls. The flames look like they're dancing with one another—it's such a pretty sight. I decide to close my eyes and just relax in the warm water.

This is just what I needed after today...

"Babe, you OK in there?" Bear calls from the door frame a while later. He has such a loving look on his face, but I don't miss that he's shirtless, or that his jeans are hanging off his hips with the button popped open—I swear to God the only thing keeping them up is his cock.

I can't help but ogle my sexy, ink-covered man. I instinctively lick my lips and look under my eyelashes at him, giving him a shy smile. He knows my innocence is bullshit now, but he loves when I go shy; I can tell by the proud, mischievous glint in his eye.

"Cupcake, do not fuckin' tempt me with that smile. You know exactly what it does to me; don't pretend you don't know what you're doing, you sexy minx. You ready to get out now? You've been in there nearly 40 minutes; you gotta be getting all wrinkly by now."

Shit! I must have fallen asleep.

"Yeah babe, can you grab that towel for me?" I ask as I unplug the bath, watching the water drain away.

I don't even get a chance to stand up before Mr. Muscles swoops in, picks me up, wraps me up in my big bath sheet and carries me back into my bedroom, placing me gently on my bed in a sitting position.

I'm determined not to fight or argue, but Bear responds to my thought process anyway.

"Darlin', I don't want you utterin' a word, OK? I need to do this, Jenna, *I need* to look after you," he insists. He softly starts drying my feet like I'm a newborn baby rubbing the towel up my legs, then over my tummy until he's face-to-face with it. He kisses it softly, and then carries on drying me. Once he's done, he slips a huge t-shirt over my head.

I slide my arms in, look down and see it's his MC t-shirt. The soft cotton caresses me, kissing my skin.

"Thank you," I whisper to him, staring down at my clasped hands sitting in my lap.

"Jenna, lay back, darlin'."

I all of a sudden feel very sleepy, so I don't argue, and obediently lay back on my pillow in a sigh, Bear places the bed sheets gently around my body as I snuggle down, rolling onto my left side.

Bear moves to the other side of the bed, and I don't hear him removing his jeans, but as my eyes begin to close, I feel him sliding in behind me and wrapping his arms around me, his palm swamping my tummy.

A feeling of contentment washes over me. I have everything I have ever wanted—I just need to listen to my body and take it a little easier at work.

I begin to dream of the future; of me, Bear, and our little one.

I can't wait to see the man of my dreams holding the child that is half of us both in his big palms. As I drift off, I hear my gorgeous man say the words I've always wished and hoped to hear...

"I love you so much, Jenna, and I'm with you every step of the way."

***

It's been nearly 3 weeks since I've been on the blood pressure tablets, and I have reduced my hours at the bakery like the nurse suggested. We're not doing too badly; I've just temporarily altered my opening and closing times slightly until the baby is here. I've been feeling good since for the most part, just tired now and then, but that's to be expected.

On August 29th at 4:02am, Ryker Xavier Cole came screaming into the world—which Dani was so grateful for after her 48-hour labor. At first, they thought she may need a C-section, but luckily it didn't come to that. He's definitely got his Daddy's dimples, and it already looks like he's going to have his Momma's greeny-gray eyes as well as nearly a full head of dark blond hair. He's absolutely gorgeous, and seeing him makes me so excited for when our little bear cub comes along. Watching Bear hold him set me off blubbering like a little baby myself, and I know he feels the same way I do—he keeps talking about our little one running around and causing mayhem with little Ryker. Watching my man coo over Axe's son just makes me fall deeper in love with him.

"Bear, stop being silly! You don't need to carry me upstairs, it's only a few steps! Put me down, you big lug. Just you being here and making me dinner is all I need."

He eventually decides to place me down on my feet and lets me walk up the stairs to my apartment, settling for guiding me. There on the stove are freshly cooked vegetables and a pot pie ready to be served up on two of my cornflower-blue plates. Even the table is set with candles on it.

"All right, beautiful, you go sit down at the table and I'll serve dinner. D'ya want water or OJ to drink?"

"Hold up, Bear. When did you have time to do all this? And *how*? I thought your specialty was an omelet and toast, big guy?" I chuckle.

"Well, maybe I wanted to surprise you and do something nice for my beautiful woman. I also may have got cooking lessons from Sue," he tells me, shrugging like it's no biggie.

Just before he goes back to my kitchen, I grab his forearm and tug him toward me, then gaze up into his eyes. My hands wrap around his shoulders, meeting around the back of his neck. His eyes instantly soften, and he looks at me so intently it's like he's looking right to my very soul.

"I can't believe you did all this for me! You are full of surprises, Bear Jameson. I am the luckiest girl on the planet; I love you so much."

***

After devouring the dinner that Bear made from scratch—which was comfort food at its best, with crumbly pastry and perfectly tender chicken and bacon—we are just chilling on the couch watching reruns of The Office. Bear's not paying too much attention to the TV, but I think I'm slightly addicted.

My phone vibrates, and I reach over to where it sits on the coffee table in front of us, but I can't grab it, thanks to Bear giving me a heavenly foot and calf rub.

"Want me to get that for ya, darlin'?" Bear asks.

He kisses the pad of my big toe and places it down, then shifts in his seat to grab it for me.

I unlock it and see a message from Dani:

Dani x: - *Hey babe, how are you feeling? I hope you're doing OK? If you're free tomorrow, how about* coming over to the club? I need some girly time, and I haven't seen you in a while. Luv ya BBF ;) x

Me: - *Hi hon, that sounds perfect! I can head over just before lunchtime if that's OK with you and lil' Ryker? Is the testosterone getting too much over there? BBF? Luv ya too xx*

Dani x: - *Yeah, that sounds good to me. Ryker will be napping most probably. UGH, yes! Axe has turned into The Incredible Alpha atm. Just wait, Bear will be the same. HA! Big Boobie Friends! ;P Xxx*

Me: - *HAHAHAHA! 1 - Axe, the Incredible Alpha – fudgin' hilarious! 2 - Big Boobie Friends! It's a good job I luv ya ;) see ya tomorrow doll xx*

"Let me up Bear, I'm bursting to pee."

He places my feet on the plush living room carpet, and I get to my feet and walk hurriedly to my bathroom. I'll change into my PJs—AKA shorts and Bear's t-shirt—afterwards; I don't think it'll be long until I fall asleep snuggled up with my big Bear.

I finish up on the toilet, and something tells me to look down. What I see on the toilet paper stops my heart, and I freeze as it leaps up into my mouth.

No, this isn't happening. Please, God, no!

"BEAR! BEAR!" I scream at the top of my lungs.

I look back at the toilet paper I have in a tight fist, at the blood spotted on the stark white that makes it seem even darker and more menacing.

Bear kicks the door open, sending it smacking against the wall. "Babe! Babe, what is it?" he shouts as he comes barging into the room.

His eyes dart over me before landing on the tissue in my shaking hand, his body freezing to a stop once he sees the blood.

"Shit! All right, babe, everything's going to be OK. We'll go straight to the maternity unit. Don't worry, baby," he informs me with a set jaw and furrowed brow.

I can't move, I'm in pure shock. "Bear..."

I can barely choke out his name before he swallows me up in his huge hold, cradling me tightly. "Baby...I got you. Here's what we're going to do, OK? Darlin', are you with me?"

"'Kay," I manage shakily.

"I need you to go put your PJs on and put your sliders or something you can take on and off real easy on your feet, then we're going to get in the car and go straight to the maternity unit. Don't worry about anything else, just you OK? I will take care of everything else. Can ya do that for me?" he asks, giving me a curt nod of encouragement.

"Y-y-yeah, I can do that," I respond, shakily pulling up my panties and walking back into my bedroom. I change on autopilot, not really knowing what I am putting on until I look down after dressing. I've shoved Bear's shirt and some leggings on and pulled out my sliders from underneath my bed.

My heart still feels like it's in my mouth, and it's pounding—I think I keep forgetting to breathe. I have never felt so sick with worry in all my life, but I don't get to think about it anymore before Bear comes in and drops down onto his haunches directly in my eye line.

"Come on, beautiful. You ready to go?"

Some women would find the whole alpha male thing annoying or brash, but this is exactly why Bear is my strength in this moment. He's calm and collected, and he has everything under control.

"Yeah, I'm ready, babe." I whisper in response. I look into Bear's eyes, and he may be showing me how strong he is, but I can see he's as terrified as I am.

Bear escorts me out of the apartment and down the stairs, locking the doors for me on the way. I'm in such a complete daze that I don't even realize he's opened the passenger door for me to get in the car before I slide into the seat, instinctively trying to keep my legs clenched together.

Bear reaches across over the console and helps me buckle my belt. "You OK, babe? You in any pain? Cramping?" His voice sounds flat, and I can tell he dreads the answer.

I just shake my head in answer—I don't think I could say a word if I tried. My mouth feels dry, and even though I'm trying to swallow, it's just not working.

***

The drive to the hospital is a painful one. I've hardly said two words to Bear the whole time, although he's trying—really trying. He's been asking questions to distract me, but I can't seem to focus. In my heart, I know he's not just doing it to distract me, but himself; I know how much our child means to him. He hasn't moved his palm off of my thigh since we got into the car, even though the journey seems to be taking so long it feels like we are going in reverse.

Bear drives fast the whole way, but the moment he sees the sign for the hospital, he floors it and drives like a madman through the entrance. We skid to a stop in the parking lot, and he lets out a big sigh.

"OK darlin', you ready?" he asks slowly, trying his hardest not to stumble over the words.

"Yeah."

Bear helps me out of the car and wraps a protective arm around my shoulders, keeping me as close to his body as possible. We weave through the shoals of people that seem to be going every which way possible, yet somehow all push against us until we finally make it to the maternity unit.

As Bear pushes through the doors, the wave of sterile cleaning fluid mixed in with the faint odor of alcohol gel hangs in the air, instantly making my stomach roll.

We walk up to the desk, and I try to acknowledge the receptionist, but find myself just standing there with my mouth hanging open. I try to talk, but nothing seems to be coming out.

Thankfully, Bear helps me out, tightening his arm around me. "This is Jenna Smith. She has some spotting, and she's 20 weeks pregnant."

"OK, sweetheart, let me get you all booked in. I will get you a cubicle and a nurse as soon as possible, all right?"

The receptionist—Holly, a sweet-looking girl with light brown bangs and rectangular glasses—turns to Bear after acknowledging me. "Are you her husband?"

Bear hesitates slightly for a second, then spits, "No, but I'm her man and the baby's Daddy!"

Realizing what he sounded like, he lets out a huge sigh. "I'm sorry, I didn't mean to be rude. It's just..."

Holly gives him a sympathetic smile. "Don't worry sweetheart, I understand. All right, I have you all booked in Jenna, would you like to follow me?" She leads us into the third cubicle down the pale gray corridor, which is so brightly lit you can make out the tiny pink squiggles on each tile of the dull, drab floor.

"If you just sit yourself on the bed, sweetheart, I'll go let the nurse know you are here. She will be into you as soon as possible. If you need anything, please just press the bell by your bed or come to the desk."

With that, Holly leaves us both sitting on the hospital bed, not knowing what's happening, Bear hasn't let go of my hands, or me in general, since we got here, and I'm clutching him so tightly I don't think I could peel myself off of him if I tried. Bear's foot won't stop bouncing on the floor, and I can feel the tension rolling off of him. He's wound up so tightly I swear he's going to uncoil like a spring any moment now.

We don't have to wait too long before the cubicle curtains are swung back and I see Ania, an African American nurse with a gorgeous mini-afro tied up in the cutest little bun on the top of her head. Her skin is a deep shade of tan, and there are a light sprinkling of freckles on the bridge of her nose—she is absolutely darlin'.

"Hi there, hon, are you Miss Jenna Smith?" she asks me, her voice so soft and smooth it soothes me like warm honey on a sore throat.

"Yeah, I am."

"OK. My name's Ania, and I'm going to be your nurse for tonight. I've had a quick look at your notes—

could you put this gown on for me so we can run a few tests? I'll give you a moment," she says, handing me a hospital gown before leaving us alone again.

Bear turns to me. "Babe, you are in the safest hands, OK? It's probably just our lil' cub wanting to test us already."

I hold onto that thought as I'm undressing and putting the godawful scratchy gown on again. I slide back onto the hospital bed with the help of Bear—I'm so glad he's here, even though we are both anxiously waiting for Nurse Ania to get back. It feels like hours have passed in these couple of minutes, but eventually I hear footsteps approaching from down the hall, standing out against the sounds of talking in the background and the buzz and beep of several machines.

"Are you done, Jenna?"

"Yeah," I gasp out, relieved.

Ania comes back in, accompanied by a middle-aged man in dark red scrubs. He's got close-cropped dark hair, and is quite average looking until he smiles— he has a lovely smile, but it has no effect on me; my head is spinning with so much doubt and worry that I don't realize I've made my bottom lip bleed until the coppery taste hits my tongue.

"Hello, Miss Smith. My name's Dr. Hardman, I'm the Consultant in Obstetrics and Gynecology. I've been informed you have had some spotting. Are you still bleeding? This can happen in some pregnancies, but as you have been treated for high blood pressure, I want to run some tests and examine you, if that's OK?"

"Errrr, y-yeah, that's fine. There was some blood in my panties." I stutter nervously, wiping my sweaty palms down my legs over and over. I hate the thought of an examination; I know what that entails.

"All right, Jenna, are you ready for me? I need you to take some deep breaths in and out when I tell you to; I'm just going to gently see what your cervix is doing, OK?"

"Yeah," I barely whisper, squeezing Bear's hand tightly. I shift and spread my legs, ready for the doctor to get it over and done with.

"OK Jenna, are you ready?" Dr. Hardman asks me.

"Y-y-yeah." I can't look anywhere but at Bear, his free hand covering mine reassuringly as he holds my gaze.

"OK, take a deep breath in for me."

I comply, and am struck by a sharp burst of hot, agonizing pain. I can't help the internal scream escaping my lips in a whimper as the pain literally takes my breath away.

"OK Jenna, you can relax now," Dr Hardman informs me.

"You did so well baby, I'm so proud of you," Bear whispers, gently placing a kiss on my forehead that lingers there for a moment as I bask in our little bubble again.

"OK Miss Smith, we are going to ask you stay in overnight to monitor you and the baby. Nurse Ania is going to check your baby's heartbeat now. Everything seems fine at the moment, but we do think it's best to keep you in to make sure, especially with your high blood pressure as well as the spotting. Do you have any questions?"

"N-no, I don't think so," I manage.

"Well, if either of you do, please don't hesitate to ask either myself or Ania here."

As he leaves, Ania busies herself with getting the baby heart monitor strapped against my tummy.

I lay there unmoving as Ania shifts the pads around, but before long, a faint thump fills the room, and tears spring to my eyes. She checks the printout and marks it, then turns to us both. "Do you need anything?"

"Nah, darlin', I'll look after Jenna. We'll call ya if we need ya," Bear answers for me—I'm still in a daze.

"I'll be back in 30 minutes to check on you, but in the meantime, just try and relax. Jenna, if you need to go to the bathroom, just press the orange buzzer and either myself or one of my colleagues will come and unhook you."

Ania leaves, and our cubicle is filled with the amazing sound of our lil' bear cub's heartbeat. In that moment, it's the most comforting sound in the world.

"Sounds amazing, doesn't it, darlin'?"

"Yeah, it does...hey, Bear? Thank you."

Bear brushes my hair back from my face. "Darlin', what are you thanking me for?"

"For being here. I don't know what I would have done without you earlier, you took control when I completely froze. I'm so glad I'm having a baby with *you,* Bear, you are my rock. I l-love you s-so much," I burst into tears, all the emotion from the past couple of hours pouring out.

Bear's strong arms envelop me, and he just lets me cry it all out, stroking my hair from root to tip like I love. He doesn't let go until I've stopped crying and pull back to grab a tissue from the box on a stand by the bed.

"Darlin', there ain't anywhere else I would rather be than with you; I love you to the fuckin' moon and back. Do you want me to call Jade?"

Yup, this man melts my heart, and is definitely a fudgin' keeper.

"She's going to panic when she finds I'm not home—she went with Kelly to a new club in town," I go to sit up and grab my phone out of my jacket pocket on the back of the chair, but Bear gently grabs my shoulders before I can.

"Hold up, Cupcake. Sit your sexy ass back down, OK? I'll call her from your phone so she doesn't worry. Do you want me to call your Momma too while I'm at it?" He asks, waggling his eyebrows to break the tension.

I giggle despite my fear. "Um, no. It's enough that she nearly fainted when you met her just from looking at you, big guy. Remember how you had to try and charm her? Let Jade call her; she won't get all hot and bothered with you over the phone that way."

He just chuckles, shooting me his panty-dropping smile, "OK babe, whatever ya say. Just remember that there is only one woman for me. I'll go call your sister, and when I get back you're gonna praise your man for not laughing at the Doc's name. Doctor Hardman? Seriously? For an OB/GYN? Shiiit!"

I burst into fresh giggles— only this man could get me to break into a smile after today, and I love him for it.

***

"Ooh girl, he's cute! Don't you dare tell Flex I said that!" Zara exclaims from the dark gray plastic hospital chair.

My sister and Kelly burst into giggles, and I shake my head.

"We won't, but Zar', you got a man! Leave some for the rest of us. I could eat him *up*; do you think if I told him I have an ache between my legs he would be willing to look?" Jade inquires, a dirty grin on her face and a mischievous twinkle in her eye.

"Jeez, really woman? No man in their right dang mind is gonna fall for that," Tinhead grimaces with a smirk as he comes in.

He turns to me, his lightly tanned face softening drastically as he does. "How ya doing, doll face?"

"Other than being in here, I feel fine. As you can hear, the baby's heartbeat is OK, they just wanna keep me in to see how we both are."

"Yeah, just a precaution, ain't that right, Cupcake?" Bear calls as he and Flex come waltzing back through the curtain. Bear comes straight to my side, and Flex hauls Zara from the chair and sits in it, placing her in his lap.

The sight makes me smile at the memory of the last time Bear did that to me, and I instantly reach out for his hand.

"Hey Bear, how did you pull it off?"

"What's that, Kelly?" Bear asks.

Kelly is still dressed in her evening wear—a dressy black top with sparkles all over it and some black jeans.

Jade's gone for the opposite vibe in a short denim skirt and an off-the-shoulder flowy white top. She seems to have sobered up—apparently when Bear got ahold of her, he could hardly hear a word she was saying, but she was slurring something about some beef she had with someone in the club.

"How did you manage to convince the nurses that we could all be here together? There are only meant to be 2 visitors at a time," she tells us, pointing to the sign above the bed.

"Hmm, well let's just say sometimes it pays to look like this and be called Bear, especially when I end up growling at them," he chortles. Tinhead and Flex start laughing along with him.

"Bear Jameson! You better not have?!" I say, playfully slapping the hand that's covering mine.

"Darlin', of course I did! My woman needs her girls, so I gave her her girls. Whatever you need, I will make it happen, OK?" he tells me, cupping the side of my cheek and rubbing my bottom lip with the pad of his thumb. He leans in and gives me the type of kiss that reaches down into your heart and sinks into every fiber, taking root inside of you and consuming you.

Bear's marking me, I know, but it's not like he even needs to. I've been his ever since I had my picnic in the woods with my very own Bear.

Chapter 25

Bear

"Darlin', I really don't think you should be going back to work so soon; we only got back from the hospital this morning! I think you should at least rest for the rest of the day."

Why does the one woman I fall in love with have to be stubborn as hell? As soon as we got home this mornin', she had a cat nap and then got up about thirty minutes ago to have a shower and start getting ready for work.

"Bear, baby, I know you mean well, but I feel fine. You heard Dr. Hardman, they were happy with me and my readings. Please can you be on board with this?" she begs, her eyes so wide and pleading I swear she's trying to kill me.

I sigh in resignation; I hate this. "OK, Cupcake, as long as you're sure."

"I'm sure, sweetheart. If I feel funny or anything, I will come straight up to the apartment, and I'm doing less hours anyway."

Damn straight she is! I wanna wrap her up in cotton wool.

I peel myself out of her bed—which may as well be mine too, but I don't want to push her, as much as I'm dying to tell her that I'm moving in and that's that.

As she busies herself with blow-drying her gorgeous hair, I grab the jeans that I dumped on the floor next to her bed, stand up, and shove my legs in, tucking my semi in with them. It's her fault for looking so fuckin' sexy with nothing but a tiny little bright pink towel wrapped her body.

How she can call that a towel is beyond me, it's like a motherfuckin' napkin!

I'm buckling my belt when I look up and catch my sexy-as-sin Cupcake gawking at me in the mirror, her mouth hanging open. As she reddens, I can tell the little minx knows I've caught her.

"Jenna...you like what ya see, baby?" I waggle my eyebrows up and down at her, and her mouth snaps shut, her lips rubbing together as her eyes fill with desire.

A moment passes before she finally finds her voice. "Mmhmm, I sure do, babe. Did I tell you how much I love your tattoos? I love the letters on your knuckles, the huge gun on the inside of your bicep, and the gorgeous red rose on the back of your hand. Maybe...just maybe...I would love to...trace my tongue...along the letters of your '*Legend*' tattoo again."

I bet she fuckin' would, as the tat happens to be right in the space below my belly button and above my fuckin' '*jam jar*'.

Sweet fuckin' hell!

I stalk up to her, our eyes not wavering from each other for a single step. I can see her breathing hitch as I finally reach her chair, and I turn it at a snail's pace and bend over so I'm face to face with her.

She's trembling, and her luscious lips have parted ready for mine—it's like second nature now, she's my prey, and I'm definitely the motherfuckin' predator.

Her tongue darts out to lick her lips as I reply, lowering my voice to a near growl.

"Cupcake, if you're a good girl today, I may reward you with just that. Carry on getting ready, OK? I'll go make you something to eat."

***

Jenna

"I can't believe he's been here all day. Do ya think he's staying to the end?" Jade asks, making me a cup of tea for my break.

I sigh in exasperation. After breakfast, Bear announced he'd called Axe to let him know he'd be with me until church tonight. There was no point arguing with him, and I secretly loved that he was being all alpha male and didn't want to leave me when I'm still anxious and scared about yesterday.

"He's going to the club soon for church, but he'll be back tonight. Is that OK?" I ask her. I feel bad; I haven't thought to ask if him coming over all the time is OK with her before, even though it is her apartment too. Sure, the apartment is just as big as the 3-bedroom townhouse we shared before I started up the business, but we don't have the luxury of separate floors anymore.

"Kelly invited me out tonight, so I'll crash at hers anyway, but of course it's all right! I've grown fond of the big brute, but don't ya tell him that, you hear?" she jokes, impersonating my Momma—she said the exact same thing about Bear when she first met him. She gave him a real hard time about getting her baby pregnant at first, but as soon as she saw how happy Bear made me, she was so happy for us.

"I won't, don't worry! All right, I'm going to go give my man a kiss and say bye to him, then I've got some accounting to do. If you need me, just come grab me, but remember we are closing up soon."

"Yeah, I know, chillax. Go smooch ya Old Man, and make sure you get an early night, missy!"

"Yes Mom, sorry Mom!" I snigger, giving her a mock salute as I march off to Bear's booth.

"Hey beautiful, you OK?"

Bear gazes up at me as I reach him, and I can't help but get lost in those teddy bear eyes of his. As my eyes travel down, I admire the way his navy-blue t-shirt is stretched and molded perfectly against his immense chest. I can see every dip and ripple of the 6-pack he's hiding under there.

I decide to carefully place myself on his lap, winding my arms around him so they flop at the back of his neck, then lean into the crook of his neck and say in a breathy voice, "Have I told you today how much I love you? Have I told you today that I can't wait to have your lil' bear cub?"

His arms swoop around my torso and he dips me back so he can capture my lips sweetly. Before long though, his tongue domineers mine, spearing it passionately like we're making love to one another. We pull apart with a gasp of breath, and he rests his forehead against mine, lovingly staring into my eyes.

"Damn, darlin', you're makin' it *very hard* for me to leave right about now. I love you more than anything, and I can't wait to spend the rest of my days with our little family either. I best get going, but I won't be too late. I'll call ya when I leave, OK sweetheart?"

"Sure. Just ride carefully, OK?"

***

The rest of the afternoon proves to be pretty uneventful—I update the ledger, help the girls finish cleaning up, and box up the last of the peach cobbler and lemon loaf for Maggie and her Dad. After saying bye to Maggie and locking up, Jade and I make our way up to the apartment.

I hope it's time for dinner, I'm ravenous.

As if reading my mind, Jade guides me to the couch and says, "Sis, you sit down and relax, and I'll make us something nice. Pasta and meatballs OK?"

I flop back onto the couch and put my feet up on the coffee table, absolutely exhausted and feeling suddenly unwell.

"Yeah, sounds good, but I don't want too much meat; I don't feel too good. My legs feel all weak, and I'm achy and tired."

"You're not bleeding are ya? Go check please!" Jade says, paling slightly.

"No, I'm not. Stop stressing, my legs are just tired! I had a long day yesterday, and I was poked and prodded like a motherfudgin' pin cushion. I'll be fine; I'll have dinner and probably just get into bed and wait for Bear."

"OK babe, as long as you're sure. If you start to feel worse, tell me right away."

As Jade heads off to start on dinner, I grab the remote and flick through the channels before settling on reruns of *Friends*—our go-to when we have a girls' night in.

***

"Oh my God, Jade! I don't think I could eat another bite, but it was absolutely wonderful." The tomato, garlic, and onion aroma lingers in the air, still smelling divine, but I really am full.

We sit on the couch at either end like bookend slobs, but all that food has made me so sleepy I can't even keep my eyes while we watch *Friends*.

"Babe, if I don't get into bed now, I think I may pass out on the couch. Thank you again for the yummy dinner, night night." I swing my feet off the couch onto the ground and head to my bedroom. On the way, I slide my phone out of my pocket and send a message to Bear:

Me: - *Hey big guy. I'm pooped, so I'm gonna get into bed. Ride carefully home. I love you xx*

"Night Jenna. Hope you feel better tomorrow; you probably just need to sleep." Jade calls after me as I enter my bedroom.

I proceed to strip out of the clothes I wore to work today, flinging them haphazardly here and there. I'm normally neat, but tonight I don't care. I grab Bear's big t-shirt and shove it over my head, then slide into bed, the cool fresh sheets welcoming me as Bear's scent drifts over me, making me feel right at home. Before long, my eyes start to grow heavier, and it's hard to keep them open. I snuggle down and lay on my side, tucking my legs into the fetal position, and eventually let sleep take me under.

***

"I love you, baby. I love our little baby too..."
I don't know what time it is, but I wake up to feel Bear's warmth and his arm draping around my midriff, pulling me tight to his body.
Ahhh, this feels perfect...so right.
I try to fight my fatigue to speak to him, but my eyes grow heavier again and begin to droop.
I'll be on my A-game tomorrow...

***

Around 2am, I wake up with an uncomfortable feeling in my tummy I can't really describe—like a kind of fluttering in the pit of my stomach.
I unwrap myself from Bear's tight hold gently— relieved when he keeps snoring softly, now lying on his stomach—and shove my arms into my hoodie, creeping out of my bedroom so I don't disturb him. I'm gonna grab something to eat; this weird sensation feels like the sickly hunger feeling I get sometimes.
I decide to just keep it simple with toast, then I pour myself an ice-cold glass of water and go to take it back to bed. On the way, I have a sudden urge to use the toilet, so make a quick detour to my bathroom and sit on it.
The longer I think about it, the more I realize the feeling in my lower stomach is not pain, but more like an ache.

I wonder if I have a bladder infection again? That would be just typical...

Once I've finished, I decide to run a bath to ease the discomfort and hopefully relax myself. I sprinkle lavender bath salts in the warm water, the smell instantly calming me as I take off my clothes and sink into the bath with a sigh. The water eases my backache and the strange fluttering feeling right away.

***

I don't know how long I've been in here, but my fingertips have gone all wrinkly in the water. I pull the plug on the bath, and as soon as I stand up, I hear a pop.

Shit! What the hell was that?

I grab my bath sheet to get dried, but feel a lump between my legs as I towel off.

No, no, no! This isn't right; it just can't be! Bear! I need Bear...

"Bear!" I can barely get his name out between panicked breaths at first. "BEAR!" I scream at the top of my lungs with all the strength I have.

I hear his feet thump onto the floor, and he runs from the bed. "JENNA! Where are ya?!" he yells, instantly wide awake.

"Bathroom! I'm in the bathroom!"

He swings the door open, letting it bounce off the wall.

"Something's not right, babe. I-I- h-h-have a l-l-lump in-between my legs, and I swear I heard a pop. *Oh G-God Bear!*" I scream, the tears running down my face freely.

"Shit! Fuuuck!" Bear bellows.

He turns his back for a second, and then back to me, and it's like he's flicked a switch—he is calm, collected, and simply amazing, running back into the bedroom to grab his phone and call for an ambulance, only to be told a first response EMT will call us back.

"WHAT THE FUCK?! Don't you realize my woman is 20 weeks pregnant?!" Bear rages.

I am a quivering mess, a mix of the chill from being out of the bath and the fear gripping hold of my heart. Whatever is happening to me, we both know it isn't right.

2 minutes pass, but it feels more like a lifetime. Bear calls again, only to be told once more that someone will call him back.

At this point, I couldn't give a shit if someone called back or not. The tears stream down my face, dripping down my neck and onto my chest.

Bear, being as calm as he can and my absolute rock, grabs me some clothes to put on and helps me into them when my vision swims too much to see. As he drives us back to the hospital like a madman, we sit in silence, dread filling us both.

Chapter 26

Bear

When the doctors have done the scan, they tell us both exactly what we have been dreading. Grief squeezes my heart like a vise as the doctor says the 5 words that would make any expecting parent's heart stop.

"We can't find a heartbeat."

My stomach plummets, hitting the fuckin' floor, and my hands tremble uncontrollably. I peel my eyes up to Jenna, who's laying there with her pale blue spotted hospital gown still up under her breasts, her little bump still on show with ultrasound gel smothered all over it, taunting and haunting us...

Jenna's face has dropped, her skin now a deathly shade of gray. Her eyes hold nothing. There's no life, no sparkle; just a complete abyss of pain...they are fixed on the doctor at first, then flick to me, and then down at her protruding belly with our unborn child still inside.

"Jenna..." I rasp, trying to stop the tears dripping down my face as I pull myself up to her side and wrap my arms around her, wishin' like fuckin' anything that I could undo this and protect her like I couldn't protect our child.

I cocoon her in my arms, and she doesn't move an inch at first, but then within the space of a few seconds, she buries her head right into my chest and grips onto me so tight it's like she's scared I'm going to slip away too. Her nails bite and dig into my skin, and it hurts, but it's nothing like the pure pain and anguish inside our hearts right now and for what I'm sure will be a lifetime...

Her whole body starts shaking uncontrollably from her silent sobs. I feel her mouth open against my chest, and they become wails of anguish as my own tears flow freely.

"I'm so sorry. I'll give you some time together and come back later," the doctor says softly, leaving us locked in each other's arms with one another.

I caress her back gently. "Babe...I know...fuck!"

God, I don't know what to fuckin' say! This whole situation is fucked up...

I go to pull away to lift her chin up so I can get a good look at her, but she just holds me tighter, trying to pull me closer to her. I get into the hospital bed with her, and we lay there for what feels like hours just holding each other and crying. In this moment, we are each other's life preserver in a sea of grief and pain.

***

Our time is cut short as a team of doctors arrives to take Jenna into surgery, leaving me alone with my devastation. The news our little bear cub has died is absolutely heart-wrenching; I think having my heart actually ripped out would be a lot less painful than this.

All our hopes and dreams for the future have just vanished in an instant, as fleeting as the feeling of a snowflake in the first snowfall of the year. As much as you try to hold on, it just melts away, and there's nothing you can do about it.

***

When Jenna comes out of surgery, we find out that we had a little girl and have a chance to hold her precious little body—she's absolutely beautiful. We take pictures of her, and the midwives help us do foot and handprints for memory boxes they give us.

Never did I think we would be doing this in a million years. Things like this don't happen to regular people—it's something you see in movies, on TV, and in magazines, not happening to us. It's left me completely empty; nothing else matters, my other fears seem so trivial now.

When they leave Jenna and I alone to process the news in our own private room away from the rest of the maternity unit, it feels like it's just us in a black and desolate hole, left with nothing but the misery of knowing that we've lost a part of ourselves. I don't think I have ever cried so much in my whole 35 years of life, even as a child, but it's all I can do at the pain and rage slicing through my heart over and over until it's in shreds.

Jenna struggles to catch her breath between sobs from where she lays next to me in the hospital bed. She has a fist tightly curled in my shirt, and the other rubs vigorously at her chest, trying to ease the matching pain that's searing through her heart too. She pulls herself off of me and looks up at me, her eyes full of sheer, raw pain that I hope I never have to see there again. She closes her scarlet, puffy eyes again as her face crumples, and she screams into the room until her voice sounds hoarse.

I've never heard a sound like it, and it twists my heart to witness the woman I love in so much pain and know I can't do a thing to ease it. I hope to fuckin' God—if there is one—that they take away her pain. Seeing my brave, funny, gorgeous woman reduced to a husk of herself is killing me.

"B-B-Bear, w-w-w-was it m-m-m-my fault?" she croaks with a stutter, her broken voice cracking.

"Fuck no! Never! It. Was. Not. Your. Fault! You hear me? It's no one's fault, darlin', I swear to you. Don't you go thinking that shit. OK?" I choke back tears as I speak, holding on to the last bit of strength I have. I need to stay strong for her—for us.

She can't meet my gaze and just stares down at her stomach, tears swimming in her eyes. Eventually, she blinks, sending a shower down onto the top of the gown that rolls onto her empty stomach. We don't have to see any babies or new mothers and fathers here, but it doesn't stop us from hearing faint cries, and I know the sound is torturing her.

I shift to get the nurse to come and give her something to help her sleep. "Jenna, I'm just going to go—"

Jenna grips my arm. "NO! No, don't leave me! Please, Bear."

I pull her into my embrace. "OK darlin'. I ain't going anywhere OK? I ain't going anywhere, I promise," I whisper into her hair as we cling to each other, desperate for what we have lost today.

Questions whirl around us, echoing out loud and in our hearts on a loop.

Did we do something wrong?
Is this our fault?
Why us?

***

"She should be out for a couple of hours at least, are you sure you don't want anything?" Nurse Ania asks me with a look of sympathy. That's not what I pushed the call button for, and I'm sick of it already, even though it's only been 3 hours since our world was turned upside down by the death of our beautiful baby girl.

I grunt my decline, and Ania gives me a small smile and leaves the room.

I didn't think it was possible to hurt right down to your very soul, but here I am. I want to rip my fucking heart out to bring my gorgeous little baby girl back and take her place, but I know I can't—I have to endure this pain, and everything that comes with it.

I watch my beautiful woman drifting in and out of sleep, and I realize that we've been so wrapped up in our pain that no one else knows what's happened. I can barely bring myself to think the words, and I dread saying them—making the whole thing true—but I decide the best option is to do it while she's asleep, so she hasn't gotta go through that too. I couldn't give birth to our child, but I can bear this burden for the love of my life.

I watch her sleep for a bit longer—procrastinating, as Jenna would call it—then gather my strength and place a soft kiss on her forehead as I pull away, gazing down at her eyes and lips, which are red and puffy from all the crying.

She stirs, and I hear her mumble the words, "Don't leave me..."

Fuck, I don't think I could if I wanted to. She's rooted deep within the very bones of me, and I know I have to be strong enough to pull us both out of this. In truth, I need her more than she needs me—she just doesn't realize that yet.

I grab her phone from her purse, checking the time—almost 5:30am—and decide to call her Momma first. I let the nurse on the nurse station know that I'll be back soon and am just going to make phone calls, then walk out of the maternity unit and into the pretty much desolate hallway. As I unlock Jenna's phone, I feel physically sick—I wish I didn't have to do this.

I find her Momma's number and hesitantly hover over the call button for a few minutes, before clenching my eyes shut, pressing 'Call' and holding the phone up to my ear. It nearly rings out, and I dare to hope I won't have to say the words out loud just yet, but then her Momma picks up—clearly life has other ideas.

"Hiya hon, y'all OK?" she answers so cheerily I have to swallow down hard on the thick lump that forms in my throat.

"Hey Mrs. Smith...I mean, Maria. It's...it's Bear," I can't stop my voice from cracking, and Maria instantly knows something is wrong, panic and concern rising in her tone.

"Bear? Where's Jenna? What's happened?"

"I-t-t-'s the b-b-baby, we've l-lost the b-baby." I don't realize I'm crying again until I see the teardrops run down the window my forehead leans against, shimmering in the orange and yellow sunrise.

The line is deathly silent for a second, and I think I may have lost connection until I hear the godawful scream, almost as raw and guttural as Jenna's. "OHHH GOD! Where are you? I'll be there as soon as possible. Is my Jenna OK?"

I can barely get the answers out through my sobs, "C-county Hospital maternity unit, we're in a private room. She's sleeping now, they gave her something to help her. I'll...I'll call Jade, OK?"

"O-OK Bear." Sobbing fills my ears. If I could, I would try and give Maria comfort, but I don't have it in me—not yet. "I'll leave now. Love you, son," she whispers, and the line clicks as she hangs up.

My mind whirls at her words, sending fresh pain right through me.

Son...daughter...our daughter, our beautiful angel daughter.

The window I stand at overlooks a zen garden in the courtyard of the hospital, and I stare at it, concentrating on all the tiny gray pebbles inside.

Everything in this fuckin' hospital is fuckin' gray, but maybe that's because all color has drained from my world. I brace myself to make the next call to my own family, but I can't bear to tell Axe—even the thought of hearing another baby in the background makes my heart break all over again. I call Jade next instead, and she cries so hard I think she'll never stop. I have to cut the call short, and probably sound like an ass, but I need to get back to Jenna's side.

Flex is last, and he yells at me for waking him and Zara up, but he's remorseful as soon as I tell him why.

"We've lost the baby."

The words are the hardest I have ever had to say, and each time stings as badly as the first. I ask him to let Axe know, and tell him not to come to the hospital, but I know he and the rest of the club will be here to grieve with us.

My brothers in the club are family, and they and Jenna are all I got now.

Jenna

I never wanted to wake up from my peaceful sleep. I lay still for a few more minutes, my eyes squeezed shut. I know Bear is in the room, lying next to me, but I'm not ready to face him yet; not ready to stop blocking out reality.

The doctor's words swirl around my skull again and again, and I know they will haunt me forever.

'We can't find a heartbeat…I'm so sorry…'

I feel Bear jolt against me and remove himself carefully from my side, then I hear him go over to the other side of the room.

When I hear my Momma gasp, my eyes spring open.

I can see Bear's devastated, forlorn face, and my Momma holding him as he stands there, unmoving. She looks awful. Although she usually never has a hair out of place, she's here in no makeup and her "loungewear".

I want to reach out for Bear, but I physically can't, so I just watch as my Momma holds him. She pulls him back at arm's length, and even in the dim lighting of the room, I can see the silent tears streaming down their faces.

I try with all my might to call Bear, but nothing comes out. He must sense my eyes on him, though, as he turns and meets my gaze a moment later.

"Jenna..."

In three strides he's at my side, pulling me into the crook of his neck and burying his face in mine as we cling to each other. I feel his tears slide down my neck, and I know my big strong alpha Bear is breaking along with me.

"Baby girl...I- I can't believe it. I'm so sorry, Jenna. *So* sorry honey," my Momma murmurs into my hair as she wraps her arms around us both, just holding us, as we all sob uncontrollably.

She holds us just like a Momma trying to comfort her child would—just how Bear and I held our little angel. She was perfect in every way, and looked so peaceful, just like she was sleeping. We are so glad we saw her, but heartbroken we had to say goodbye.

***

The rest of the day is full of people coming to see us and wrapping their arms around us just like my Momma did, showering us with their love. Before long, as much as we appreciate them, it becomes too much, and I ask them to give us some space. I can see Bear getting antsy, and I'm exhausted.

Jade, Kelly, Zara and Flex nod and get up to leave, and I can see even Flex fighting tears. Jade cries as openly as she has the whole time, completely speechless, and Momma rubs her sympathetically on the back as she comes over to us.

"All right, you two try and get some sleep, I'll head to the bakery and grab you some clothes, Jenna, and I'll see you both in a few hours," she says gently, placing a kiss on both our cheeks and squeezing our clasped hands.

As the door closes after my Mom, Bear snuggles into me, pressing his forehead on mine. "Darlin'...I can't get my head around all of this. 24 hours ago, our baby was safe inside you, and now she's all alone down the hall."

I can't help the waterfall of tears that come from me upon hearing the rawness in his voice.

He's right, she was safe; we heard her heartbeat...

It's hard enough to know that we have lost our beautiful baby girl, but the hurt I hear makes me hope I don't lose my Bear too. I really don't think my heart could stand anymore pain, anymore anguish, or anymore love lost.

That's exactly what our gorgeous girl was—our love in the tiniest of bundles.

~ Chapter 27 Jenna ~

We named our sleeping princess Sophia...

4 weeks after...

I haven't dared—or even wanted—to go back into the bakery yet. Bear's moved into the apartment unofficially, and I don't think everyone at the club took it too well—I think they wanted us both there, but I couldn't give a flying fuck! I need to be at home, and *we* need each other desperately; our days are all about trying to keep everything going, and our nights are filled with tears and questions and anger. Every time we talk about it, it slowly burns away at my heart.

Bear is seriously struggling too. He hasn't truly broken yet, but I can see the anger and hurt inside of him through the look in his eyes. I've tried talking to him, but he just shuts me down at every turn. He thinks he has to stay strong for me, but he doesn't. What I want—no, *need*—him to do is to actually break for me so we can do this together. Grieve together.

What does that word truly mean? If it's the way I feel now, the definition should be, 'Pure devastation; the sense that it would be easier and less painful to cut out your own heart with a blunt, rusty knife'.

"Morning sis, I made you some breakfast. Do you feel like coming down to the bakery today? You don't have to do a whole day—just for an hour maybe?" Jade asks me hesitantly as I pad into the kitchen to grab a cup of coffee. I think it's the only thing I've survived on for weeks; Bear tries to feed me anything and everything, but the thought of having food makes me sick.

Jade has been amazing to Bear and I since we came home, although I can see she's still hurting too. I see she's made me my favorite blueberry pancakes and manage a weak smile. She hasn't stopped apologizing that she couldn't come into the hospital for long—she was too distraught—but I know it hit her hard, and she hasn't broken yet either; she's just keeping quiet about it.

"Thanks Jade, that's lovely of you. I'll try and eat, but my appetite still isn't right. The pancakes look yummy though." I sit down at the kitchen table and try to force myself to swallow them. I know they taste amazing, but I can't taste anything. Everything is bland, boring, and gray.

"Do you know what time Bear left this morning? I didn't hear him leave." It's only 8.30am, so I should have heard him, but I put it down to how tired I am. To be honest, I didn't hear him come in last night either—I was asleep by 10. Part of me doesn't think he was here at all. Even with the help of the herbal sedative Kelly suggested, my sleep is still light enough to feel when he puts his arm around me, and I couldn't even smell him on the sheets this morning.

"Jenna, I've been up since 7 getting ready and making breakfasts; I don't think he was here last night. I mean, I was still awake reading after 11, and I didn't hear him come in," Jade says, shaking her head sympathetically. "Sis, I need to talk to you about something. You don't have to yet, but..."

I know exactly what she's going to say—Zara and Kelly both started the question the same way last week. "Dani wants to come see me, doesn't she?" I finish.

Jade's shoulders drop, and she nods. "Yeah, she does. She knows you're hurting, and you know that girl, she wants to come and comfort you. She said she'd come alone."

As Jade heads over to the bathroom, I decide I've put it off long enough. As much as it hurts, I want to see my friend; she has sent me flowers, chocolates, pamper treatments, and is constantly reaching out to check on me.

"Jade!"

"Yeah? I'll be back in a min—"

I cut her off before she can finish—or I can change my mind—and my next words make her freeze in the doorway. "Jade, tell Dani she and Axe can come over today—or tonight, whatever's easiest for her—but I want to her to bring Ryker too."

"Are you sure, JJ?" Jade replies as she walks back to the kitchen. "You don't have to; she will understand if you need more time."

I give Jade a small smile when I hear our shared nickname. "No, I want to see them all. I'm going to have to see them sooner or later, so why wait?"

"OK, I'll message her in a little bit. I'll be here, and Bear should too."

I wander aimlessly around the apartment cleaning for a while, but eventually, I decide to force myself to go downstairs and lose myself in some baking in the back—it's always been my way to de-stress and unwind.

Sure enough, before I know it, I look up and see I've been in the bakery for over 3 hours baking pies, brownies, and cookies.

Jade walks through the kitchen door and stops stock still in the doorway with a big smile on her face. A small teardrop forms in the corner of her eye, and she brushes it away. "It's great seeing you in here, sis! How long have you been down? I thought you went back upstairs earlier."

"I've been down for about 3 hours; I didn't realize how long until just before you came in. What time are Axe and Dani coming again?" I ask, ignoring the sudden sick feeling deep in the pit of my stomach.

"She said around 2, so in about 15 minutes. Have you heard from Bear?"

I grab my phone from my back pocket and check.

Nope, no calls, no texts, nothing.

"No, I'll call him soon."

***

15 minutes later, Jade and I are up in the apartment waiting for Dani and Axe to arrive. I've tried calling Bear non-stop, but to no avail.

DING DONG!

Jade gets to her feet at the sound of the doorbell but stops and looks at me. "You still sure about this? I can reschedule with them."

"No, it's OK. I've got you, I'll be all right."

"I'll grab the door, then," Jade tells me as she heads out of the apartment, leaving me anxiously rubbing my palms up and down my jeans.

"Hey, honey!" The door swings open, and I'm greeted with Dani's unsure smile. As soon as she gets to me, she wraps her arms around me and holds me tight. As I cling to her too, she whispers in my ear, "We love you, sweetie, and we care about you and Bear so very much." Dani's voice cracks as she speaks, and we both break down on each other.

After she's collected and trying to console me, I pull away to see Axe sitting down and rocking a fluffy blue bundle.

Ryker.

My heart skips a beat, then starts to ache. Ryker's fast asleep in his Daddy's huge arms, and the sight makes me want Bear badly.

Where is he? Why isn't he here?

Just as the thought crosses my mind, the apartment door reopens again, and there is the man in question; my Bear. His gaze softens as soon as he sees me, and we give each other a small smile.

Axe coughs dramatically, and Bear's eyes flick over to him and Ryker in shock, then back at me, confusion written all over his face. In a second, he's by my side, and I instantly melt into his arms as he holds me.

"Darlin', are you OK?" he whispers into my ear with a slur—he's been drinking. The only place I feel safe might be in his arms, but Bear has become distant with me and everyone around him—including his Prez. Jade tells me she's heard he's been keeping a low profile at the club since he started going back there.

The rest of the visit is understandably awkward and strained, but all in all it's lovely to have them here. I even work up the courage to hold Ryker—it isn't as bad I thought it would be, as he isn't a tiny newborn anymore, and it's only brief, but Bear refuses to hold him or show any interest.

Seeing him like this kills me—when we visited after they first brought him home from the hospital a few months ago, Bear was rocking and holding little baby Ryker constantly. I wish we could both be normal around babies again, but deep down I know that every child, baby, or pregnant lady I encounter is going to feel like a kick in the gut and a stab to the heart. I just have to bear it and get on with my life.

"Bear, I want to talk to you in the morning. No ifs or buts this time, OK? I want you in my office at 9am on the dot," Axe orders as we are saying our goodbyes to them.

Beside him, Dani gives me one last cuddle. "Jenna, we'll do this again, OK? I know it's going to take some time, and we understand that, but we all miss you at the club," she tells me in my ear.

"Yeah, that would be great. Soon, maybe?" I reply, although truthfully, I really don't know when I'll be ready.

Once they leave, I turn to Bear. "Where have you been all day? I called and texted you, but nothing! What did Axe mean by 'no ifs or buts this time'?"

Bear grunts. "Nowhere, and it don't matter, OK? It's club business," he spits.

I stand there in pure shock at the way he's talking to me. Bear never snaps or hides things from me; something's not right.

Did he feel obligated to be with me because I was pregnant? Does he still feel forced to stay with me even though there's no baby to be here for? I worry, panic rising in my chest.

He's slouched in the armchair on his phone, oblivious to the shock on my face.

I turn on my heel, stride into my room, and grab his shit, stuffing his clothes and anything I can grab of his into his gym bag. I swing it as well as I can out of the open window so it lands with a thud on the concrete outside the back of the bakery.

I don't give a shit anymore. I don't need him—if doesn't want me anymore now there's no baby, he can get the fuck outta my life!

I storm back into the living room, see he hasn't moved an inch, and shout, "You! Get the fuck out of my apartment! Now! I don't know what's got into you, Bear Jameson, but if you don't want to be here, you don't have to anymore! Go!"

Jade comes running out of her bedroom and to my side at the commotion. "What happened, Jenna?"

"I want him gone! He's hardly here, and when he is, I get this shit!" I wave my hand at him in exasperation.

He's still in the same position, but his face looks defeated. I don't care—I've had enough of this bullshit.

***

My alarm clock reads 10:40pm. Bear moved back to the club earlier, and I have been laying on my bed staring at the ivory ceiling and counting the tiny cracks in the paintwork for what feels like hours now. I'm not getting very far—all I can think about is Bear's hang-dog look as he left. He kept trying to explain himself, but he was so drunk he wasn't making sense at all.

My phone buzzes, and I reluctantly grab it to see a message from Zara:

Zara: - *Hey hon, r u ok? Bear's here and he's an absolute mess, drunk out of his brain and slurring about crap that don't make much sense. Something about u throwing him out. Xx*

Me: - *Hey babe, I'm all right. Yeah, I did throw him out xx*

The next thing I know, my phone is vibrating like mad—Zara is calling me.

"Hey hon—"

I don't even get through my greeting before Zara interrupts me. "What d'ya mean you threw him out? What happened?"

I hear her walking away from the rowdiness of the club and wait until the noise fades into the background before replying. "He talked to me like crap when I asked him what he had been doin' after I put up with him being gone for a whole day and night with no explanation, so I made it easier for us both."

"Hold up, you must have things confused; did you ask him where he was? And this is easier how, exactly? I can hear you've been crying, and he's drunk out of his mind thinking all kinds of shit. You're both still hurting. Hard."

I choke back the sob in the back of my throat as the hole in my heart cracks open even more. "Z-Zar', it's easier this way, e-e-even though I love him so much. We only got together because of Sophia, and now she's no longer here, he doesn't want to be lumbered with me. He would just be staying with me out of duty, and I don't want that for either of us," I manage to stutter before I break down harder—both for the daughter I'm mourning and the man I adore.

I wrap my arms around my midriff, rubbing my stomach and willing more than anything for this to be a horrible nightmare and for my beautiful long-fingered girl to come back to her Momma and her Daddy.

"Oh God, Jen, I think you have both misunderstood. Listen, he needs to sober up before you talk to him, but *trust me,* you have it all wrong. Try and get some sleep; it will be okay, I promise," Zara implores.

I can't stop the silent sobbing or the tears pouring down my face, but I eventually manage to choke out my response, "O-O-OK Z-Z-Zar', I'll try. I haven't known where he's been for the past week, and it's drivin' me crazy. I k-know he's h-h-hurtin', but s-so am I."

"Jenna, you get some sleep, doll, and I'll get Flex to talk to him. I'll come over tomorrow, OK? Night honey, I'll see ya in the morning."

As Zara hangs up, I quickly drop her a message:

Me: - *Thank you for that hon, tell Flex not to kick his ass too much* :) xx

"Oi! POOH BEAR! What the hell have you been playin' at?!" Zara screams as she storms back into the main room of the clubhouse, flailing her arms around. I can't deal with her shit, especially after my woman throwin' me out. I can't blame her after I basically abandoned her all week. It's for a good reason, but she can't know why yet.

I swivel on the bar seat I've been warming my big ass on for the 4 hours since smashing my fists into the wall outside the bakery and riding my bike back to the clubhouse to smash my fists into the punching bag in the backyard.

Dagger and Tin literally dragged my ass back into the clubhouse, and I told them what had gone down at Jenna's. They tried to beat my ass for leavin' her, so I'm sitting here with a busted lip, a bloodied nose, and maybe a sore rib or two. I didn't even stop them—I've been consumed by guilt ever since she threw me out, and I deserved the beatin' and then some.

Dagger especially was furious with me. He told me if he had a stunner like Jenna wanting his old ass, he woulda never let her go. As for Tinhead, well, I think he just enjoyed beating my ass down.

Zara Hart is the next to take her shot, and I feel a searing pain in my ribs take my breath away. Part of me is glad it wasn't her Ol' Man—they committed to each other last night, but Flex didn't want any celebrations until the timing was more suitable; I only know 'cause Wrench ran his drunk-ass mouth.

"That's for upsetting one of my girls, you bastard! What the hell, Bear? Why haven't you told her what you've done?" she yells at me.

"Look just leave it, OK? I'll deal with it, she will understand in a day or so," I reply, then neck my double shot of JD, enjoying the smoky burn down my throat.

"Yeah, if you live that long! She's over there crying into her pillow, thinking you have been distant with her all week because you don't want her if she can't give you Sophia."

Fear grips my heart at Zara's words, and I explode. "WHAAAT?! What do you mean? Did you tell her she's got it all wrong?!" I demand in frustration.

"Of course, I told her she has it all confused. But *you* need to sober up and fix things tomorrow."

"*Fuck no,* I ain't waiting until then! I ain't letting her think that shit!"

"Yo Dags, you been drinkin'? I need you to take me over to Jenna's. Now!" I holler across the room.

"I got you Bear, let's go brother!" Dagger replies as he jumps off the couch and puts his untouched beer on the bar in front of me.

"Tinhead! Put that in the fridge for when I get back!"

He turns back to me. "All right, you better sober the fuck up before you go. If you have fucked this up, you deserve to get your ass beat for leavin' her after what you have both been through."

Like I don't know that!

"Shut the fuck up and take me to Jenna, Dagger! I need to make her understand what I've been doing this week," I tell him as I run out of the clubhouse door and jump into the club's cage.

Dagger's ass casually swaggers up to the driver's side, and he gets in. "What the fuck, Bear? What have you been playing at, brother? You need each other; now more than ever." He informs me through clenched teeth, shaking his head in disbelief.

"Look, Dags, I hear ya and you're right, but I thought Jenna didn't want me anymore. It turns out she thought the same about me, but that *was never* going to be the case. You can lecture me later, but I need to talk to my girl. I appreciate everything you've done for me these past couple of months, but right now, just put your fuckin' foot to the floor and get me back to Jenna."

He stares back at me for a moment, searching my gaze for something, then gives me a curt nod and does what I tell him.

***

"JENNA! PLEASE OPEN THE DOOR!" I'm outside the back door of the bakery slamming my hand on the metal again and again. I've been standing here for at least 15 minutes, and nothing. I've only stopped to call and text her.

I go to try again when Jade swings the door open and steps aside, her hair mussed, a sweatshirt covering her PJ shirt. "Bear, she doesn't want to see you. Go back to the club and see her tomorrow when you've sobered up."

"Nah, not happening, Jade." I'm not taking no for an answer, so I take the chance and squeeze my whole body through the back door. I take the stairs up to the apartment 3 at a time before she can stop me, and reach the front door, which Jade's left wide open too. I scan the living room, not seeing the woman who fills my mind, my heart, and my soul.

"Jade, I told you to leave it, he'll—" Jenna comes to the doorway and stops dead when she sees me standing right in front of her bedroom. She looks worse than when I left her, with puffy red eyelids and ruby lips swollen from crying.

"Cupcake..."

"Don't you 'Cupcake' me, Bear, what are you doing? I don't want to see you right now!" Jenna spits at me.

She turns on her heel and goes back into her bedroom, going to slam the door in my face, but I catch it quickly with my fist.

"I know you don't want to see me, babe, but I need you to hear me out. If you still want me to go afterward, I'll go," I implore her, throwing in my most irresistible smile and wink for good measure.

Jenna's not even the love of my life—that's for small fish. No, my Jenna is the love of my whole fuckin' universe, and I can't let her go.

Her piercing glare softens as she walks back into her room and perches her gorgeous butt on her bed—I can't help but notice the screwed-up tissues scattered haphazardly over her comforter as she does.

After what feels like a lifetime, she exhales a big breath. "Come on, big guy. Tell me what the hell you've been up to all week that has made you so distant with me."

I sigh from pure relief. "Darlin', you gotta know one thing first, and you better be listening to me when I say this. I will *always* love you. I never got with you just because you got pregnant! I fuckin' love you to the end of the world, you know that. I thought you didn't want me anymore, so that's why I didn't fight it when you threw me out. I thought you didn't want a serious relationship, just sex or friends with benefits. God! This has been the biggest fuckin' case of crossed wires ever, Cupcake."

I drop to my knees in front of her, holding her calves as she gazes down into my eyes, tears streaming down her face, which is contorted like she's in physical pain.

Not more pain…Fuck! I'm too late.

~ Chapter 29 ~

Jenna

I think I've been running on pure adrenaline for the past couple of months. I get up, barely eat, try to talk, sleep, and repeat the cycle, all while trying to mourn for a daughter who is no longer with us and deal with the fact that the man I love has shut himself off from me for the past week.

After speaking to Jade earlier, I think she's right—I should go to counselling. I want Bear to go too, but I can't force him to—he has to want to do it on his own. Based on the scene before me, though, I think he's coming close.

He's the most vulnerable I've seen him as he actually cracks on his knees in front of me, keeping a death hold on my calves. He looks exactly how he did when the doctor told us Sophia had died—completely lost, devastated, and alone.

"J-Jenna, baby, despite being s-surrounded by all the men at the club, it has to be one of the loneliest places to be. Even my Dad was no help after D-D-Doc told him. I feel trapped, and I know there is nothing I can do to fix this. I want to make everything all OK…and I can't, I just can't. It's out of my control, and that absolutely kills me, babe. All I want to do is stand by you and be strong for you always, but this has changed me as much as it has changed you, beautiful. I tried talking to Dagger and Flex about it, but no one can truly understand it unless they have experienced it themselves.

"I know I have fucked up and been distant, but that's not your fault, babe, I promise. All the men at the club have been trying to get me to talk, but I couldn't. I only ever wanted to keep coming home to you and being your rock. I wouldn't even care if we weren't a couple; my love for you and our daughter will always burn bright. Always."

My fists instantly go into his hair and tug sharply on it to make him look up at me. My own tears are freefalling now, but I don't care if I look like a snotty, red-eyed mess or not. His words still make me smile— he's the only person who does at the moment. "Bear! Why didn't you tell me this? I want to be your rock too...to bring us back together and make us whole again. I love you so much, but please don't fuck around with me again...I can't bear losing you too!" I howl between silent, breath-stealing sobs.

Bear scoops me up in his arms and places me on his lap, my head instantly finding refuge in the crook of his neck, his scent soothing me like a balm. We cling to one another, basking in the love that binds us together as he rubs my back, comforting me. In that moment, I know that I'm back where I belong, with my arms around the most sweet, kind-hearted, and amazingly strong man in the world.

"So, what have you been doing this past week that made you all distant?" I mumble, my head still buried in his neck.

I instantly feel him tense up, but within a few seconds, he relaxes. "Ah, shit…OK, you're going to have to let go, babe."

I unravel my arms from around his waist and withdraw my face from his strong neck, rearranging my pajama shirt. He gets up, standing right in front of me and looking nervous as hell, swallowing hard. "This is what I have been up to this week."

Before I can ask him what he's talking about, he whips his dark gray shirt off, revealing his beautiful tattooed torso… and my heart stops.

There, right over his heart, is a stunning black-and-gray tattoo of Sophia's handprint with the smallest, cutest pair of angel wings either side of it. The wings are so intricate I can see them being ruffled by an invisible breeze and shadows where the light hits them. Sophia's name is written underneath her handprint in a delicate cursive, and faint daisies and hearts cover the surrounding skin, blending seamlessly into the rest of his ink.

Taking in the tattoo with a hand over my mouth, I cry. I sob even harder than before, making my chest ache and burn. Even though our gorgeous girl is not physically with us, this wonderful man is still being the most amazing Daddy to her by carrying her with him always.

I stand up on unsteady legs—feeling just like a newborn calf—and take the longest time to eventually reach him, but when I do, I touch the tattoo hesitantly, tracing the design, carefully leaving our baby girl's handprint until last. I press my palm over it and close my eyes, resting my forehead against Bear's as he wraps his arms around me tighter than ever.

"This week, I asked Zara to design me something, and then I had to take her the prints of Sophia's hands for her to trace. After that, she started tattooing. I wanted to wait until it was completely healed, but if I'd have done that, I would have ended up losing you. Do you like it, darlin'?"

I stroke his beard, still loving the feel as it grazes my palm despite my numbness, then reach up on tiptoes and place the softest kiss on his lips. As I pull away, I whisper, "I love it. It's absolutely beautiful, Bear, a true tribute to our baby girl. You'll never lose me, baby; what doesn't kill us makes us stronger."

Bear

10 days later...

"So, you're definitely sure he's at this place, Brains?"

"Yeah bro, he's definitely here. I've been tracking him since you asked me to 6 months ago, and his work calendar says this is the last time he's going to be here before he goes back to Nashville."

"OK, OK. All right, you going to be on the radio while me and Dags go in?"

"Yeah, damn straight! I got your back, man, just hurry up before Axe blows up my phone," he grunts out.

Me and Dags remove our cuts, leaving them in the back of the cage with Brains while we go inside this restaurant. I readjust my navy-blue 2-piece suit—we decided to drop the ties—and we jump out onto Main Street, 2 blocks away from Jenna's Bakery.

Brains tracked Brent Johnson down and set up a business deal under his real name—Robert Daniels—so we could be sure we'd meet him. Brains is the son of a wealthy businessman, so when people hear his last name, they pay attention.

As we walk through the doors of Luigi's, we find that it's a typical rustic Italian restaurant, with dark wood paneling and multicolored wine bottles of all different sizes hanging down from the ceiling. I scan the restaurant, trying to see any sign of our man, but the place is deserted except for the waiters and waitresses.

The concierge shows us to the table in the far corner, and Dagger seats himself facing towards the back exit, with me facing towards the main doors.

"How long do you think we're going to have to wait…"

"Not long," I interrupt. "There's a man being walked over here…"

Hold up, this dude looks familiar! Receding hairline with what hair he has got slicked back, red blotchy skin…

Realization hits both of us at the same time. "It's you! What the fuck!" we say in unison.

"What is it, brother?" Dagger whips around crazy-eyed, always on guard.

I leap to my feet and kick the chair from under me, not caring when it thuds to the floor. "This fucker here! He's the little prick I told you about that gave me and Jenna shit when we were waiting at the lights!"

I take a step closer to him. "You're Brent? Jesus, *you* are the bastard who fat-shamed my woman back in college? Seriously? Look at you, man!"

My phone's buzzing ten to the dozen in my back pocket, and I remember I've thrown my earpiece on the table. I don't give a fuck about this ruse now.

Backing away, the weasel stutters, "W-w-what d-do you mean? Hold up, Jenna? Do you mean Jenna Smith?"

"YEAH, FUCKIN' JENNA SMITH!" I roar, the sound of my woman's name coming from his mouth sending me over the edge. "What gives you the right to say her name, you ugly fu—"

"Bear Jameson! Leave him, he's not worth it!" demands the only voice that could stop me in my tracks and make the world tilt on its axis.

Jenna.

I flick my head up to see the most beautiful woman in the world, the orange hue of the lights casting a halo around her golden hair. She looks like an angel.

"Cupcake, this little motherfucker gotta know it ain't right to talk to women the way he did. What he did was messed up, so I should fuckin' mess him up!"

"Bear! Don't. Please. He's not worth it. You're worth a million of him. Look at him, he's a far cry from the most popular jock on the football team now. It just goes to show, what goes around comes around."

She sashays her sexy ass over to me, her deep red polka-dot flared dress hugging her all in the right places. You would never think in a million years that this stunning, strong, amazing, caring, beautiful wonder woman went through hell only weeks ago.

She eventually stands toe-to-toe with me, grabs a fistful of the lapels of the suit I've got on and drags my face down to her eye level.

"You look sexy as hell like this, big guy, but I much prefer the rough-around-the-edges, leather-wearing biker I fell in love with. You didn't need to do all this; he's my past, and he held me back from taking a chance...until I took it for you, and I'm glad I did. You're my rock; my big teddy Bear. "

4 months on...

"Sugar! What the hell is that on the base of your neck?!" Flex shouts across to Zara.

She's standing at the bar talking to my Cupcake, Dani, and Jade. It's meant to be a party, but you wouldn't think it looking at Zara's face—it looks like someone slapped it with a wet fish. Zara pivots on her heel, wide-eyed and with pursed lips flicking her chin up high in defiance.

"Flex, why don't you come over and find out exactly what it is?"

I decide to go over with him—I need to see how this is going to go down, and it's a welcome distraction from Sue holding 7-and-a- half-month-old Ryker.

As we both walk over to the bar, I wrap my arm around Jenna's waist, pulling her close as I place a gentle kiss to her temple, inhaling her strawberry smell.

"What the fuck, Zara? Who said you could mark your skin up like that?"

"Look, Flex, I thought you would be happy! It says Sugar." She rolls her eyes at him, and that's all it takes for him to grab her wrist and pull her flush with his body.

"Zara fuckin' Hart, do you know what you marking your skin with my name for you does to me? It makes me rock hard, that's what. You deserve a spanking for this."

Moments later, she's dragged off to their room with her long legs wrapped around his waist and a knowing glint in her eyes.

"Oh, God! I better go find Axe, I'll catch you all in a few minutes," Dani tells as she leaves the room on a mission to find my Prez.

As Dani strides off, she reminds me of how determined Jenna was that time she caught me in Luigi's with Brent fuckin' Johnson.

She told me once we got back to the bakery how she found out I was there—apparently, Mrs. M, being the town gossip, rushed in to announce to a packed bakery that she had just seen Jenna's scary biker man dressed in a suit heading into Luigi's while she was out walking.

Jenna thought she was makin' shit up, but couldn't help herself going down there to call me out for sneakin' around again if it was true. Fuckin' hell, does that woman have me by my big brass balls...with whistles on them too!

Axe let me and Dags off the hook for goin' rogue, but he told me straight up that if we do it again, I get my *'jam jar'* chopped off!

Yup, it seems that my gorgeous Cupcake can't keep her mouth shut about what I'm packing in my pants...

***

A half-hour later, Axe comes through to the main room, where we're all drinking and enjoying ourselves—well, we're trying to at least, but it's not easy when Brandy's trying to sing but sounding like a dying bunch of alley cats, and Jade's sticking to us like glue. I don't know what's up with her, she looks so uncomfortable being here.

I try and relax, but keep my arm protectively wrapped around Jenna as Axe yells, "All right! Can I have your attention? As you know, this is a party of sorts. Tinhead and Wrench, come up here!"

Tin puts the glass he was cleaning down and pensively walks up to Axe alongside Wrench. Flex shows his face just in time for the main event, with Zara at his side carrying a black bag.

I unwrap myself from around Jenna, and Doc, Flex, Dags, Brains and myself start to surround Tin and Wrench, stalking them like they're our prey.

"Tinhead and Wrench, you've been prospecting for us for over a year and half. It's time for me to decide whether you stay or go." Axe's face looks grim, not betraying a flicker of emotion.

The 5 of us move one step closer to them in turn until we're right behind them and practically breathing down their necks, counting down.

I remember this feeling from my own time as a prospect; how time seems to slow down and the seconds turn into minutes.

5, 4, 3, 2, 1...

We lock eyes with Axe, and a slight twitch of his nose sets us off. We punch, knee, or kick them both once each, making Tin and Wrench screech in pain.

"Argh, fuck!"

"Shit, brother!"

I grab Tinhead and Flex grabs Wrench, both taking a tight hold on their biceps. I shove Tinhead on the bar stool right in front of Zara, who's inking her tattooing gun ready to mark them both.

After an hour apiece, Tinhead and Wrench are officially marked with the Devil's colors—Tin's stands out on his bicep, and Wrench's covers his right pec, branding them as the newest members of the club.

Axe comes marching out of the office swinging the colors for their cuts, strips the cuts off their backs, and lines his hunting knife up perfectly against the prospect patches, slicing through the thread like butter.

***

The party is in full swing, and me and Jenna are standing around talking to Doc and Sue.

I look around the club, thinking about how these past few months have been some of the hardest and darkest in our lives, but also made our relationship stronger, when in reality, they could have torn us apart just as easily.

We seemed to see pregnancy and babies everywhere at first, and it hurt and drove us crazy in equal measure—after some heavy persuasion from Jenna, I agreed that the best thing for us to do was speak to a counselor about Sophia and our feelings.

The counselor explained that seeing babies and signs of pregnancy everywhere is normal, and due to the fact our brains pick up on the things that are likely to affect us more when we're in a sensitive state, whereas normally it would ignore them. I can understand the science, but it doesn't make it any easier—it feels like your own brain is mocking you, making you feel 100 times worse.

A few months ago, I even hated children and pregnant women because of it—not so much Ryker, but women and children on the street, and in the bakery. I wanted them to suffer the way we were, and I couldn't understand why they got to have something we had taken away from us.

With the counselor's help, I know that's irrational, and it's easing, but I do think it's been harder to seek and accept help because I'm a guy. Everyone looks after the women and is expected to understand the emotional and physical trauma they have to endure, but from my experience, men tend to be expected to deal with it on their own.

Even so, I know I'm very fortunate—I have an amazing network of family and friends around me, including my Dad. He's not the talkative type, but he's checked in with us both every week since we lost Sophia, and because of that the tension between us has lessened.

I don't feel isolated or mad at the world anymore, and above all, I have my Cupcake, who I love and adore to the end of the whole fuckin' universe. I know the pain will never go away, no matter what people say about it getting easier with time, but maybe that pain is also the constant reminder of Sophia's love we need.

We are slowly but surely getting on with our lives; day by day, week by week, but all we can do is keep taking each day as it comes and learning to live with the pain that still lingers in our hearts and the void that sits in our souls; a sign that we have loved as much as a sign that we have lost.

THE END

Read on for a teaser of the fourth book in the Devils Reapers MC series,

Tinhead

Coming Soon…

The name's Dylan, but my club call me Tinhead. As bikers go, I'm a friendly guy. I get along with my brothers, their women, the club girls…everyone except Jade Smith, the younger sister of Bear's woman Jenna. I don't know why, but she's been givin' me shit since the day I first walked into the bakery a few months ago after gettin' a tattoo.

I thought she was cute as hell, with sun-kissed red hair and a dusting of freckles across her nose…but then she opened her mouth. All right, I admit askin' for her 'goodies' was probably a mistake, but all I wanted was a brownie and a cup of coffee! If looks could kill, I woulda been a dead man there and then, and she chewed me out real good, screamin' about how I wasn't gonna get any from her, club member or not.

Yup, the girl sure does have a beehive up her ass when it comes to me—it's like she's got a grudge or somethin'…

***

The moment he walked into the bakery with the same arrogant swagger, I knew nothing had changed. He acts like he's God's gift to women, but this woman sure as hell won't buy it. If he thinks he has a chance with me after what he did, he's got another thing coming. I can't believe he had the nerve to come into *my* sister's bakery and hit on *me*; he deserved every word of the whoopin' he got for that.

He wants my 'goodies'? Well, he'd better keep dreamin'!

Thank you so much for reading Bear.
I hope you enjoyed it his and Jenna's story as much as me. It was one of the hardest storylines to write but as like with my other Devils books I incorporate real life stories as well as the romance side of things.
I do hope you loved Bear as much as me.

I would really appreciate you leaving a review on Amazon or Goodreads. Even if it is a one liner.

Thank you again,
Love and hugs
Ruby xx

Printed in Poland
by Amazon Fulfillment
Poland Sp. z o.o., Wrocław

57259572R00160